"Who are you?" I asked, fighting back the wave of dizziness to look up again. I barely recognized my own voice.

He reached out and tilted my chin up to face him. "I think you've always known."

"I need to hear you say it." The heat of his fingers warmed me, chasing the cold from the room, from my soul. Part of me just wanted to give in to the heat and forget the rest.

"I'm a god, Kate. Hades. Lord of the underworld, keeper of the damned."

"The devil," I said, quite clearly, before my vision fuzzed and I tipped forward, unable to steady myself, and fell straight into his arms.

TO HELL WITH LOVE

Sherri Erwin

ZEBRA BOOKS
Kensington Publishing Corp.

www.kensingtonbooks.com

ZEBRA BOOKS are published by

Kensington Publishing Corp.
850 Third Avenue
New York, NY 10022

All Kensington titles, imprints, and distributed lines are available at special quantity discounts for bulk purchases for sales
promotion, premiums, fund-raising, educational, or institu-
tional use.

Special book excerpts or customized printings can also be created to fit specific needs. For details, write or phone the office
of the Kensington Special Sales Manager: Attn. Special Sales
Department. Kensington Publishing Corp., 850 Third Avenue,
New York, NY 10022. Phone: 1-800-221-2647.

Zebra and the Z logo Reg. U.S. Pat. & TM Off.

ISBN-13: 978-1-4201-0105-8
ISBN-10: 1-4201-0105-6

First Printing: September 2007
10 9 8 7 6 5 4 3 2 1

Printed in the United States of America

For my sisters.

Acknowledgments

I count myself extremely fortunate to be surrounded by a number of wise and witty women who offer endless support, encouragement, laughter, and inspiration.

Special thanks go to Stephany Evans, my agent, for her keen insights.

To Danielle Chiotti, my brilliant editor.

To my biological sisters, Deborah Brunelle and Kristin Browning.

To the sister of my heart, Laura Jerry.

To my coffee sister, Debra Kozikowski (my 'bucks or yours?).

And to my Whine Sisters, Kathleen and Dinah: I love you, man.

Prologue

Darkness everywhere. Every day, every night, dark. The hazy half-light thrown by the eternal flame of the underworld was nothing like the sun. The environs of Hades reflected the mood and temperament of the god himself.

Religion, myth, and legend had assigned him a variety of duties and any number of faces and names. Satan, the devil, Lucifer. He preferred to think of himself in the Greek tradition as Hades, a god in his own right performing the necessary task of final justice.

It was up to Hades to decide who deserved to rise to Elysium, the heavenly sanctum of the pure. It was also his burden to send the wicked on to Tartarus, the true hell, and decide what tortures should await them. His brother Zeus's job, to give life, seemed the far favorable employment.

Just once, he would like to lead his brother's lot, to reign radiant over creation, to generate light and warmth. To feel, for once, filled with life instead of drained by death at every turn.

Hades sighed aloud, prompting a response from Byron, the nearest minion.

"What troubles you, my lord? Shall I bring Cerberus in for a visit?"

"I'm not in the mood. A dog isn't the sort of companionship I have in mind." Hades raised a thin, dark brow, leaving little doubt the sort of companion he was looking for. Between wives for centuries now, Hades was desperately lonely. Or simply randy as hell. He couldn't decide which. He merely knew he needed—a change.

Byron's face drained of color. "Not another mortal consort?"

"Perhaps." Hades rose, agitated. "I want a true partner. An equal. Not one who comes reluctantly or lacks in self assurance."

"And you think there's a woman out there both worthy of you and willing?"

Hades sighed. "Can they never think of the good I've done? The benefits they reap from my mere existence? Without me, there'd be overpopulation, famine, chaos."

"You want them to give the devil his due?" Byron said, all mischief.

"Exactly." Hades gestured with a flourish. "And why not? Am I really such a demon?"

"According to most sources."

"True enough." Hades tried to hide the depth of his concern. "But how to prove otherwise?"

"A visit, perhaps? A chance to show the real you?" Byron offered.

"It would help to start out in a place where people keep open minds, in general."

"Might I suggest Manhattan? Big city, lots of options. Single women outnumber single men by nearly two to one."

"Too easy." Hades dismissed the suggestion.

"How about Boston? New England's chock full of liberal thinkers."

Boston. Hades mulled the idea. He always liked America, particularly the Northeast. People tended to be suspicious of *strangers, making it a challenge to form relationships. But once one broke through the superficial barriers to establish trust, New Englanders were fiercely loyal, a plus. They kept faith in the Red Sox, after all.*

"Boston, hmm. Perhaps. Look at a few possibilities for me. Try to narrow down a field of women who might hold some favorable opinion of me."

"Of you?" Byron laughed. "Favorable, you say? As in, decent? Just? Promising?"

"Is it so hard to believe that someone would be singing my praises?"

"Generally, yes."

"Well, have a look anyway," Hades ordered. "Find someone who has something good to say about me. Or something slightly above negative. I'll settle for anything less than a curse."

Chapter 1

I stood outside my sister's door for what seemed like an eternity, shifting a bottle of cheap wine in my arms and wondering about the odd earthy odor I'd picked up somewhere between leaving the car and going up the front walk.

I looked down. It figured. Shit on my shoe. Caked to my pricey stiletto heel, the last pair I would buy in a while. It seemed like an omen. I should run while I had the chance.

Bennie opened the door, wearing the tight little smile she reserved for guests that blossomed to the real thing when she saw it was me and not a pair of her husband's clients or one of the endless twits with whom she tried to set me up. "Kate! You made it. On time, no less."

"Early, in fact. And bearing wine." I passed her the bottle and hoped she wouldn't recognize the label as one from the three-for-twelve-dollars bin at the corner liquor store. Since trading glamour in New York for grit in Newton, Massachusetts, I'd given up my penchant for designer shoes and fine wines to better control my expenses. Glamour paid a lot better than grit, let me tell you.

For now, I made ends meet by working retail at a Country Curtains outlet, but my long-term goal was to open my own interior decorating firm.

"Come in," Bennie said, taking the wine. "How's Mother?"

"Ugh." She loved to rub it in that I'd been bunking with our mother and stepdad, a temporary situation until I could get settled and find an affordable apartment. Since I lost my set design gig, Manhattan had become a tad pricey. I'd recently moved back home to save money. "Mother's the same as always. Why don't you visit? She never stops talking about the kids."

"She never stops talking, period," Bennie added. We shared a conspiratorial laugh as we made our way down the hall.

Bennie's Miss Clairol Strawberry Blonde hair was swept up in her usual dinner party chignon. Her elegant navy blue sheath made me feel underdressed, though I was wearing a perfectly lovely cream chiffon blouse and a violet silk skirt with hand-embroidered edges, last season's formal wear mark-downs from Filene's Basement.

"Rob's dying to meet you," she said, reaching for my hand as if to encourage me or, knowing Bennie, to force me to move faster toward the sacrificial altar. She couldn't bear to see me contentedly single.

"Rob? He's already here?" Only twits and relatives came early, an unspoken dinner party rule.

"He's smart. You said you *like* smart. A bio professor at Wellesley. And he's cute."

"And punctual." I shrugged out of my coat and hung

it on the rack. "I guess you've forgotten that I also said I didn't want any more fix-ups after last time."

Last time, Bennie introduced me to her plumber after I'd made the mistake of mentioning that I liked a man who could work with his hands. He spent all night telling me what he could do to my pipes.

Bennie wrinkled her nose, ignoring my "no more fix-ups" protest. "What's that smell?"

"We better get to the kitchen before you introduce me around," I said, pointing to my feet.

"Oops, sorry." Bennie blushed. "The gardener was trimming the backyard so I had Kristin walk Bert and Ernie out front today. I guess she missed a spot."

Bennie had wanted a small calm dog. Putting her faith in the word of an over-enthusiastic breeder, she'd ended up with both Bert and Ernie, a matched pair of pugs. And carpeted floors to protect from claw scratches, among other dog-inspired sins of design.

I followed Bennie to the kitchen, mourning the loss of my shoes before I even had a chance to view the damage up close. *Ode to My Last Manolos.* With any luck, I could wash off the shit and move on. I tried not to think of it as a metaphor for my life. I slipped off the shoe, an ivory satin slingback with mud caked over the crystals decorating the spiked heel.

"Give it here," Bennie said. "It's not too bad. I'll have it good as new in a sec."

True to her word, she worked her magic and handed the shoe back.

"Thanks," I said, checking the heel. No damage. Saint Bennie, the domestic miracle worker. "Good work."

Bennie didn't stop to acknowledge the compliment. Instead, she placed her hand on my shoulder and nudged me toward the living room. "Now let's go meet Rob."

"Give me a minute. Sheesh." I pulled away and took time to get myself together. Shoe on, hands washed, I was ready to follow her out to the formal living room.

Over at the bar, an antique cherry piece I'd salvaged for them off a stage set, Bennie's husband, Patrick, stood opening a bottle of something. A stranger who bore an uncanny resemblance to Bennie's pugs perched, not unlike the dogs, on the arm of the nearby overstuffed sofa as he made small talk with Patrick. "Hello." The stranger stood as soon as we entered. Well, at least he had manners. "Nice to meet you, Kate."

"Rob?" I said, feigning uncertainty to cover my blatant hope that he wasn't Rob.

He stood about two inches shorter than my five feet six. He had soft brown eyes and well-formed lips. Up close, his features weren't as pug-like as I'd first assumed. But the fact that he reminded me of a dark-haired garden gnome could be something of a setback. If only he hadn't chosen to pair his white oxford shirt with a green wool vest. I resisted the temptation to look around for where he may have left his pointed red cap.

"Rob. That's the name and the game," he said, reaching for the hand I'd yet to offer. "Consider yourself warned."

"Warned?"

"Be careful or I might just steal your heart." He winked. "Rob, as in steal?"

Oh. God. I endangered my Manolos for a pun-spinning gnome? I smiled at Rob and cast a sideways glance at Bennie.

"I have to get back to the kitchen," she said. "You two

amuse yourselves until the other guests arrive." Then she ran off.

I thought of ways to amuse myself. They didn't include Rob. They did include a slow, painful torture of my little sis.

When we were kids, she used to trick me into playing Barbie dolls with her by crying until Mother forced me to play. As a subtle form of revenge, I buried her Barbie dolls in the backyard. I figured that if I was trapped into acting out scenes with picture-perfect plastic dolls, I was calling the shots and Barbie's funeral had it all over Barbie's dream date, in my opinion. Bennie didn't agree. She cried all through Skipper's touching eulogy. But it was *Night of the Living Dead: Barbie's Return* that gave her nightmares for weeks. Those were the days.

By inviting me to her dinner parties, Bennie still managed to force me into play-acting. Fortunately for Rob, it was a whole lot harder to bury the guests in the backyard.

"Bennie says you've just moved back from Manhattan?" Rob asked. "I'm not cut out for city life. I like it right here, close enough to enjoy Boston but far enough out of the rat race."

"I've always liked a good rat race," I said, ignoring the way he patted the couch next to him as an invitation to sit down.

"So why'd you move back?" Rob asked.

"Work."

"Interior design." He nodded, as if Bennie had handed him my entire résumé in advance. "I'm in genetic engineering, with worldwide recognition in plant research."

"Wow." I needed wine, but a glance at Patrick proved he wasn't exactly hurrying. He stood, poised over the bottle, taking time to clean his fingernails with the corkscrew. Ew. "Patrick, need a little help with that bottle?"

Patrick startled and looked up, a fierce blush spreading over his cheeks. "It'll just be a minute."

He reminded me a little of a potential love child of Laverne DeFazio and Richie Cunningham, streetwise with a boyish charm, not to mention the thinning red hair. Normally, he was more adept at hiding his inner DeFazio.

"My work is destined to impact the entire future of agricultural enterprise. But enough about tomatoes. Tell me more about what you did in the Big Apple." Rob, caught up in his own lame attempt at a humorous segue, punctuated his sentence with a snort-like laugh.

"I was a set designer for *Darkness Eternal.*"

"*Darkness Eternal*?" he asked. "Was that on Broadway?"

Most people had heard of it. Most people found my work on a daytime drama a fascinating angle of conversation. Rob was not most people. He looked to be the sort whose television didn't get much use with the exception of Home and Garden Television, from which he undoubtedly picked up fashion advice from the other garden gnomes.

"All My Vampires, as we liked to call it around here," Patrick joked, approaching with glasses of wine. "It was a soap opera."

I snatched a glass and took a sip. An earthy Merlot. *Nirvana.*

"Vampires?" Rob looked lost. And a little frightened.

"It was a great show," Patrick said. "We got addicted around here."

"Alas, we got cancelled after a six-year run. The writers said their creativity had been sucked dry." Oh no,

I'd made a pun. I hoped Rob didn't get too excited. "After that, all the other soaps were staffed and I didn't want to work an endless chain of stage shows. I like steady employment."

I *needed* steady employment. I wasn't getting any younger and the desire for stability grew stronger with every tick of my biological clock.

"Plus," I added, "something about starting over back on my home turf appealed."

I could hardly think what it was. The quiet charm and reliability of the suburbs that drew me back was now the very same thing pushing me away. Too quiet. Too reliable. I needed a shake-up. I needed . . . something.

To be frank, some great sex would be nice, which was why I never protested too loudly when Bennie launched another of her set-up attempts. I kept hoping she would introduce me to the right guy and I'd at least get some action out of the deal. And if it led to more, so much the better. I wanted what Bennie had. House, husband, kids. A place to belong. A place of my own, with people who needed me as much as Bennie's family needed her. I'd almost given up on the idea of finding a suitable love match, but a family was not out of the question. So what if I didn't have a man? I could do it on my own, with the help of modern science.

Tradition be damned.

Unfortunately, one look at Rob and I knew the dry spell would persist. Tonight wasn't the night.

"The thing with tomatoes is . . ." Rob had begun to explain the complicated process of growing the perfect tomato.

The doorbell rang, signaling the arrival of more guests. More guests meant less Rob, as far as I was concerned. I decided to make a break for it.

"I better get that," I said, and darted off to answer the door.

It was Paul and Rhonda Wiskowski, the owners of a mortgage company with whom Patrick, a realtor, did a lot of business. Fortunately, the Wiskowskis were late and we sat down to dinner almost right away, cutting down on the necessity for more pre-dinner small talk.

Patrick took his usual seat at the head of the table with Bennie at his right. Paul settled in next to Bennie and Rhonda assigned herself what she probably thought to be the next most important seat up near Patrick. I sighed and filled in near Paul, saying a silent prayer that Rob would choose to not stick dutifully by my side. When he sat down across from me, I was relieved, until I realized this meant I had to look at him all night. So much for prayers.

Bennie, a Martha Stewart aficionado, had set the table with a harvest theme. Dried autumn leaves interspersed with tea lights formed a line down the middle of the pumpkin orange tablecloth, a perfect match with Rhonda's hair.

Once we were all settled at the table, Rob attempted to start the conversation with a discourse on tomatoes. Rhonda, not one for polite listening, cut Rob off with an inquiry into Patrick's latest real estate development.

"Nothing's selling," Patrick said with a heavy sigh. "Twelve brand new houses with wooded backyards all clustered around a cul-de-sac and no one wants in."

"If only you could sell one. After one family settled in, the rest would go like that." Rhonda snapped her fingers and sent a long red nail extension flying into Rob's soup. No one seemed to notice. "Give it time."

"The problem," Patrick went on, "is that open floor plans are the new rage, but they make a house look too empty. Houses used to be divided into more rooms. It made it easy to picture a home life within the enclosed space."

"An established comfort level there is, to see a house that is actually a home." Paul channeled Yoda, complete with gray hair flying out his ears, between slurps of soup.

"So why not stage the houses with furniture accents?" I asked. All heads turned to me. "The Wyndham Park houses must be going for what? Half a mil?"

"Seven hundred grand and up," Paul said.

"Way up," Rhonda added.

"So what's a little extra investment? Maybe fifty thousand or so to do some superficial decorating, make the place look a little less empty." And that's when it dawned on me. Who needed stage sets when I had entire houses at my disposal?

"Why don't I come by tomorrow morning, take a look around?" I asked Patrick. "Give me a few days and I could have the place looking like something out of *Better Homes and Gardens.*"

On their dime! If it worked, I could start my own business much sooner than I'd imagined. Good-bye Country Curtains, hello success! More important for my immediate satisfaction, good-bye Mom, hello chic city address. South end? Back Bay? The more family-friendly Beacon Hill? The sky was the limit. Provided I could work out the details. The sooner I set up residence, the sooner I could move ahead with satisfying my maternal instincts. Even seeing baby diaper commercials made me stop dead in my tracks lately, my heart racing in a way that only ads for sample sales had been able to inspire in the past.

"What's in it for you?" Bennie chimed in.

"Commission," I answered without a second's hesitation. "If I do the house up and it sells within three days, I take a thirty percent cut of your profit."

"Thirty percent?" Patrick's face flooded with color.

"We can work something out," I said. A few commission checks and a small business loan and I would be on my way to owning my own business.

"I work out." Rob injected himself back in the conversation, interrupting my reverie. "Kate, you should meet me at the gym sometime."

"Gym? I'm allergic." No way in hell. I rose to escape, er, to help as Bennie started clearing dishes.

"Have a seat, Kate." Bennie took the silver right out of my hands. "*Patrick* is going to help me in the kitchen."

Matchmaker Bennie was on the job. I sunk back into my seat and plotted my revenge. Fortunately, Paul took over the stalled conversation.

"If you could have dinner with anyone in the world," he asked, "past or present, who would it be?"

My first thought? Yoda. And here I was. Lucky me. My second thought was to ask Yoda to bring Han Solo. I was about to ask if fictional characters were allowed when Rob piped in first.

"Jesus." No surprise that he answered with the standard safe response for Christians everywhere.

"Good one," Rhonda said. "Let me think. Anyone in the world?" Seconds passed while Rhonda contemplated. "Ooh, I know. Neil Diamond."

"Neil Diamond?" Paul laughed. "Figures. At least you didn't say Tom Jones. I was going to choose Gandhi or Mother Teresa but since you're bringing Neil . . . I guess I would say Jaclyn Smith."

"Jaclyn Smith?" Rhonda's voice reached a nasal zenith. "The Charlie's Angel?"

"Yeah." Paul smiled. "I always liked how she looked in that white string bikini."

Rhonda reached across to slap Paul's hand. "I doubt she fits in it anymore."

"I don't know. I bet she's still got it." Paul rubbed his fingers. "So we have Jesus, Neil Diamond, and Jaclyn Smith. I think we need someone else to round out the pack. Kate?"

Yeah, like someone born after Woodstock, perhaps. I didn't dare mention there was a more recent version of *Charlie's Angels* with younger babes and skimpier bikinis. Paul might not be able to handle the temptation.

Who to choose? I looked around the table in time to catch Rob's sanctimonious smirk. That's all it took. He didn't think I could do better than Jesus?

"I choose the devil," I said with a wicked, playful grin.

"Satan?" Rob's gnome cheeks reddened. "But wouldn't you fear for your immortal soul?"

I shrugged. "It's only dinner. My soul would set him back more than a mere meal. I'd hold out for dinner and a movie, maybe a weekend away. No soul until three dates at least."

Rob looked alarmed. Fortunately, Bennie and Patrick appeared with the main course, putting an end to the discussion. And to think, I'd almost bailed on Bennie when she'd invited me for yet another fix-up dinner. I didn't need Rob. I didn't even need to date the devil or sell my soul. I'd saved myself. First the business, then if all went well on that front, the baby. Who needed a husband? I was on my way.

Chapter 2

One year later . . .

"What time do I have to show up?" I cradled the receiver in the crook of my shoulder so that I could fluff pillows and talk at once. Multitasking had become second nature since I'd opened my own business, Curtain Call Designs. I'd found a unique niche in a crowded home interiors market and made myself a small fortune. I was back in designer heels. Life was good.

"Come by around seven," Bennie answered.

"Do I have to bring anything?"

"Only your scintillating conversational skills," she quipped.

"I was thinking of bread or dessert, but wit will do. Easier to carry."

"Wear something pretty," Bennie said. "The last time you came over, you were a mess."

"I look fine," I said. I would throw a little scarf on over my simple black dress and voila—day wear dresses up for dinner. Then it hit me. *Oh, no.* "I thought we'd put an end to this. You know I hate it when you try to fix me up. Who is it this time?"

"Marc Ramirez." I could hear the sly smile in her voice.

I racked my brain to put a face to the name. "Ramirez, the linebacker? From the Patriots?"

"The very one. Remember last week, when you were here watching the game? You said he had the most perfect ass you'd ever laid eyes on."

"Just because I admired his, um, physique doesn't mean I want to have his babies."

"It has nothing to do with babies. You meet, sparks fly, you go on a few dates, and who knows. For now, it's all about the sparks."

"The sparks," I repeated, dread growing.

"Sparks. Physical attraction. Leads to wanting to know more about each other which leads to—forget what it leads to. That's your problem, Katie. You're too goal-oriented. You need to forget planning ahead. Relax and let life unfold."

"That's your life philosophy, let it unfold. If *I* waited for things to unfold, I'd be home alone unable to move from all the cartons of ice cream it took to keep me occupied until the phone rang."

"You're so funny. Bring that trademark wit to dinner and maybe you'll score a touchdown with Marc. See you at seven."

Click.

Bennie hung up before I could offer an excuse to miss the party. In some ways, we knew each other too well. In other ways, Bennie hardly knew me at all. She didn't understand my business-over-pleasure approach to life. With Bennie, it was all about hearth and home.

Everything she'd ever wanted had fallen right into her lap—loving husband, adorable children, beautiful home. For me, it was work that came easy. Relationships required Herculean effort to develop, let alone to maintain for any length of time.

Fortunately for Bennie, she didn't remember our parents' relationship nearly as well as I did. I'd been an impressionable age twelve when our father walked out on the family. Bennie had only been eight. I remembered what it was like to witness a marriage going bad—the fights, the accusations, and finally the numbing sense of helplessness. I didn't want to land in a mess of my own. Years later, I still doubted any man could restore my faith in long-term relationships. Especially not any of the men Bennie found for me. I was better off on my own.

I had a thriving business, a South End condo, a growing financial portfolio, and my health. Why did I need a man?

"You're needed in the nursery," my assistant, Val, came downstairs as if on cue. "The men can't figure out how to set up the crib's canopy."

"Figures. Let me finish in here and I'll be right up." I surveyed the living room furniture to try to figure out what was needed to pull the room together. Two club chairs bookended the fireplace. A sumptuous couch sat across from them, an antique chest serving as a coffee table in between. "It still needs something, don't you think?"

"Yes, but what? Maybe some throw pillows? A few more candles on the table?" Val squinted as if assessing, then set to work on rearranging a few knickknacks.

"Was that your sister on the phone?"

"Yes. She's throwing another dinner party and she

didn't give me the chance to back out. I know she's trying to fix me up again, but I'm so tired of pointless dates."

"Poor baby." Val rolled her eyes. "To be courted by countless eligible bachelors, wined, dined, and generally adored. Oh, the suffering."

No sympathy. Val was a divorced fifty-something who dreamed of romance-novel heroes coming to life to sweep her off her feet. She was probably the only woman alive who'd actually recorded Fabio's I Can't Believe It's Not Butter ads and replayed them on a weekly basis. The ads gave her hope there was someone out there for everyone, she'd say by way of an excuse. I should learn not to bitch about my love life, or desire for lack of it, to Val.

With Val doing her thing with the decorative touches, I excused myself and went up to check out the problem in the nursery.

Setting up a crib was something I could handle. It was filling it that might be my problem. I'd recently discovered that my first insemination attempt had failed and the news left me feeling lonelier than ever. Would I ever be a mother? I wasn't ready to accept that it wasn't meant to be.

Bennie's kids were practically teenagers, but I still felt a painful stab in my heart every time I remembered watching my sister cradle her firstborn, Spence. The way she'd looked at him, as if the whole world was caught up in that one tiny bundle in her arms. It was the first time I could ever recall envying my sister. Not that I'd wanted to be a mother back then. But to have that bond, a connection with someone that ran bone deep. *Soul deep.* Unconditional love. Would I ever know the feeling?

At thirty-four, I told myself I had plenty of time left for motherhood. It had only been a year since the business had really taken off, and I'd just been through my artificial insemination. Many women went through four or five attempts before getting the good news of implantation.

I climbed the stairs, turned the corner, caught sight of the white crib in the corner, and felt the familiar tug of longing. Plenty of other women had chosen single motherhood. Jodie Foster, Meg Ryan, Elizabeth Hurley— if they could all do it, why not me? I had plenty of money and nothing but time to keep trying. Later in the week, I could call my gynecologist and ask about looking over the lists for a new anonymous donor. For now, I had a party to attend.

By the time I finished up at the Elmwood house and prepared to head over to Bennie's, it was half past seven. Good thing I kept a few bottles of wine in my showcase, a handy kitchen accessory. Nothing said "lived-in" like booze. I grabbed a spare bottle and made for the Lincoln Aviator, my most recent extravagant gift to myself.

Traffic was a mess, but I leaned back in my seat and sighed instead of cursing out my fellow drivers. I needed to learn some stress management techniques. What had my yoga instructor said this morning? *Breathe in, breathe out, be the ocean, flow like the tide . . .*

Outside of class, it simply sounded idiotic. Flow like the tide. Get real. After a twelve hour day, the only thing I needed to hear flow was wine into my glass.

Deep in thought, I almost didn't notice until too late the sleek black sedan that shot across two lanes of traffic in a last-minute effort to make the upcoming exit.

My exit. Adrenaline pumping, I hit the brakes in time to avoid rear-ending it as it slid into line in front of me.

Through the darkness, I could barely make out the driver's shape, a silhouette framed by the streetlights' glow. Tall, broad shoulders, close-cropped hair. Almost definitely a man. Figures.

He drove a nice car. An expensive car. I recognized the pricey VW Phaeton from my own car shopping weeks earlier. Mr. Hell on Wheels picked the wrong woman to trifle with tonight. I decided to stay on his tail. Directly on his tail. Finally, he pulled into the parking lot of a local florist and I breathed a sigh of relief. Good riddance.

When I pulled into Bennie's driveway a couple of blocks later, my heart was still racing from the near-accident. I grabbed the wine, got out, and tried to regain my composure. My nerves tingled with a mix of fear and excitement. Strangely enough, it was the most alive I'd felt in weeks. Maybe Bennie was right about one thing: I needed to get a life.

"Where have you been?" Bennie asked as soon as I slipped through the side door off of the kitchen. She stood in the midst of dirty dishes and boiling-over pans, madly chopping parsley on her enormous butcher-block island. "You're late."

"No kidding."

She looked up from chopping. "My God, have you been having sex?"

"What makes you say that?" I laughed to hide my shock. Sex? She knew I hadn't had sex in over a year. Not that I liked to brag.

"You're blushing. You *did* have sex. Who is it? Don't tell Marc you're seeing someone after I had Patrick drag him here to meet you. Pretend you're interested."

"I'm not here to pretend anything," I said. "And I'm not having sex with anyone. Not even myself. I'm out of batteries."

"Ew." Bennie grimaced. "TMI! TMI!"

"It was a joke, Ben. Jeez. You told me to bring my wit." I grabbed a carrot off a half-devoured tray of crudite. "I'm flushed because some yahoo in a black Phaeton cut me off on the highway, that's all."

"I notice you didn't make time to change." She crossed her arms and gave me the once over, a gesture she could have stolen right from our mother. In fact, ever since Bennie had gone ash blond, she reminded me of Mother. Too much. Same hair, same dramatics, same superficial concerns.

"What? I look fine." I'd wrapped a shawl, silk with velvet burned-out flowers, over my shoulders and thrown on a strand of pearls in an attempt to dress up my plain black knit dress.

Bennie wore an off-the-shoulder plum cocktail dress with delicate sandals. Her guests, I knew from experience, would be dressed down in comparison. I would fit right in while she basked in her role as Lady of the Manor. It suited her. She'd always been the dreamy-eyed princess growing up. I was the tomboy realist.

"So what's this about Marc Ramirez having to be dragged here?" I said, before she could get back to criticizing. "I don't want to be offered up as a mercy mission."

"You're not, believe me." Bennie arranged a bed of greens on a crystal platter. The catering staff she employed for such events stayed conveniently out of sight while Bennie played chef, but I knew that they would swoop in and work magic any time now. "Marc is getting over a bad breakup. If anything, you're doing him the favor."

"Rebound men, my favorite."

"Come on, be a sport. You two might hit it off."

One thing I hated was to be called a poor sport and Bennie knew it. She was determined to get her way and I was too tired to fight.

"Maybe I'll get an attack of the clumsies and oops, keep dropping my fork. At least I can enjoy the view of him bending over if all else fails."

"That's the spirit. Now help me arrange the stuffed mushrooms and we'll introduce you."

"Look who's here." Patrick put down his corkscrew and came over to greet me with a half-embrace, cheek kiss, and smile. "My late sister-in-law."

"*Fashionably* late," I corrected. "Good to see you, Patrick."

"I believe you know Paul and Rhonda." He gestured toward his former business partner and wife.

"Hello. Good to see you again." I made the rounds with Patrick, careful not to look over-interested in Marc, the hulking stranger holding up the corner bookcase. Patrick introduced me to another couple, the Skinners, before delivering me up to Marc as if I were one of the hand-passed appetizers. *Care for a mushroom? Scallop wrapped in bacon? How about a Kate?*

"Marc, this is Kate."

"Hey," he said, offering his hand for a shake. Hey? So much for smooth conversation.

He was bigger in person than I'd imagined, tall and so dense with muscle it was a wonder he could move all that body mass. His neck was as thick as one of my thighs, and that was saying a lot since I'd been surviving on a steady diet of fast food and brownies lately. But he had thick, dark hair and a warm smile. I would try to think positive.

"Hey," I answered. "Nice to meet you."

He nodded as if he expected as much. Oh boy.

"So you're into football?" he asked after a second.

"Football's okay," I said, pleased to have proof that he could string words together to form a sentence. I'd been half afraid he might grunt his answers or simply say *yes*, *no*, or *hey* all night. "I like to kick back and watch on the occasional Sunday."

"Only Sunday?" He arched a bushy brownish red brow, which reminded me of a caterpillar, the striped furry bear kind I used to hunt as a kid in the field behind my house.

"Sunday, sometimes on other days. Depends on my work schedule." Maybe our first official date could be at a spa for a good waxing. I tried to forget the eyebrows.

"That's cool. You have a job."

"Yeah." I laughed. Didn't everyone? "Is that a surprise?"

"My ex didn't work," he explained. "But then, she didn't do a lot of things."

"I see."

"But what's past is past," Marc said. "These days, I'm looking for a more intellectual sort of woman. Someone more my speed."

"An intellectual." I smiled. "I'm not sure I measure up, but I can read." Score one for Newton public schools.

"I got a soft side, you know. Most women don't expect that. You look like you might get me."

Was that a threat? "If I got you, could I give you back?"

"Give me back?" He looked puzzled for a second. "Oh I get it. Funny. Your sister warned me about you."

Conversation stalled. Lost for words, I nudged a book off the corner of the shelf. "Oops."

It fell a little behind Marc's feet. He leaned to pick it up. My gaze followed. To my disappointment, his suit jacket partially obscured my view of his taut, athletic behind.

"Here you go." He handed me the book, allowing his hand to linger on mine.

I waited for the spark but none came. Maybe I was truly incapable of feeling a spark. Marc seemed like a nice guy and all but—

His cell phone rang. To my surprise, he answered it.

"Hey you," he said, holding up a finger as if to say it would be a minute.

I wasn't here to play games or wait around for potential dates to get off the phone. I drained my glass of wine, waved good-bye, and headed to the kitchen for a refill.

Chapter 3

In the kitchen, a bottle of Australian Shiraz stood unopened on the granite counter. I preferred a nice mellow cabernet but . . .

"Love the one you're with," I deadpanned, heading for the corkscrew.

"Lucky me," a throaty male voice answered.

I jumped and turned around. A second later, a man emerged from behind the corner coatrack near the door.

"You startled me." I caught my breath, only to lose it again when I caught sight of him. Tall, dark, lean, muscular, and handsome all wrapped up in a designer label suit. *Calgon, take me away.* "I thought I was alone."

"Even better. May I watch?"

"Excuse me?"

He wanted to watch me? In a very sexual, downright dirty kind of way? Perhaps the downright dirty was all my invention. His tousled hair and bedroom eyes put me in a dirty frame of mind.

"I'm all for self-love." He smiled. "Very empowering. And sexy."

"Actually, I was about to love the wine," I confessed, feeling the heat rush to my cheeks—and other less frequently used body parts.

"Tough day?" he asked.

"The toughest." I reached for the corkscrew to give me something to still my nervous hands. Innuendo from a stranger made me a little uneasy. Especially from a stranger who looked like he'd walked off a *GQ* cover.

"Allow me," he said, reaching for the corkscrew at the same moment.

Our hands touched. Sparks flew. I jumped. It was an actual electric spark.

"Sorry," he said. "It must be something in the air."

Definitely something in the air. I met his gaze, enthralled. My first real spark! So what if it was a fluke of physics, static electricity in the dry indoor heat? I was ready to believe.

"You must be the sister," he said. "Kate?"

"Yes. How did you know?"

As if it wasn't obvious by looking at me, a taller, blonder, more sophisticated version of Bennie. Okay, sophisticated was up for grabs, but I *was* taller. And though I was naturally blond, I had Elaine at L'Air du Temps Day Spa to thank for my subtle golden highlights.

"I know everything." His smile was smug but charming. Sensuous lips parted to reveal straight white teeth. He had a delectable mouth framed with a well-trimmed black mustache and the shadow of a beard.

Intrigued, I leaned casually on the counter, watching as he expertly maneuvered the bottle. He had long fingers, not too thick but nimble. Strong, capable hands. Very sexy.

If I dreamed of men, he would be the man of my dreams. Unfortunately, I tended to dream of more symbolic things. Snakes, horseback rides, an occasional dancing monkey. I knew the first two represented sex. I still couldn't figure out the monkey. But this man, appearing out of nowhere? Had I fallen asleep? Was I dreaming? Was Val rubbing off on me?

"I can't believe it's not butter," I said out loud before catching myself.

"Excuse me?" He handed me a glass.

"Butter." I fought off a stinging blush and tried to smooth things over. "Bennie sent me in for butter and I just realized that all she has is margarine. The nerve."

"Everyone's become far too health-conscious these days." He poured himself a glass. "I say give me butter any day. To butter." He raised his wine.

I clinked his glass, careful to meet his gaze. "To butter. And other culinary sins."

"You like to sin, Kate?" he asked, his voice low and deliberate as he leaned over the counter toward me, our faces nearly close enough to brush noses.

Whoa. My heart raced faster than it had in the car earlier. Twice in one day. I'd better take it easy. Wit, don't fail me now.

"You tell me. I believe you claimed to know everything?" I arched a brow, my best impression of flirtation.

"Ah, touché, Katie Beth."

Katie Beth? No one had called me that since my father left, so many years ago. Katie Beth, his own special shortening of my full name, Katharine Elizabeth. How could he have known?

I stared him down, intrigue now mixed with the slightest hint of alarm. "Katie Beth?"

"Your nickname." He shrugged, matter-of-fact, no attempt to make excuses. "From your childhood. But we were on the topic of sin, I believe."

"Sin," I repeated, unable to move my gaze from his. Who was this guy? How did he know? The thought of sinning with *him* charged my brain, offering up a potent temptation. Just how much did he know on the topic of sin? And how much did he know about me? His arrogant awareness made me all the more drawn to him. Women liked bad boys. I felt myself sucked right into the cliché.

"Of the culinary kind. I bet you sneak a little treat at the end of the day. Let's say ice cream. Dripping with chocolate syrup. Though your figure shows no signs of it."

His gaze dropped down to my cleavage and back up again. Thank goodness I wore the scoop-neck black and not the turtleneck. At least I had something to my credit besides boring basic black. Cleavage, my new favorite accessory.

"Aha, you *don't* know everything. I'm a purist. No syrup."

He nodded, took a sip of wine, and said, "Because it would be wrong to mask the pure taste of Ben and Jerry's Vanilla."

"My reasoning exactly," I said. I gave him what I hoped was a mysterious smile and decided against telling him that I preferred Häagen-Dazs.

He leaned in closer, his breath heating my neck as he dropped his voice to an intimate whisper. "But it's Ben and Jerry's you have in the freezer," he said, and

I wondered if I'd spoken aloud after all. "On sale at the market. You couldn't resist the discount."

A thrill ran up my spine. I spent so much time trying to be all things to all the people in my life. I'd carefully constructed a false image of security and stability to hide the mess deep in my soul. As a result, intimacy didn't come easily for me. The thought of a man *knowing* me, without me having to take the effort to lay my soul bare, without the games and the pretense that came with building relationships, tempted me beyond anything I could imagine. Even vanilla ice cream. Who *was* this guy?

Then it dawned on me. My sister was getting smarter at this fix-up game. She'd made me think Marc was my date so that I wouldn't automatically reject her real candidate, Mr. *GQ*, here. That's how he knew so much. My sister had obviously told him a few things. "Bennie."

"Your sister? I should go say hello." He stood to full height, ready to walk out of the kitchen. "Oh, almost forgot. I brought some flowers." He gestured to the sink, where a still-wrapped bouquet sat among the soaking pans. "Be a love and put them in water for me, hmm?"

With that, he turned and walked through the doors to join the guests in the other room. I stood, stunned. *Be a love?* Did he want a date or a servant?

Men. Even when they looked perfect on the outside, there was always something dark and undesirable lurking underneath. At least he wasn't serial killer dark and undesirable. A control freak I could handle for a night, as long as he looked like that.

Meow. I could feel myself getting hot all over again.

Hot enough to reach up to the shelf over Bennie's fridge where I knew she kept the vases and start arranging. Not because Bond, James Bond, had told me to, but because I needed to take a minute to cool down before facing the guests. Or so I told myself.

Bennie walked in as I snipped stems, mid-arrangement.

"Oh God, they're beautiful," she said, admiring the oversized pink daisies and freesia.

"Like the man himself. You finally got one right. Or close enough. I mean, I'm not sure how long it'll last, but I'm all for one night of magic." I waggled my brows.

"Really? You like Marc? You bailed for the kitchen so fast that I figured—"

"Not Marc. Come on, Ben. I'm onto you."

"Onto me? What do you mean?"

"You faked setting me up with Marc so I might actually fall for your real prospect, right? Mr. *GQ*?"

Her face drained of color. "No, Kate. Oh, no."

"What, no?" My thoughts were more yes, yes, yes, YES!

"You met Owen."

"Owen?" I crinkled my nose. Okay, so it wasn't such a *GQ* name, but I could make it a point to think better of Owens.

"Owen *Glendower*," she said. "Patrick's *investor*." She folded her arms across her chest and shook her head. "He's off-limits, Kate. I don't want you anywhere near Owen Glendower."

Instantly, he became all the more appealing. Forbidden fruit. "Then why are we both at the same party?" I asked.

"I didn't think there'd be a problem. Geez, Kate. I try to fix you up for two years and you've never shown a hint of interest."

"You've never fixed me up with anyone worthy of note. Owen Glendower is definitely worthy."

"Forget it." Bennie gave me the same look she had

when we were kids and I'd used her Easy-Bake Oven to heat my mud pies. "He's evil, Kate. Keep away from him."

"Telling me to keep away from him is like daring me to take him home and give him a test-drive."

"Then you're an idiot." She put her hands on her hips, no-nonsense. "I'm not trying to make him more appealing. I'm trying to protect you. I mean it when I say he's evil. The man is the devil himself."

"The devil? Of the pointed tail, staff, and red horns variety?" She looked so serious, so frightened, that for a minute I almost believed her. Almost. Then I remembered that the kids were still home, sent to bed early with Kristin, the nanny, keeping watch so the grownups could have a nice meal. Bennie would never let evil within a mile of her house when those kids were upstairs. Not to mention Bert and Ernie, her precious little pugs. Bennie was nothing short of fierce when it came to guarding her kids and her dogs.

"Don't be ridiculous. He's the devil for forcing Patrick to abandon his family. Patrick is basically at his beck and call to scour potential real estate investments. He's like the boss from hell."

"The devil, hmm?" I said, trying to test her playacting skills. "An intriguing choice of dinner guest. So if I do end up taking him home, I have an excuse. The devil made me *do it*."

"Ugh. Katie." She rolled her eyes and abandoned me in favor of the fridge. Either she had been acting or she wasn't all that concerned. How quickly salad assembly had replaced saving my soul on her to-do list.

"Besides," I said, using a stray lily for a pointer. "If you *really* didn't want me to see him, you wouldn't have told him all that stuff about me."

"What stuff?" She looked up from sprinkling crou-tons over a bed of romaine.

"He called me Katie Beth." I narrowed my eyes at her. "Come on. He didn't just happen onto that from out of nowhere."

She sighed and went back to her croutons. Salad was a science to Bennie. One part crouton to every three parts green. I think she actually had a mathematical formula to help her keep the balance.

"I told you," she said. "He's the devil. He knows things without being told."

"Right," I said. "And I'm the Easter bunny."

"You always were a little overly fond of jelly beans." Bennie brushed her hands free of crumbs. "The staff will be here soon to finish off the meal. Let's go back to the guests. I recommend you stick close to Marc. *He's* a keeper."

I didn't want a keeper. What I wanted was a really good one-nighter. As we moved to the dinner table, I rearranged myself so that I would end up sitting next to Owen Glendower.

"Sorry," I said, as my thigh "accidentally" brushed his trouser leg as I slid into place beside him.

As dinner was served and the guests made small talk, I had plenty of time to start piecing together what I re-membered Bennie saying about Patrick's new investor. He was indeed rich, something like Boston's version of Donald Trump. And like Trump, he lived for his own publicity and generated gossip as often as he changed supermodel girlfriends. Fortunately, unlike Trump, he listened to his stylist, if he had one. Decent haircut, no comb-over.

I stole a glance at Owen's perfect profile. I didn't

have a chance. Bennie had nothing to fear. Still, there was no harm indulging in a little flirtation over dinner.

"Isn't there?" he asked, the husk of his whisper sending a thrill up my spine.

I hadn't said that bit about flirting out loud, had I?

"Isn't there what?" I answered hesitantly.

"A nice complexity to the shrimp? The combination of fruit and spice works well together," he said, apparently in response to something Melanie Skinner, to his left, had asked.

"It's a mango chipotle glaze," Bennie answered. "But I left yours plain, Melanie."

From the subtle eye roll of the server plating the shrimp, I got the impression that Bennie hadn't exactly been the one doing the glazing. The caterers rarely got any credit at Bennie's affairs.

"South Beach diet," Rhonda explained for Melanie. Melanie shot such a menacing look across the table that Rhonda shut up immediately, far from her usual habit of going into intricate detail.

Owen entertained Melanie with a short anecdote about his last trip to South Beach.

"South Beach in August? Wasn't it hot?" She fluttered her lashes in a move more reminiscent of Melanie, Southern belle from *Gone with the Wind*, than Melanie, married suburbanite.

"It must have been hotter than hell," I piped in with a sly smile in Bennie's direction. "But I like it hot, don't you?"

Before Owen could answer, Melanie jumped in again. "I hear Kate Hudson sits in the sun without a top."

"You might be thinking of Jennifer Aniston, but she

has sworn me to silence on the whole affair." Owen replied with a wink.

"Then you're quite the devil to even bring it up," I said, drawing a glare from my sister. "But I'm sure you never joke about investments, Owen. Is it true that you're trying to buy a football team?"

Oops! I'd completely forgotten about Marc, who was seated directly across from me, looking sullen. But he perked up at the mention of his favorite sport. "Football? Which team?"

"European football," Owen said. "A soccer team, actually. But that didn't come to pass. I backed out of the deal and decided to invest in a restaurant chain instead. Food has always interested me. The dinner is amazing, Bennie."

The servers collected plates and the second dish was served. As the portobello ravioli made the rounds, I couldn't find an opening to work my way back into the conversation.

Owen was clearly the center of attention. We had a bona fide NFL superstar at our table and all anyone seemed to care about was asking Owen's opinion on everything from spices to Spice Islands, where he'd recently bought some land.

I let my gaze slide down his lean body to his lap. I couldn't help wondering . . . *Hello. Is that a corkscrew in your pocket or are you just glad to see me?* From the rise in his tailored trousers, I could guess that he wasn't overcompensating for anything. Apparently, Owen Glendower lived up to his press. He really did have it all.

When I looked up again, he was staring at me with a wolfish grin, as if he knew exactly what I'd been looking at *and* what I was thinking.

Nervous, I reached for my glass. Without thinking, I

took a long, slow sip and savored the subtle flavors of chocolate and currant. And then it hit me. My glass had been nearly empty. Now it was full and I couldn't recall anyone filling it. I didn't see the bottle anywhere at the table. In fact, the catering staff was only coming around with a dry white to accompany the next course.

My gaze went straight to Owen's. The conversation continued all around us, but once our eyes locked, it was all about the two of us. Finally, he seemed to be taking great interest in me, and me alone.

"The wine," I said. "My glass was empty."

"Was it?" he asked, taking a sip from his own glass, which I could have sworn he'd left in the other room. "I suppose it's all a matter of perspective."

"Perspective? Are you suggesting it's a glass-half-empty, glass-half-full kind of thing?" I asked, arching my eyebrow. At least I hoped I did. I never could master that one-eyebrow arch.

"I deal in possibilities, not suggestions. Drink your wine. Or perhaps you've had enough." With a shrug, he turned his attention away from me and back to his ravioli and Rhonda's pictures of her new bichon frise. I'd been dismissed.

Perhaps I'd had enough, indeed. Without another glance at Mr. Glendower, I started on the glass of white just poured. If he thought I was smitten, he was sorely mistaken. Just because a woman shows some interest doesn't mean she'll spend the evening caught up in flirty games. Ha. Owen who? I'd forgotten him already.

I hoped that the two hours of dinner proved to Mr. Glendower that a) I didn't care for him or his opinions and b) I certainly had not had enough to drink. I could hold my wine. In fact, I was holding my fourth glass on the way to the parlor, where Bennie led her guests for after-dinner conversation.

The "parlor" was actually Bennie's prized four-season porch. With the return of warm weather, she'd revert to screens and to calling it a porch. Nonetheless, the wicker furniture brought to mind lazy summer evenings. I could almost hear the crickets chirping. Or was that the high-pitched drone of Melanie's voice? She hadn't stopped talking since she sat down on the loveseat, right next to Owen. And for his part, Owen hadn't stopped listening. Intently. He looked downright amused.

Fine. I decided to make the best of getting to know Marc "reach out and touch someone" Ramirez, who seemed to be finishing up yet another very important call on his cell.

"So tell me, don't you usually get to escape this horrid winter chill for training in Florida or something?" I tried to interest him before he dialed again.

"We're in the middle of the season," he said, looking at me as if I were some kind of moron. "We train right here. You're thinking of baseball. Wusses. *They* can't stand up to snowstorms and ten below, hazards *we* face regularly."

"Right. Being a New England team and all, I suppose you can perform in any weather."

"I can perform, all right." He smiled, a large self-satisfied grin that made his eyebrows dance. It made me want to name them, his eyebrows, so I did. Ace and Lola. Yes, that fit. I sipped my wine, preparing myself to cozy up to Marc a little, in case Owen ever decided to pay attention. Not that I wanted him to pay attention.

"So after the season, what then?"

"Then we get a little time off. And then training starts again." Marc slid his arm around my waist. "I see where you're going with this. Don't worry, babe. I won't skip out on you before we get to know each other a little."

"Oh. Good." I laughed lightly—more of a stifled groan, actually.

Ace and Lola did another dance, an intimate tango. I shifted closer to Marc in case Owen was looking. Not that I could tell. My back was to him.

"Ooh, is that a draft?" I said. "Maybe we should go sit with the others?"

"No." Marc shook his head. "I'm waiting for a call. I get the best reception here by the windows."

Ugh. "Okay."

"I love the stars," he said, pulling me into the solid plane of his body. "There's Wen-chang."

"The eighties band?"

"No, the great bear. From the Chinese."

"Oh. My knowledge of astrology is limited to the Greek and Roman myths, I'm afraid. I minored in Classics." And majored in Art History. Two great useless subjects that went great together.

"Well, there's Orion then. You must know that one."

"Yes, the hunter," I said absently. I could see Owen's reflection in the glass.

And hey, good news, Owen *had* a reflection. He wasn't a vampire, how evil could he be? Well, actors had reflections and they had it all over vampires as far as evil. I'd learned as much while working on *Darkness Eternal.*

I took advantage of the lull in conversation to stare at the night sky—or I pretended to stare as I studied Owen and Melanie. They were seated even closer than they had been earlier, and Owen rested his hand dangerously close to her knee. She leaned into him as she spoke, practically giving him a look down her dress, and look he did. I followed his gaze to her ample chest. How could he? Melanie was married. And she made nasty faces. And, hello, she was married. I would expect him to ignore me for supermodels, sexed-up heiresses, maybe the Olsen twins. But Melanie Skinner?

Her husband sat in the corner, deep in conversation with Bennie, Rhonda, and Paul while Melanie made the moves on Owen right there in the middle of the room! As if to confirm my suspicions, she tossed her platinum curls back and laughed at something Owen had said. Likely, she was trying to channel Marilyn Monroe, but she reminded me more of Miss Piggy.

Behind me, Marc stirred and I felt a sudden, distinct throbbing near my bottom. Oh-oh. Houston, we have a problem. Or in Marc's case, perhaps I should say New England.

I turned around, ready to explain that I was by no means ready to take it to the next level, as he apparently was. But as I turned, he whipped out his phone and answered it.

"Hello?"

So it was his *phone* going off on me. I narrowly escaped the embarrassment of admitting I'd mistaken his phone, set to vibrate, for er, his receiver of another kind. At least he didn't have me on speed-dial. Yet.

I needed another glass of wine.

As if four wasn't enough.

What was I doing? Owen showed no signs of interest in me, despite our initial meeting in the kitchen. Marc was only interested in his phone, and I wasn't interested in Marc. No amount of wine was going to liven up this party. I didn't need wine. What I needed was to go home, before I made a fool of myself.

I made my way over to Bennie and issued apologies and group good-byes. My sister followed me out and hunted for a more in-depth excuse.

"But it's early," she said. "You and Marc seemed to be hitting it off."

"Marc is hitting it off with his *phone*."

"He's in the middle of contract negotiations," Bennie explained. "I'm sure he didn't mean to offend you."

"I'm not offended. Really. But I don't think he'll miss me. The phone seems to be all the company he needs for tonight." I meant it. I'd felt the vibration on that sucker. Powerful stuff.

"You do have your early showing tomorrow. I guess you need your sleep."

"Yes. Big showing. Very important." The showing *was* important. My commission increased significantly when buyers made an offer on the day of a Curtain Call open house.

Bennie followed me to the door. "Shall I give Marc your number?"

"Why not? I might have better luck with him on the phone." And I had caller ID. It was easier to screen calls than argue with my sister about my high standards and bad attitude. Again.

"Okay. Drive safe."

An air kiss later, I was free. Free to sit in the driveway and call a cab. I'd spent half the night lusting after an unattainable egomaniac. Clearly, my judgment was impaired. No way was I driving myself home.

I headed straight for my car to get my cell phone. Halfway there, I stopped dead in my tracks. A black VW

Phaeton had blocked me in at the end of the narrow driveway. I scanned the bushes but saw no one. Had the Phaeton driver come back to get me? *Holy crap.*

"Nothing holy about it," a voice said from behind me. A voice that made me feel warm all over. Owen Glendower's voice. "But if you choose to see it that way, be my guest."

Chapter 4

"Excuse me?" I turned on my heel. "*You're* the Phaeton?"

"No, that would be my *car*," he said. "*I'm* Owen Glendower. I believe we've met?"

I should have been relieved, but Owen's voice inspired more of a frenzied response. Suspicion. Surprise. *Lust.*

I didn't take his offered hand. "Funny. But if you came to move your monstrosity out of my way, don't bother. I'm about to call a cab."

"Monstrosity?" He laughed. "My car? You drive an SUV. I fail to see how mine ranks as monstrous."

"I suppose it's harmless without you behind the wheel."

"You take issue with my driving?"

"I take issue with *you*."

"I thought we'd rather hit it off." He closed the distance. "Or was the seventh-grade courting ritual all for naught."

"Seventh-grade courting ritual?"

"You pretend to ignore me. I pretend to ignore you. Meanwhile we can't keep our eyes off each other. Very junior high, don't you think?"

I blushed. He'd caught me under a waning wine buzz. My mind was slow with the sharp comebacks. But whoa, back up. He couldn't take his eyes off me?

"I saw you staring at me," he said. "You cast a reflection too, you know."

I still didn't know what to say.

"Your sister's about to look out the window any moment now," he said, with enough conviction that I believed him. "She'll see us together and wonder what we're about. Why don't you let me drive you home?"

"You?" I half-laughed, a pitiful effect since we both knew there was no levity behind it. "No thanks. I can have a cab here in minutes."

Forty-five minutes, if I was lucky.

"If you like." He shrugged. "I'll wait with you."

I'd expected more of a fight. "No need. I don't want to inconvenience you."

"Then be a love and get in my car, will you? I don't bite."

"Hmph." I wasn't so sure. In fact, I'd rather been hoping he might. "How much wine have *you* had?"

"Not near as much as you," he said.

"Fine." What the hell. A clean car beat a smoky cab any day. "But I'm in the city, South End."

"I know where you live, Kate," he said, opening the passenger door for me.

I paused. "You what?" I'd never realized danger had an aphrodisiac effect on me. My body practically convulsed with an unexpected throb of desire, mixed with slight uneasiness. "You're on my payroll," he said, "in case you haven't noticed those occasional commission checks from Glendower Enterprises. You've done a few houses for us."

It seemed logical, and yet . . . "As if you have time to examine names and addresses on every little check sent out. Don't you have staff to handle that kind of thing?"

He leaned in close. "I pay attention to detail. My ability to hone in on the seemingly insignificant is what put me where I am today."

Seemingly insignificant? Ouch. I got in, no more questions. His car smelled of leather and old money. Or was it cigars? I felt light-headed in a way that made me want to let loose and drift away, as if caught up in a smoky haze.

My brain began to buzz anew, a pleasant tingling that made me feel better all over and reminded me why I liked wine. I closed my eyes to savor the magic while it lasted, but being so close to Owen, somehow I couldn't relax.

We rode in silence for a few minutes, and I stole a glance at him. He sat straight behind the wheel, nice posture, hands at ten and two. He could have been a textbook perfect driver. But he wasn't fooling me.

"So if you know everything, how come you almost missed your exit earlier tonight?" I asked, turning to face him.

He shrugged, not taking his gaze from the road. "I did it on purpose. To get a rise out of you."

"You didn't even know me then." I laughed. "Aha, see? You really *don't* know everything."

He offered no defense. "I know that if I asked you to invite me in for a drink," he said, after a minute, "you wouldn't say no."

Damn, he had me. I didn't want to say no, but I had

the option of proving him wrong. The question was, did I want to be right or get laid? I was leaning toward the latter. I could be right any time I wanted at work. I was the boss. But sex? It had been so very long for me.

"My sister warned me about you," I said, buying time to mull my options.

"Did she now?" He glanced at me, the smile playing about his full lips. "Let me guess. She told you I'm the devil."

"In fact, she did," I said. "Should I be afraid?"

"What do you think?" He glanced at me. "Do I scare you?"

"Not really." I yawned and looked out the window, all for effect. Of course I was scared. Scared that I would like the way he felt in bed next to me. Scared that I would want to see him again. Scared that I would start to need a man just when I had my life all worked out.

But did I have it worked out, really? If the right man came along, who was I to deny him a chance? I wasn't sure about finding Mr. Right, or if there really was such a thing, but Owen felt right for now. Too right. It was almost frightening how right.

"You don't have to be frightened, Kate." He reached across the seat and placed his hand on me, his warmth radiating through my cotton dress right down to my bones. In that second, I believed him. I probably would have believed anything, he felt so good. "I'm not a bad guy. Despite popular belief."

One look at him with his rumpled Colin Farrell hair playing against his suave Pierce Brosnan self-assurance told me that I didn't have to worry about a second date, or even a call back. By all accounts, Owen Glendower was not the kind of man who played for keeps when it came to women. A hot and sweaty one-night stand chock full of earth-shattering sex and he would be on his way. What was the harm? I owed it to myself to indulge in all he had to offer. I thought of the one-liner from the hair dye commercials.

Because I'm worth it.

I decided that being right was totally overrated. I gave Owen what I hoped was my sexiest smile and said, "Do you want to come in for a drink?" as he turned the Phaeton onto my street.

He looked at me, his eyes dark as a midnight sky lit by the glow of the moon, and smiled. "I thought you'd never ask."

"So tell me about Kate Markham," he said, gesturing with the empty glass in his left hand just enough to make the ice cubes clink.

Silhouetted by the city lights outside my townhouse parlor window, he looked like he'd stepped right out of a magazine ad for the perfect life. He oozed sex, charisma, and a deeply vested interest in me. At the moment, it was good to be Kate.

"No need to dwell on what we both know," I said, reaching for the bottle and crossing the room to refill his glass. The Laphroaig, a peaty single malt Scotch, was a gift from a client, not something I would normally buy. I'd barely sipped at mine, desperate to hang on to whatever brain cells remained intact for the evening. "Tell me about Owen Glendower."

"The tabloid version or the reality? I'm afraid the tabloids make me sound far more interesting."

"I can pick up a *People* magazine at the grocery store, thank you." My aim had been to get him away from the window and settled on the buttery leather sofa behind us, but he seemed content to stand, so I played along.

"Tell you what," he said, moving closer. "Let's not talk about us at all."

Less talk, more action. Now we were getting somewhere. My gaze caught on the dark shadow of new beard surrounding his lush lips. Just enough growth to provide some velvety friction. *Purr.* I could appreciate a man with the sense to keep a trim fringe of facial hair. But then, there was a lot to appreciate when it came to Owen Glendower.

Smooth as the Laphroaig, he set our glasses on a corner table and pressed his body close to mine. The scent of Scotch on his breath was far more intoxicating than what had been in the glass. Any second now, I expected him to kiss me. Instead, he traced the outline of my lips with his finger. My lipstick had long worn away so it did not leave a smudge, thank goodness.

"Exquisite," he pronounced, right before he leaned in for the kiss.

The taste of him tingled over every inch of my skin. His lips were still cold from the Scotch's ice, but his breath was hot enough to melt me on the spot. I wanted to climb into his mouth and make a home there, but he'd already ended the kiss. Still, his body was lean and hard. And, oh yeah, hard.

"Kate," he said. "Oh, Kate."

Oh, oh, Owen. Just being near him was enough to make my body throb with need. More. Please more.

He could have had me right there on my newly polished pine floor. But he didn't. He backed away.

"I really should go. It has been a lovely evening," he said, regret in his voice.

"You don't have to go," I said, probably too fast. "I

mean, you're welcome to—" *Stay, please stay!* "Hang around and finish your drink."

"I'm driving."

"Right." Was he waiting for an invitation? "Um, well, I do have—" *A spare bed? A spare space in my bed?*

"Big meeting tomorrow." He waved me off before I could make any embarrassing offers. "I really do have to go."

"Tomorrow," I repeated. "I've got the showing, too, so—" So, phew, good thing I narrowly escaped an evening of mind-blowing sexcapades. *Yeah.* "Well, thanks for the ride home."

"Hm," he said, dark eyebrow arching.

"Hm?" Mine wouldn't arch. Dumb eyebrow.

"How are you getting to work tomorrow? We left your car behind."

"I'll have an associate pick me up." Damn. Did I blow a chance to see him again?

"No," he said. "No need. I'll have a minion drop your car off for you."

"A minion?"

"They're good for that sort of thing." His mouth curved in a mysterious smile.

"Right. Minions. Must be nice."

"There are advantages."

"To being rich?" I said, and wished I could take it back. Stupid. The last thing I wanted was for him to think I had any interest in his wealth.

"No," he laughed, a throaty rumble. "*To being the devil.*"

I caught his gaze in time to fix on a fleeting fiery spark. The devil? A thrill ran up my spine and cascaded in hot tendrils down the length of me. A night with the devil sounded like such wicked fun. Besides, I wasn't ready for it all to end.

He headed for the door, but I reached for his hand to ease him toward the sofa. "The devil wouldn't be in such a hurry to leave." I tried to muster a sultry femme fatale moue.

The second he turned back to me, he had me pressed up against him. He smiled down at me. "Oh? Suddenly you seem so well acquainted with the devil. So tell me, what would he do next?"

I sucked in a breath. "Surely the devil would stick around to make an effort to steal my soul."

"Ah." He slid his hands to capture my wrists and urged me past the sofa, pinning me flat up against the wall behind the door, my arms raised up over my head. Slowly, his hands traveled down, heat searing my skin straight through my thin cotton sleeves. He paused at my shoulders, hands poised above my breasts. My nipples puckered in sweet anticipation, but he stopped there. He lowered his head to trace my collarbone with his tongue, adding light nips with his teeth when he reached my throat.

His tongue slid in and out of his mouth, tracing slow circles along the column of my neck. I rolled my head back and inhaled deeply, desperate to slow my breathing and linger with him pressed solidly against me, his knee begging entry just between my eager thighs. By the time his lips found mine, my hips rocked against him, seeking him, leaving no question of what I wanted. He deepened his kiss until I thought I might die from a combination of desire and lack of air.

My knees buckled. He caught me around the waist as my hands dropped limply to my sides.

Wow, I thought. I still didn't have enough breath to actually speak.

"Not bad," he said.

Not bad? Ouch.

"But I'm not sure your soul's worth all the effort of stealing. You've been a very bad girl."

"What?" I mocked offense. "Me? Bad?"

"Very bad." He nodded. "So bad, in fact, that I rather think I'll need more than merely your soul."

"More?" My knees got weak again. It was a good thing I was still in his arms.

"All of you." Playful, he tapped my nose. "In due time. I imagine you'll need a fair amount of courting first. Your soul would cost more than dinner and a movie, after all. You're sure to drive a hard bargain for the entire package."

I grew weak in the knees a third time, and this time it wasn't from lust, it was from déjà vu. Why did the conversation seem so familiar? Then it hit me: Bennie's dinner party, the fix up with Rob the Garden Gnome, my smart-assed comment about dinner with the devil. I looked up at Owen. He *couldn't* have been there. How did he know?

"Sleep well, Kate," he said. And before I could say anything else, he was out the door.

Thoughts of Owen kept me awake all night. Stronger than a double shot of espresso, he coursed through my veins, buzzing, whirring, making me higher than a kite. Higher than the space shuttle. No matter how hard I tried, I couldn't come down. Instead of fighting it, I got up and paced.

I'd need a fair amount of courting, isn't that what

he'd said? As old-fashioned as the concept of courting seemed to be, it had a very exciting ring to it. I imagined me at the balcony in a diaphanous nightdress, Owen serenading from below. Presents of flowers, candy, and the odd strand of pearls. No, pearls were bad luck as a gift between lovers. Diamonds would suffice. Hey, he was Owen Glendower. A girl could expect the best.

I imagined picking up the phone to hear his velvet purr coming down the line, but he hadn't even asked for my phone number. Not that he didn't have ways to obtain it. My pulse raced. I tried to stay calm, but all sense of reality flew out the window and I was a dreamy-eyed girl again. The high school Katie Markham, jumping at every ring of the phone thinking Bart Haywood was calling her at last.

Poor girl. She'd given up on Bart by the end of junior year and ended up dating shmucky Tommy Moriarty. Not one to let go of a dream, she ended up breaking up with Tommy and losing her virginity to Bart after drinking too much at a kegger. Bart told everyone and never called her once after the fact. Humiliating.

Had I not learned a thing after all these years? The perfect man did not exist. Even if he did, he wasn't for me. And even if he was, he would prove himself not worth it in the end. I was better off on my own. Owen Glendower could stick to his supermodels.

Still, cheap sex had its appeal. In brief doses. Every now and then.

I breathed deep. Nothing about Owen Glendower said cheap. If he'd stayed, he would have given me the Rolls-Royce of rolls in the hay. Sex with Owen would be like flying in first class. Once you've done it, you never want to go back to coach. Owen represented unparalleled comfort, luxury, and endless indulgences. Upon comparison, all other men would be reduced to standard service, no leg room, and a backache upon arrival.

At just past four A.M., I traded my Owen rush for the real caffeine buzz of a pot of coffee, showered, and got ready to face the day. Some men were meant to remain wild fantasies, nothing more. I needed to put him out of my mind. There were more important things to focus on.

The holidays loomed. My finances were sound, but a sale would serve to boost my visibility. Realty was not a winter business. If I could manage to keep the market hopping through the Christmas slump, I would be worth my weight in gold to sellers everywhere. Considering my recent habit of late-night snacking, my weight in gold was a pirate's wet dream.

Unfortunately, there were not many pirates around to claim this booty. Owen Glendower was out, but I hadn't given up on Johnny Depp. Jack Sparrow, take me away.

Chapter 5

By eight, I was ready to hit the road. Fortunately, I looked out my window before calling Val or a cab. My Aviator was parked outside along a prime spot of curb by the building's front door. Talk about service. I had to look into getting my hands on some minions. I didn't even want to think about how they moved my car without keys. I trusted that when Owen Glendower hired minions, he went for the best.

True to my suspicions, the Aviator was spotless inside and out. No sign of forced entry or crossed wires. The engine started without incident, and everything was right with the world. Besides the fact that I thought I could get used to the idea of being Owen Glendower's girlfriend. My pulse raced again. I didn't even need to stop for coffee on the way. My Glendower high still rated above any caffeine source for stimulation.

On the way into work, I dialed Mother on my cell phone. If I didn't check in with her at least once every twenty-four hours, she would start leaving frantic messages for me, worried that I'd fallen victim to some horrible tragedy. The morning drive to work was the perfect time to check in with Mother, with the handy excuse of traffic to end the call early.

Mother answered the phone, her voice overpowered by high-pitched squealing and laughter in the background. "Hey Mom," I said. "What's going on over there?" Activity at Mother's house at—I checked my car clock—eight-thirty was almost unheard of since she'd retired from her bank job two years earlier.

"I've got the kids today," she said, sounding distracted.

"The kids? *Bennie's* kids? Why?" When I'd left the party last night, everything had been fine. I couldn't imagine why Mother would have Spencer and Sarah on a school day unless something had happened.

"You mean you don't know? Oh, it's *won*derful! Patrick's investor, that delightful man, decided that Patrick isn't spending enough time at home with Bernadette and the kids. So I have the kids this morning while Bennie and Patrick get them all packed. They're going to Disney World. All expenses paid."

"All expenses? You've got to be kidding."

"Patrick's investor set the whole thing up for them. He called this morning and told them to start packing, just like that."

"Wow, he must have really put the minions to work," I said, before I thought the better of it. A whole week's vacation planned in an hour? "I mean, that's really nice of him."

"Isn't it? The article they ran on him in *People* magazine made him sound like a real hothead, but I guess it was all lies. You can't believe everything you read."

Mother *always* believed everything she read, and she

read a lot. She had lifetime subscriptions to *People,* the *National Enquirer,* and a few other tabloids.

"No, you can't," I said absently. I was happy for Bennie, but frustrated. How was I supposed to pump her for valuable information about Owen if she was on vacation with the Mickey Mouse Club? I had to act fast. The car behind me honked, and I realized I'd been sitting at a green light. "Look, Mom, I have to go. But I'll call you later."

I dialed Bennie.

She answered on the first ring, a flustered "Yes?"

"Bennie, it's me. Mom just told me the good news."

"Isn't it wonderful?" Bennie, breathless, was obviously rushing around in haste to pack. "Owen just called up with the flight information and told us to get going."

"Out of the blue? Or did you know last night?"

"I had no idea. I guess he thought it up over dinner. He said he was giving us the gift of family time."

"Family time." Okay. But why? "So just like that?"

"Just like that. He's arranged *everything.* We don't even have to pack if we don't want to. He has an account set up at the hotel boutiques. Incredible."

"Incredibly generous. I guess he's not the devil after all?"

"Oh, he is. Trust me. He's up to *something.*" From her tone, I knew now wasn't the time to bring up our little make-out session the night before. "But I don't care. The kids are so excited. We're going to leave our worries behind and have a good time."

"Good for you, Ben. You deserve it."

"You don't know the half of it." She huffed. "Patrick's run himself ragged for Owen in the past year. He keeps an inhuman schedule and expects everyone else to follow suit. We definitely deserve this. Listen, I'm expecting a call from the vet. Kristin's on vacation and I can't find Bert and Ernie's vaccination papers in case Mom decides she needs to kennel them. And I have to call the school." Click. She hung up, just like that.

Inhuman. Bennie's word choice stuck in my mind.

If only I could get my mind off Owen's last kiss. Just thinking about it made me hot enough to percolate coffee. So much for the October chill. I had to cool down before the windows started to fog. I flipped on the AC, cranked up the stereo, and drove the rest of the way to work, praying that singing along with "Tainted Love," would take my mind off Owen Glendower once and for all.

Normally, my morning coffee buzz delivered the appropriate jolt of energy to combat the stress of morning traffic. This morning, caffeine seemed a weak alternative to a bigger better buzz, the Owen tingle. If only I could bottle the feeling. I dreaded to think that I'd become dependent so soon. I probably just needed more coffee. I was lucky I made it to the Elmwood house before I had a traffic-induced meltdown. Next time, I would get a bigger cup, and maybe a straight espresso chaser.

I got inside, poured myself a refill from the jug of coffee I'd brought to serve guests, and took a look around. Natural light filtered through the big picture window over the family room, bathing the whole open floor plan, from the back porch to the front door, in a soft ethereal glow.

With earthy wood, rugged stone, soft fabrics, and the flowers to add a delicate nuance, the place looked gorgeous. I was grateful I'd stayed late last night to get mostly everything done for today's showing.

My cell phone rang as I was heading up the stairs to check out the bedrooms.

"Curtain Call, Kate speaking." I tried to answer in professional mode between the hours of nine and five. It was ten minutes to nine, but close enough.

"Kate, hi. Glad I caught you." It was Debby, the Realtor who'd called me in to handle today's showing. "I'm sorry for your trouble, but I need to cancel today."

"Cancel?" I stifled the wave of dread. Canceling meant rescheduling. With my appointments tightly booked for the next two weeks, rescheduling could be a problem.

"I've sold the house! Can you believe it? Sight unseen. We had a drive-by early this morning, some corporate bigwig. He fell in love with the house and bought it on the spot. For full asking price!"

Debby could barely contain her excitement. I tried to match her enthusiasm, but the fact was that I'd lost the commission.

"Great news." With the holidays coming, a lost commission left me less than thrilled.

"Yes, but don't move the furniture out yet," Debby said. "I'll be taking the buyer around later today and I have a feeling he'll want to buy a few pieces."

"Sure." I agreed. "I'll keep it all as is. Let me know what he wants. Congratulations again." I hung up.

At least I could pick up a few bucks out of the furniture sales. Still, I hated to lose a chance to prove my worth. Houses were supposed to move after I'd worked my magic, not before the buyer even stepped inside. Damn.

I called the florist, to cancel that morning's order,

and Val, but she wasn't answering her cell phone. She was probably en route, which gave me time for more coffee and a conciliatory donut. Or six. It was gearing up to be a half-dozen donut kind of day.

While I sucked down the sugar fix, I broke out my laptop and Googled Owen Glendower.

Pages of links came up: business profiles, acquisitions, developments, advice for fledgling investors. I clicked one that boasted a biography. Odd, it listed his accomplishments of the past business year but nothing else. No birth date, no education or previous experience, no mention of family. It was as if Owen had popped, fully formed and Armani-clad, out of the womb and into the boardroom.

Before last night, I hadn't paid much attention to his name but I *had* heard it. Surely he'd been around longer than a year. He couldn't have just dropped out of the sky and landed his company on the Fortune 500.

I continued to click links in search of information but couldn't find any reference to Owen's previous history. He couldn't be much older than forty, I decided. But who knew, with plastic surgery, good nutrition, and fitness regimes? Maybe he had a shadowy past. It was possible he'd spent time in jail. International investors got into all sorts of trouble.

Other links referenced an Owain Glyndwr, a fifteenth-century nobleman and leader of a Welsh rebellion often accused of—*mental brake screech*—being the devil.

Bennie's words came back to haunt me. *The man is the devil himself.* I laughed out loud. *The devil.* In *my* apartment? Sure. But on some level, it scared me. A thrilling tingly sort of scared, the kind adolescent girls got at slumber party séances. I was freaked out, intrigued, wishing it would stop, and wanting more all at once. I took a second to indulge myself with supposing it could be true. I'd dated Republicans, why not the devil?

But what would the devil want with me? My soul? Doubtful. With some of the stunts I'd pulled in college, my soul wasn't much of a catch. My sister was the more likely target. She'd been a perfect child, now a perfect wife and mother. I didn't think she'd ever slept with anyone but Patrick. Bennie actually served on a few charity boards, for goodness' sake. Barring a tendency for high drama and the need for regular attention, Bennie had no serious flaws. What devil would pass up a chance to corrupt Saint Bennie?

I tried to imagine him with red skin, horns, and a pointed tail. No, it didn't fit. Devils didn't dress in designer suits and walk around Boston buying up land and building million dollar developments.

Our last kiss sprang to mind. His soft lips. The taste of him, cloves and mint and exotic spices. And the heat, the odd radiant heat that seemed to roll off him in waves and warm me down to my toes. What was that?

It was magic. Something I couldn't name. A thrill I'd never felt. Odd and new to me, yes, but there was nothing evil about it. The sex could be good enough to border on supernatural, but that didn't mean any mysterious forces were afoot. The man was skilled. He had the wealth and experience to build a reputation, perhaps hide some less flattering things from his past. Maybe he'd even renamed himself to better match his circumstances as he climbed the corporate ladder. Who could blame him? If the devil had used Owain Glyndwr, the name held some panache. And it all made me wonder whom he had been before, and what brought him to where he was now? It made me curious in a dangerous way, the way that made me want to get to know him and really understand. I doubted he had that kind of relationship in mind.

I had to face facts. Even if he wanted to see me again, what would happen? We would go out a few times, have some amazing sex. Before long, amazing sex would turn to predictable sex that would fade to occasional mundane couplings and he'd move on, unfazed, with my heart hanging in the balance. I could get all too caught up in the game, and I didn't have time for games. I had big plans.

A few days ago, I'd been ready to head back to my doctor to try a second insemination attempt. Was I really willing to put it all on hold and contemplate a new direction all because I'd met a man?

Not that I could help taking an extra second to *imagine* being with the man. Candlelight dinners, star-studded movie premieres, long weekends in a secluded beach house filled with servants to cater to our every whim. Servants? No. He'd called them minions. Minions. Very devilish of him. I smiled at the thought.

"Kate, you here?" Val usually beat me to appointments. She sounded appropriately surprised to see my car out front.

I shook it off and shut down the computer before she could make it to the kitchen. *The devil?* Right. I needed to get some sleep.

"Just checking on some assessments."

"The place looks great," she said, ducking in around the breakfast nook. "Now all we have to do is wait for the florist and we're in business."

"No business." I met her gaze. "Debby sold the house this morning. I tried to call to tell you but you didn't pick up."

"Dang," Val said. Not that it mattered so much to her. She got paid the same regardless. "There goes my day. Well, I guess I could get a start on my Christmas shopping. Unless you need me at the office?"

"Take the day off." I shrugged. "We'd planned on being here all day anyway. Nothing at the office that can't wait 'til tomorrow."

"You should go home and get some rest." Val studied me through narrowed eyes. "What happened?"

"What do you mean?" I stifled a yawn.

"You look like crap is what I mean. What did you do last night? Anyone else, I would say you stayed out drinking 'til dawn. Considering it's you, no. Are you coming down with something?"

"That must be it." Owen fever. Or withdrawal. Or maybe Val was right. I was probably just coming down with something. "I think I will go home and straight to bed."

"Good idea. Do you need anything? I can bring you some soup later."

I laughed. Val was such a mother hen. "I'll be fine. Thanks anyway. See you at the office tomorrow morning."

By the time I navigated my way through traffic to return home, I was exhausted. Absolutely spent. I'd come down from my Owen high and slammed back to earth with a thud. Which was all well and good. I probably needed a good thud to rouse me from ridiculous daydreams of dangerous men. I only hoped Val didn't shop herself ragged because we had some major shopping to do at work later in the week.

It was my favorite part of the job, but scouring antique stores and retail outlets for just the right piece took tons of energy, and I was already on empty. A day in bed would do me some good.

But when I stepped through my front door, all thoughts of sleep fled. On my parlor table, right inside the entry hall, was a huge bouquet of peonies arranged in a stunning crystal vase. I knew without looking that it was Waterford. It matched the pattern I kept on display in my dining room cabinet, the crystal that I'd inherited from my great-grandma—my father's mother. I didn't have to read the card to know who they were from.

Breathless, I leaned forward and inhaled their sweet scent. The large, luscious blooms spilled over the edge of the vase. I'd always hated roses, too clichéd. Peonies were my favorite. How did he know? How did he get them here?

A chill shot up my spine. My door had been locked. Securely. It was late autumn, so all my windows had been shut tight and locked against the coming cold. Minions, I thought to myself. Those tricky little minions of his. Impressive.

Scary.

I reached for the card. Eager. Excited. Desperate to confirm what my heart already knew.

The devil *may* care.

I hugged the card to my chest, almost afraid to look. When I opened it at last, I read with interest, but growing alarm.

Once you have found her, never let her go.

It was cryptic, odd, but intriguing. No signature. Never let her go? A sharp stab of panic accompanied the quote. Never? What did he mean? He'd been in my apartment, for goodness' sake. When I wasn't even home. My heart pounded faster.

My knees shook. I couldn't decide if I was frightened or thrilled. I only knew that I was suddenly over-whelmed. Who was this man? If not the devil, then who? How did he know me, the real me, the hidden me. The me that remained unknown to over ten years' worth of men, hundreds of dates later. He'd hit on just the thing to stir me only hours after making my acquaintance.

I took a calming breath, deep, steady, as I'd learned in my one day at yoga. My gaze shot to my dining room cabinet, great-grandmother's Waterford. Dusty, but all there. He could have studied it while he was here and taken note that I had almost a full set of stemware and a candy dish but I was missing the vase. He'd warned me that he paid attention to detail.

A framed print of Manet's *Peonies* hung in a dusty corner near the china cabinet. Aha. Details. He hardly had to guess that I loved peonies. He'd simply observed my framed print and taken it from there. Smart man. I had nothing to fear. What did I expect? He was a man with drive, resources, and a determination to "court" me properly. Isn't that what he'd said? Perhaps he'd meant it after all.

The breaking in was a bit much, but the result was worth it. The Owen tingle returned, sending a jolt of energy and pure heat straight through me. Had I been tired? I could scarcely recall. I only knew the sudden, unadulterated enthusiasm of being pursued by a desir-able man. His feelings had to be mutual, didn't they? Else why would he go through the trouble?

I couldn't wait to see him again, even though my instincts warned me to be cautious.

Cautious? If Bennie knew about this, she would accuse me of thinking too much. She would tell me I should run with it, throw caution to the wind. I wished I could call her, ask her opinion, but I remembered that Owen had sent her out of town.

Convenient. The stab again, a quick pulse of panic.

I wanted desperately to relax and go with it, but I just couldn't. I studied the quote again, certain I knew it from somewhere.

I read it again, out loud: "Once you have found her, never let her go."

"Some Enchanted Evening!" It came to me at last. From the Rogers and Hammerstein classic, *South Pacific,* one of my favorite movies of all time. Rossano Brazzi's Emile broke my heart with his mooning over Mitzi Gaynor's Nellie Forbush. How many Sunday afternoons at Gran's had I spent watching *South Pacific* on TV? I hadn't seen it in years but I remembered it well. It all came back to me.

One of my first impressions of love and romance came from watching *South Pacific.* Cornball Arkansas girl, tortured heroes, and taboo affairs of the heart.

Owen couldn't have been more endearing, and yet I was still skeptical. Was I falling for a wonderful guy, or did I want to wash that man right out of my hair?

Hours later, the phone rang.

"Kate. I've missed you." His voice shot through my veins like a drug, an instant rush.

"Owen. It's only been"—I checked my watch and did the math—"ten hours."

"Eleven," he corrected. "I restrained myself until the eleventh hour."

"Okay." He had to restrain himself? My heart surged. "Thank you for the flowers. And the vase. Oh, and the car delivery. It made it much easier to get to work this morning."

"No need to thank me. I practically forced you to leave your car last night. It was the least I could do."

"You're quite the gentleman."

"Some say."

"Only some? What about the others?"

"It isn't fit for a lady's ears." I could hear the smile in his voice.

"Who told you I was a lady?" Meow.

"Mm." He purred back. "I wanted to take you to dinner tonight but I'm afraid something's come up."

"Something?" My heart sank. I was reminded of an old *Brady Bunch* show, Greg coaching Marsha how to politely turn down a date. Something suddenly came up . . .

"A problem with a recent acquisition," he clarified. "Not to worry. I'm sure it will pass. I'll call you in a few days."

Click. Just like that, he was gone. The peonies, the vase, the note. Surely it wasn't a brush off? Still, I knew what I was going to do with the rest of my night.

I was going to wash my hair.

Chapter 6

I didn't hear from him for a few days. Then, one morning while getting ready for work, I put my blow dryer down just in time to hear the doorbell. I ran to get it, but no one was there. Instead, a small package sat waiting for me. I looked left and right; no sign of anyone. Minions?

I carried the package inside and ripped into the brown paper like a kid at Christmas.

A DVD of *South Pacific*. No note, but I didn't need one to know who it was from. I couldn't wait to watch it, but work beckoned.

My latest Curtain Call venture was an ultra contemporary and ultra hard-to-furnish house that I'd taken to calling Viva Las Venus, straight from the *Jetsons*. I didn't have anything in stock, so Val and I were going shopping. I was only grateful that the previous owners were leaving some custom-made pieces behind. It made my work that much easier. Most of our showings were in brand new constructions, but occasionally we got an established residence or a hard-to-sell larger estate.

I hummed "Some Enchanted Evening" as I bundled up in my new cashmere coat over a simple silk blouse, slim black trousers, and spike heeled boots. The temperatures were unusually low for this time of year, and I was prone to chills. Lately, though, I had been feverishly warm, and I had a feeling it had nothing to do with the weather.

Once you have found her, never let her go. The lyrics echoed in my mind as I stood in the foyer watching out the glass storm door for Val's arrival. Dried brown leaves blew past the door, down past the shop windows and restaurants, and across the street to the T station. Just last week, it seemed, the leaves had been a brilliant orange, and not long before that, green. Time flew by with the wind, and I could hear the ticking of my own clock over the sound of rustling leaves. Maybe Owen was going to try to hold on to me after all. I didn't exactly mind the idea. I couldn't help imagining the baby we could make together. His dark hair, my light eyes. Or maybe his eyes. He had that mysterious spark. But I was getting way ahead of myself. Val pulled up, beeping her horn and saving me from my own nonsense. Val's most prized possession was a covered-cab pickup truck, perfect for hauling furniture, which had previously belonged to her lowlife cheating scum husband. Her husband had called it the Matterhorn, but Val had renamed it Waltzing Matilda, Mattie for short.

"Sorry," I said as I climbed my way into the truck's high cab, where Kirsty MacColl's "In These Shoes?" blared over the truck's stereo system. "I left my mountain-climbing gear inside."

"S'okay," Val said. "Just don't scuff ol' Mattie's hide with them fancy boots."

"You ready for some serious shopping?" I asked as she pulled into traffic.

"Born ready," Val said, then went back to singing along with the CD. In my head, I heard a different tune. "Some Enchanted Evening" played a constant rotation on my internal stereo. I couldn't tune it out. Just like I couldn't stop thinking about the man responsible for putting it there in the first place. The tingle came again, filling me with instant energy.

"Okay, fess up," Val said when the song ended.

"Fess what?"

"Last time I saw you, you looked like crap. Today, you're radiant."

"Radiant?" I knew I'd been blushing, off and on, mostly when I thought of Owen in the role of Emile, the sexy French planter. But radiant?

"Absolutely glowing. You're gorgeous. And the outfit? Come on. Who are you planning on running into? Don't tell me you've finally converted Julio."

Julio was the dashing but all too gay owner of La Flat, one of several stores we were visiting that day. "No dice. I'm an ottoman short of a full living room set for poor Julio's liking."

"Come on, girlfriend." Occasionally, Val forgot she was a middle-aged white chick. Too much Jerry Springer. "Spill. Who's your daddy?"

"Who's my daddy?" I laughed at Val. "What do you mean?"

"You're seeing someone. The angst, the mood swings, the new clothes. High heels, for shopping? I don't think so. You're supposed to be the sensible one, remember?"

With Val as a partner, it didn't take much to rate as the sensible one.

"I felt like heels today. That's all. As for the mood swings, well . . . you know."

"Know what?"

I blushed. "I'm retaining water. I figured I would dress up a little to try to counterbalance the water weight."

"Hm." Val seemed to consider whether she believed me or not. "So there's no hot new Latin lover waiting in the wings?"

I was tempted to tell Val everything, but I just wasn't ready to share my Owen fantasies. Yet.

Still, he was on my mind all day, and once during the afternoon, when Val and I were negotiating the price on a red plastic bench sofa for the Viva Las Venus library, I glimpsed a figure across the crowded room who looked like Owen. Dark hair, tailored suit, six foot something.

"My God, is he following me?" I blurted without thinking.

"What? Who?" Val looked around, eager.

Then he moved out from behind the room divider column and I could see clearly that it was not Owen. Same height, same pleasing build. Wrong tattoo. This guy had a tattoo across his neck that said something in Chinese script. It was not Owen. I was being silly.

"Sorry." I laughed it off. "I thought I saw Julio. Heaven forbid he catch us shopping at a competing store."

"You got that right." Val rolled her eyes. "We could forget our twenty-percent discount. But that's not Julio."

"Right you are."

"Like he would even be caught dead here. They sell plastic."

"So does Julio," I defended. "But he calls his Plastique."

We laughed. I was saved.

Still, the Owen buzz lasted me the rest of the day. I could barely calm down.

At lunch, I had to forgo my normal midday diet coke in favor of something decaffeinated. Wine.

The next day, after I spent hours furnishing Viva Las Venus, the realtor called to cancel the open house. Out of the blue, Viva Las Venus had sold without even making it to list on the market. It was unusual for two listings to sell without showing, even in the soft market that came with the holiday season. Still, I braced myself for the worst when my phone rang again. Not another cancellation?

"Bali Hi," said a voice, low and melodic. I breathed a sigh of relief when I recognized the voice as Owen's.

"That's Bali Ha'i, silly." That he could make me smile on such a wretched day was a big point in his favor.

"No matter. Did you enjoy my gift?"

"Very much. I haven't had a chance to watch it yet but it looks like my schedule is freeing up."

"Oh? Business isn't good?"

"Business is great, for real estate agents. For me, not so much. Everything seems to be selling the second it hits the market." Or, in the case of casa Viva Las Venus, even before.

"A hot market is a good thing." Easy for him to say. "You'll reap the rewards soon enough. Besides, this gives you more time for personal affairs."

Affairs? My heart banged against my ribs. Hard.

"Not much," I said, reluctant. "I have two more open houses to set up over the next two weeks."

"So a little jaunt to the South Pacific is out of the question? I was thinking we could find our own little Bali Ha'i."

I laughed. He *was* kidding, right? "Sounds like heaven. I'm afraid all jaunts to Bali Ha'i will have to wait until after Thanksgiving. Until then, I'm pretty much booked."

And thank goodness. I didn't need business to get any worse.

"Until then, hm?" He sounded distracted. "Fair enough. I'll be in touch."

Click.

"Hello?" I spoke into blank air space. Just like that, he was gone. Was it something I said? Men. I'd never been able to figure them out.

I picked up the phone to dial Bennie for advice, then snapped it closed when I remembered she was still away. Damn. My sister always knew how to handle crises with men. There must be a relationship gene that skipped generations and totally bypassed firstborns. For now, I had to live with that fact that I'd Bali Ha'i'd myself right out of a date.

Like most highs, the Bali Ha'i didn't last. The next day, a third showing cancelled for an early sale and I was feeling pretty low. Owen called as if on cue.

"Are you sure you can't make time for one dinner?"

"For you, anything." I wasn't about to risk losing a date this time. Plus, just hearing his voice made my heart thunder. He was better than caffeine *and* exercise. A good thing, since exercise wasn't on the agenda.

If he had this effect on my heart, I wondered what he could do for my thighs. "As it happens, my weekend is suddenly free. Which night?"

"Now. Tonight. I can pick you up in an hour." A pause. "I really need to see you, Kate."

His urgency brought my mind back to our first kiss. My hand reached up to follow the line of my collarbone and trace slow circles at my throat, a wasted effort as my fingers lacked the heat and magic of his tongue. My mouth went dry at the vivid recollection, but I managed to say yes before hanging up the phone.

By the end of an hour, I was ready. I'd just hooked a dangly crystal earring through my ear when I caught sight of the stretch limousine pulling up out front.

"Wow," I said out loud. Was it too late to run and change? Not knowing where we were headed, I'd pulled on a pale silk blouse with dark tailored trousers. Safe, I'd thought. An outfit that, with the right jewelry, could fit in as dressed up or down.

But a limousine? I needed bigger jewelry.

My breath caught as Owen stepped out of the car. He never failed to amaze me. Simply looking at him filled me with a hollow hunger, the same way hearing his voice made my heart go wild. Much to my relief, his outfit was almost the male equivalent to mine: dark pants, white shirt, leather jacket. Doing my best to check the sigh that rose to my lips, I walked out to meet him.

"Hey, handsome." My range of flirty nicknames was limited at best. I didn't get out much.

He smiled as if he didn't mind. "Kate." He leaned in for the cheek kiss. "Good to see you."

I broke away from his leather embrace and allowed him to help me into the back of the car, pleased that I had avoided the dilemma of making a graceful car entrance in a skirt. His scent, male as rutting boar but ethereal as mountain clouds, lingered on my skin where he had kissed me.

I loved that smell, something by Escada if I guessed right.

"Magnetism?" I asked.

He laughed. "I try. Is it working?"

"I mean the fragrance you're wearing. Is it Escada's Magnetism?"

"Fragrance?" He seemed puzzled. "I believe the magnetism is all my own."

Right. Well, fine. He wasn't required to give away all his secrets. For my part, I had no plan to tell him that my Estée Lauder matte foundation concealed a small pimple forming on my chin. Some secrets were good.

"So where are we headed?"

"That's a secret." He smiled knowingly.

It was maddening the way he seemed to know what was on my mind. Maddening, but a little intriguing. And somewhat appealing, the more I thought about it. If we stayed together, I could work on mind control techniques. How cool would it be to never have to tell him to put the seat down?

"Some things are simply out of your control," he said. "How does it feel?"

"It feels tempting." I referred more to the fact that he had begun to gently stroke the back of my hand with his thumb. Still, the more I thought about it, the more losing control gained in appeal. Just a little. Just this once. I *wanted* him. That darn tingle.

When something looked too good to be true, I generally believed that it was, and the Owain Glyndwr Google connection had stayed in the back of my mind.

Maybe I had to stop being so cynical. Or maybe he really *was* the devil. He definitely ranked in the "too good to be true" range.

"What have *you* been up to?" I asked. "Destroying civilizations, wreaking havoc, tormenting souls?"

I was only half-kidding.

"The usual devil business." He nodded, playing along. "And you?"

I ignored the small twinge of alarm. This was one relationship I was not ready to kill early out of fear for the long haul. "Digging my way out of hell. What a coincidence."

"What could you possibly know of hell?"

"Believe me, plenty. My business is apparently headed there right now."

"It can't be that bad. The market is booming."

"That's the problem. No one needs me. Houses are selling very well, thank you."

"*I* need you," he said, lacing his fingers with mine.

"Thanks." It didn't help my business any, but it sure perked my spirits.

Sitting beside him in the back of the limousine, I resisted the urge to rest my head on his shoulders as familiar landmarks whisked by the window. Boston Common. Beacon Hill. We didn't head out of the city, as I suspected we would.

"I'd thought you might be taking me to Blue Ginger."

"Is that a favorite of yours?"

I nodded. "Their brandied lobster is to die for."

"Then cross that one off the list. We can't have you dying."

"So, where are we headed?" I leaned across his lap to look out the opposite window. Okay, and to get my hands on those incredibly solid thighs. "Looks like Commercial Street?"

"You're catching on."

I couldn't think of anything out this way. Except the airport. My stomach did a flip. "Logan?"

"Don't worry. You won't need your passport."

I gulped. "Um, okay. Somehow that doesn't reassure me."

"Relax. I can have you back by morning."

"Back by morning?" I nearly shot out of my seat. "You said dinner. You didn't say anything about flying off somewhere."

"You're not afraid of flying." It was a statement, not a question.

"No." I conceded.

"Come on. I know a beautiful place. Our own little Bali Ha'i. It will be an adventure. Say you're up for it."

"And if I'm not?"

"Kate." He turned toward me, a dead serious look in his eyes. "You know I would never do anything against your will. Trust me."

I looked at him, weighing my options, trying to see inside his soul. His eyes held a familiar gleam, a warmth like the radiant glow of a fire burning deep within. Devil or no, I felt I belonged right by his side.

"I trust you." I finally gave in to the urge to rest my head on his shoulder and when I did, he laced his fingers with mine. "Let's go."

Power offered an aphrodisiac effect that even *I* couldn't deny, and power radiated from Owen. He was the bug zapper on a hot summer night. I was the mosquito who was about to get fried for flying in too close to his deadly ultraviolet core. If not careful, I might end up a little black shell of my former self. But I was done with being careful. I wanted to be with him, skin to skin. The temptation was too great to ignore.

What exactly did he have in mind for tonight, anyway? Just in case, I'd donned my new fancy underwear while getting dressed. Silk, lacy, seashell pink. I wished I had opted for red. All of the sudden, I felt a little racy. I think it was the revving engines of the plane. The private jet of Glendower Enterprises.

Inside, it looked less like a plane and more like a luxury trailer from a glamorous movie set. Or at least like the trailers I'd seen on *E! News* when Ryan Seacrest did on-location interviews with the stars. Posh taupe furnishings arranged for comfortable conversation, plush cerulean carpeting, a corner bar. I settled in next to him on a cushy loveseat facing a narrow window that looked out on the sun as it set over the airstrip. I gripped his hand and breathed a sigh of relief that I didn't disintegrate on the spot from excitement. Still, something *was* starting to catch fire. Heat seeped between my thighs. I could go down in a very slow burn.

I welcomed the possibility.

"Are you nervous? About flying?"

"Not at all," I said honestly. "I love taking off. That second when the plane first lifts off the ground? What a feeling."

"So then it's me?" He moved in closer, cradling my cheek in his palm. "I make you nervous?"

You make me high as a kite. A supersonic kite. Had anyone invented a kite that could reach the moon?

"Not really," I slid off my shoes, tucked my feet up under my bottom, and leaned closer to him. "It's more excited than nervous. I can't believe you're whisking me away. But maybe I should be nervous, considering I hardly know you."

"I feel like I've always known you. Deep down, I think you feel the same about me." He leaned in for the kiss and his lips met mine in a slow, erotic exploration. A tender kiss, no pressure, no insistence. It was as if our mouths barely touched, and yet I could feel the heady heat of him straight down to my core.

Without even touching me anywhere else, he made my body come to life. My pulse throbbed. I had to take a deep breath just to steady the sudden ache between my thighs. I met his gaze. The same heat that rolled in waves over my body seemed to center in his deep brown eyes, which were glowing as if lit with a mysterious spark—or perhaps it was mere amusement at my predicament?

I was surprised at how my body reacted to his closeness, even though he hadn't made a move. My nipples hardened to rock-solid nubs. I arched and nestled closer to him, my breasts rubbing against his sleeve. I resisted the potent desire to climb onto his lap and straddle his thighs. My clitoris pulsed as if an invisible tongue slid across it, slowly circling, winding me up to a frenzied euphoria. A feral moan formed at the back of my throat and, trying not to be obvious about my sudden state of heightened arousal, I buried my burning face in Owen's shoulder as I climaxed.

Seconds later, the pilot casually strolled across the cabin to pause in front of the loveseat.

"We'll be taking off in just a minute. If you'd like to get buckled in, I'll get us in the air and then you can resume your, um, normal activities." I managed an embarrassed smile, but Owen seemed completely unfazed.

"Safety first," he said, and reached across my lap to

find the safety restraint somewhere underneath my bottom. All business, Owen strapped me in and flashed a smile that belied his innocence in the matter of my enflamed passions.

Had I really just had an orgasm? Had he tricked out the seats with massage and vibration? I didn't even want to know. I put my feet back on the floor and settled in for the ride.

"I've never sat sideways on a plane before," I said, to cover my confusion with innocent conversation.

Owen nodded. "Good. I hoped to give you a night of firsts."

My cheeks flamed again. Contact-free orgasm had certainly been a first. What else did he have up his sleeve?

"It's dark," I said, staring out into the night, a distraction. "We won't be able to see much."

"Like where we're headed? Aren't you dying to know?"

I shrugged. "Paris, Hawaii, whatever. Same old, same old."

"We'll be there in a little over an hour."

"That rules out Hawaii. You said I won't need a passport, so that rules out Paris. Just tell me it isn't Canada."

"Why? You have a problem with Canada?"

My problem with Canada, besides that it was colder than Massachusetts in autumn, was that it didn't have an exotic ring. "He took me to Canada for dinner" just didn't have the same verve as "we flew off to Cancun."

Conversation paused while the plane taxied down the runway. All I could think about was sex, and if he planned to get down to business and make me a member of the mile high club. Unfortunately, after the momentary rush of liftoff, he seemed determined to keep the focus on making conversation instead of making love. Once the pilot gave the all-clear, Owen undid our restraints and got up to get us some champagne. While watching him pour, not spilling a drop, I grilled him on his favorite things.

"Mountains or beach?"

"Depends. Am I with you?"

"Trees or water?"

"What kind of trees? What color is the water?"

"Beef or fish?"

"You're leaving fowl off the list?"

"Why, is that your preference?"

"I'm a man of diverse tastes and interests."

He remained deliberately evasive.

"What about you? What are your little idiosyncrasies?"

"That's not fair. I asked you for preferences and you want me to list my flaws?"

"Your flaws are readily apparent. I was merely playing along with your little game."

I gasped. "Oh. Well then. No need to discuss further."

He flashed the mysterious half-smile and sat down next to me, handing me a glass. "I propose a toast," he said, lifting his glass in the air. "To reaching dizzying new heights."

"To reaching dizzying new heights together," I added, with a clink of the glass, hoping he planned to join me the next time he sent me off to trip the light orgasmic.

Chapter 7

An hour later, after a little more conversation and lots more champagne, we arrived at our destination.

It was dark so I couldn't tell much but that we'd flown over a stretch of water dotted now and then with lights. When we got off the plane, it was warm, a delightful bone-seeping warmth, with the smell of hibiscus in the air.

"Where are we?"

"Hilton Head. I have a little retreat not far from here."

"A retreat?" Retreat brought to mind monks. Owen Glendower seemed far from holy.

"A place at the beach. The staff at Glendower Enterprises gets most use of it. They come here for long meetings, strategy sessions, or entertaining the occasional corporate client."

"I can imagine," I said, following him away from the plane to the waiting Town Car. Steam rose off the damp blacktop around us, as if it had recently stopped raining just in time to welcome us to the island. "Is that how you'll write me off, then? Corporate client?"

"I'll never write you off. I think you're shagedelic, baby! You're switched on! You're smashing!" He turned, chucked me on the chin, and winked.

I stood frozen. Owen? Joking? Acting goofy? It was a side of him I'd never imagined possible, much less expected to see.

"What?" He shrugged. "It's my Austin Powers impression. I do have a sense of humor, you know. Mike Myers makes me laugh."

I rolled my eyes. "Good to know. But if you're going to start doing impressions, you're far more suited to James Bond than Austin Powers, for future reference."

"What? You don't like me shagadelic?" He asked, suavely taking over door-opening duties from the chauffeur.

"I have no problem with it," I said, getting into the car. In fact, I liked it. It made him seem more human, less superior corporate bigwig. At least he hadn't asked if he made me horny. I think our moment on the plane may have made it all too obvious. "It's just that if I'm going to be playing the role of female sidekick, I would much rather be Fatima Blush than Foxxy Cleopatra, thank you."

"Are you sure?" He slid into the backseat beside me, so close that there was barely any space between us. Of course, I didn't mind. "I believe Fatima dies a rather nasty death, whereas Foxxy lives a long and happy life."

"Are *you* sure? Did you see her hair?" I asked. Owen smiled and issued orders to the driver. As the car started and began to roll away from the airstrip to the unknown, I felt the pressing need to keep up a light banter in order to distract me from my desire to launch into another round of twenty questions. The last thing I wanted was to pester him with childish prompts of "are we there yet?"

"You don't think you'd look good in a fro?"

"I know I wouldn't. I'd take a flaming pen bomb in the gut before I'd get caught without a flat iron."

He reached over and ran his hand through my hair. The sudden intimacy caught me off guard. "You haven't flat ironed a day in your life. You used to pray for curly hair."

I did. I'd prayed for it nightly when I was about eight years old. I wanted long, glorious, curly hair instead of my own hair, which remained stick straight no matter how long I spent in curlers. In adulthood, I wore my hair straight to my shoulders, no bangs, but fortunately it always kind of swooped over to one side on good hair days. "How do you know?"

He shrugged and moved his hand away, back to rest on his own lap. I fought the temptation to grab it and put it back. As much as I longed for more physical attention, I felt it was better to put off coming on strong until we were at least near a couch. Or a bed. Or simply not accompanied by chauffeur or minion. I caught the driver's gaze in the rearview mirror and smiled politely until his attention turned back to the road.

"Women always want what they don't have. Your hair is fine and soft. It doesn't seem to be the kind that would hold a curl."

"So now you're Warren Beatty from *Shampoo*?"

Owen chuckled. It was the first I'd seen him blush, and probably the most endearing moment I'd spent with him yet. "I don't know. You just look like a straight hair kind of girl. It flatters you. Besides," he added, "I've seen a few of your girlhood photos at your sister's house."

Mental shriek. "Which ones?"

"There's a rather fetching one of you in a purple bikini. I think your top is falling off on one side." He raised his eyebrows in lecherous approval.

"You perv." I playfully slapped his arm. "I must have been ten years old. I don't think I've owned a bikini since then."

"You were cute. Despite the missing teeth."

We pulled off of the main road and through an imposing security gate. Lights dotted the long, winding driveway at intervals, and we rounded a small bend in the drive, which revealed a house that could have been a small resort hotel. The outdoor lights reflected off the clapboard exterior and enormous wraparound porch.

Owen got out and came around to open my door. As I stepped out on the driveway, I breathed in the warm air and took in my surroundings. A brick walkway wound through perfectly manicured lawns lined with expertly trimmed hedgerows and the occasional flowering shrub, quaint touches that lent a homey Southern feel to the grounds.

"Lovely," I said.

"I find it relaxing, a nice break from the New England chill."

I shrugged out of my jacket. It was more than warm and I'd begun to fear breaking a sweat, and not from mere proximity to Owen this time.

We headed inside. The interior was no less impressive than the outside. The parlor opened to a larger sitting room. Hardwood floors were covered with occasional rugs. Plush furnishings were artfully placed, set off by solid wood accents. It all showed a more rugged, down-to-earth side to the man who portrayed himself as an international jet-setter type to the media.

There were no personal photographs lying around, only paintings and prints, all landscapes and ocean views. "So what about you? Don't you have any embarrassing boyhood photos you could share to even out the playing field?"

"Even the field?" He stared me down. "You've had me at a disadvantage from the moment I looked in your stunning green eyes. It will take a lot more than a few charming photographs to raise me up to competitive level, trust me."

"A private plane to dinner at your beach house in another state isn't competitive?"

"It's extravagant, perhaps. Showing off, to tell the truth. I'm not ashamed to admit it. You make me want to be my best, Kate."

Hubba. "You're off to an excellent start."

"And I haven't even opened the wine. The night seems promising indeed."

"You have plied me with champagne. I believe that counts for something."

"Are you feeling it yet?"

"Is this the part where I'm supposed to crinkle my nose, giggle, and say the bubbles all went to my head?"

"Most assuredly not."

"Good, because I don't have it in me. I will concede to the designer stereotype and say that I love what you've done with the place." Lack of photographs aside, the setting revealed more about him than he could possibly imagine, unless he had left the design entirely in the hands of a professional. "Who's your decorator?"

"Are you honestly interested or angling for the job?"

he asked, heading to the bar area and opening a bottle of something red.

"I have enough on my plate. It's honest interest. Although a few weeks a year working at the beach wouldn't be the death of me."

"I designed it myself." He poured and handed me a glass. "Perhaps it might have come out better in the hands of someone with experience, but I like it. Feels like home."

I smiled. It felt homey to me, too, but I wasn't about to confess it for fear of feeling too much at home too soon. The more time I spent with Owen, the more he made me feel relaxed and all too ready to imagine future outings and a more permanent sort of togetherness. For now, I struggled to keep the conversation away from more intimate topics to avoid revealing too much of myself in the midst of the new sorts of feelings Owen stirred in me.

I sipped the exquisite cabernet, which was definitely not from the three-for-twelve bin at the corner store. "So do you golf? I think I made out the sand traps of a course on the landscape as we rode here, but it was too dark to tell for certain."

"We did pass a course or two on the way here. I golf. Not well. But I've been known to pick up the clubs now and again. You can't very well live on Hilton Head and avoid the sport."

"You're being modest." I gestured with my glass. "I'll bet you're good. You're the type who's good at everything." I was already a little tipsy, but not unpleasantly so. The Owen tingle recharged me and made me a little less cautious. Maybe it was time to be less guarded after all.

"It's true, I'm very accomplished. I don't like to brag."

"Fine." I slid my feet out of my shoes and curled up, getting comfortable. "But I have to tell you, things are looking a little too good to be true from my angle. You're handsome, athletic, smart, filthy rich. You have good taste in décor. There's got to be something underneath it all, a hidden chink in the shining armor?"

"I wouldn't hide anything from you. You want to know something, just ask." He smiled slyly, as if offering a dare rather than simply laying himself bare to my inquisition.

"Okay, devil man." Excited by the invitation, I sat up straighter and tucked my feet under my bottom. I steadied the glass in my hand just in time to avoid sloshing wine on the nubby brown fabric of the couch. "As I'm certain you're aware, the name Owen Glendower has a rather sordid history. How did you end up with it?"

He shrugged. "I suppose that depends on what you consider sordid. To be honest, I named myself. I was in Wales at the time, traveling, feeling a little rebellious, and it seemed to fit."

"You changed your name? So you *do* have a secret past. I knew it." I was thrilled at the prospect of uncovering secrets about Owen. He was like my own private mystery to unravel. My heart raced. I sat, literally, on the edge of my seat, eager for each new revelation.

"So what was your pleasure? Raising hell? Stealing souls?" I asked. I was feeling amorous and I hoped to ease him into a wicked frame of mind.

"I don't actually steal souls." He removed his jacket, tossed it on a nearby chair, and approached me, his every move lean and economical, a jungle cat ready to pounce.

My pulse went wild. I breathed deep, an effort to steady myself and shake off some of the wine buzz. Suddenly, I wanted all my wits about me. But the dizziness, the heady intoxication, seemed to come more from being with Owen than from the wine. I backed off the teasing and went back to the light, breezy questioning until I could recover my bearings.

"No souls? How about candy? Do you take candy from babies?"

He shook his head. "I don't have much of a sweet tooth. Do I look like I need to steal?"

"It's the kittens, isn't it? You torture kittens."

"Only the ones who've been very, very bad." He sat down next to me. The mere action of watching his taut, perfect ass lower into the seat nearly sent me over the edge. He had an incredible body. It made me weak to remember the feel of him against me.

"There has to be something." The memory of burning for him on the plane left me a little hesitant to start playing with fire until I was certain he was ready to join in. "I'll find it. Just give me time."

"Take all the time you need. I'm at your service."

At my service and sitting so close? I had the feeling he was playing with me, deliberately testing my resolve. I almost gave in. What resolve? Why fight it? My mouth went dry, despite the fruit-forward wine. I gave in just enough to reach for his hand, lace my fingers with his, when he pulled away and stood up.

"It's time to eat. I've arranged for a light meal out on the terrace."

"Oh. Great. I'm starving." I hid my disappointment

as I followed him outside. I wasn't the least bit hungry for food.

The dinner was so incredible that I managed to eat as if I'd been starving myself for weeks. I never got a glimpse of his minions, but they did amazing work, laying out a spread fit for visiting royalty. We'd had grilled mahimahi over a creamy lobster risotto, a light spinach salad with spiced walnuts, and now a decadent dessert. The delicate aroma of walnuts still lingered, mixing with the ocean breeze.

"Earlier, I asked about your childhood photos," I said between spoonfuls of the most delicious crème brûlée I'd ever eaten, served with macadamia nut brittle and grilled pineapple on the side. "Do you have any? I'd honestly like to see what you were like as a boy."

We sat across from each other at a candle-covered round table set up on the patio overlooking the ocean. It was still warm enough that we'd left our jackets inside. In almost matching plain white shirts, we might have been two blank slates. Owen finally spoke, filling in a little color.

He sipped his wine and seemed to think a moment before he answered. The breeze rumpled his dark hair, much the way I wanted to with my fingers. "I didn't have much of a childhood. If you're still looking for that chink, that might be it. I come from the ultimate dysfunctional family."

"We all think we had it bad growing up."

"My background is beyond bad, Kate. When you're ready, you'll hear every gory detail."

Beyond bad? Maybe he was right. I wasn't ready. I wanted to know more about him, but every gory detail?

Perhaps a discussion best left for another time. Appetite sated, bearings regained, my mind turned back to the physical.

"I'm ready to walk off that incredible meal," I said, rising from the table and heading for the low interlocking stone border that framed the patio. I stood at the edge, stared off to the stars twinkling out over the rolling ocean, and mentally beckoned him to join me. The anticipation built until I felt him hovering just over my shoulder. I could barely breathe with the force of my yearning for his touch.

"The beach is beautiful at night," he said, and reached for my hand.

My shoes were still inside, so I walked barefoot, relishing the feel of the cool sand between my toes the second we stepped off the brick steps. I loved the beach, the feel of my heels sinking into the soft sand with every step. I hadn't walked on a beach in years, though I'd never been far from the coast. He took a second to kick off his loafers before we strolled the few feet down to the water's edge. White-capped waves rode in, breaking up the inky blackness of the ocean. The water would have appeared to go on forever if not for the moon hovering on the horizon.

As we strolled near the water, I stole a glance at him. He'd rolled up his sleeves to reveal strong, lean forearms lightly covered with dark hair. Such masculine arms and such a firm grip. He was perfect.

A wave rushed up and grazed my ankles. I jumped at the unexpected chill.

"It's a little cold this time of year," Owen said.

"It's nice. It just startled me. My family used to vacation in Maine, so I'm accustomed to cold water."

"You don't like to be cold," he said, and something

in his voice gave me a chill. It was more a statement than a question.

"That's true. Why I've stayed in the Northeast all these years is beyond me."

"You stay for the smell of autumn in the air, for picking fresh apples right off the tree, for that first snowfall of every year." He listed my thoughts nearly as soon as they came into my mind.

"Right. All those things." It didn't take a mind reader. He'd just hit on every New England cliché. "Plus, my family is there. As much as they drive me crazy, I like to be close."

"This feeling of family, of being connected, it warms you?"

"I guess so. It's nice to have people who accept you no matter what." I paused, not quite sure I wanted to put the rest into words. I picked up a shell and tossed it out into the surf. It landed with a small splash only a few feet away. The simple action grounded me, made me ready to say something I would normally keep inside. I stared out at the water with my back to Owen. "But, you know, they're family. Sometimes you put aside who you are, what you want, to be who they think you ought to be."

I didn't tell him it was also the reason I'd decided it was time to have a baby. I hadn't been able to pin it down until that moment, but I craved the chance to make something new, to have someone who loved me unconditionally, without preconceived expectations or demands. Unlike my mother, sister, or grandparents, my baby wouldn't want me to be any smarter, cuter, thinner, or more successful. With one special person in the world, I could be completely at ease and free.

At last, I hazarded a glance back. Owen nodded but

he had a vacant look in his eyes, and I thought again of his dysfunctional family. The lost look in his dark eyes made me ache, but not where I normally ached for Owen. This ache was centered closer to my heart. I closed the distance until I stood pressed right up against him and reached up to stroke his face. The skin beneath his stubble was so soft beneath my palms, a contrast to the sharp contours of his sculpted features and rugged jawline. My fingers itched to stray to his delectable mouth, those lips, but I held back.

Save for the few lights on in the oversized houses dotting the shore behind us, we could have been the only two people in the world. "Don't you have anyone to care for you?" It didn't sound quite so grandmotherly when I thought it in my head. Fortunately, Owen didn't flinch.

He took my palm and kissed it. Slowly. Erotically. Until I felt as if I'd melt on the spot, right there on the sand.

"I have you," he said, pulling me into his arms.

Arms around each other, we walked back to the porch and nestled in a cushioned chaise, our bodies curled right up against each other, face to face and closer than ever. I could feel his heart racing. I could feel his breath on my neck. I could feel the start of something else growing solid against my hip. Hello, gorgeous.

He kissed my mouth as slowly as he had my palm, but within seconds, a frantic urgency overcame me not unlike what I'd gone through on the plane. Only now, I had him at my mercy. I sucked on his tongue, drawing him to the back of my mouth, wishing I could draw him all the way inside me.

"What you do to me," he moaned.

"I can feel it," I said, letting my hand take a wanton journey south.

"Not yet." He pulled my hand back up to his chest. I rocked against him, curved my hips into him and wrapped my legs around him to draw him as close as I wanted—needed—him to be. My breath caught as he flicked his hands over the buttons of my blouse, undoing them with one fell swoop. I worked at his, the heat of his chest nearly scorching my fumbling fingers, hardly able to contain myself.

He kissed me again, hard and fast, as if to appease my longing, but he only managed to feed it, and apparently his own in the process. I couldn't figure out how he'd managed to unhook my bra so quickly, and the sudden breeze whisked across my bare breasts. He cradled me in his warm hands.

"So beautiful." His thumbs grazed my hardened nipples, sending a jolt of heat right through me. At last, his hands on me, and it was better than my imaginings on the plane. When I felt his lips replace his hands, I nearly erupted on the spot. His tongue, liquid glass, rolled over my swollen buds, stirring the ache down lower. I hooked my leg around his backside, desperate to pull him into me. I wanted him inside me. His rock-solid erection proved he was as ready as I was. I writhed against him.

"Easy," he said. "Let's not get carried away."

"No, let's." I straddled him, careful not to upend the narrow chaise, and leaned to kiss him once I found my balance. On my knees, I centered my damp heat over his erection and rubbed erotically, my hips finding a steady rhythm that fired, not soothed, my enflamed ache. His cock throbbed with a force I could feel even through his trousers and my pants. I wanted to strip bare and feel him, skin to skin. I wanted him. Here, now, hard, fast.

Bending low, I teased his mouth with my breasts, brushing their pink tips light as a whisper across his parted lips.

"Kate." He sat up under me, easing me back, holding my shoulders to steady me so I wouldn't slip off the chaise to the bricks. "We're moving too fast. I think it's time we went to bed."

"Good idea," I whispered between kisses. I would have been perfectly happy to do it out on the porch like a couple of wildcats, but Owen had neighbors and I felt the scream, the one that had gathered during the plane trip, begging for release in the back of my throat. "But I won't be too loud. I promise."

I lied, a little white lie.

"No." He held my shoulders. "Separate beds. I mean it. We're not ready to jump that far ahead."

"You *feel* ready. I know *I'm* ready."

Without even a hint of regret, he flashed a winsome grin. "I'll show you to your room."

Chapter 8

Reader, I didn't get any.

I failed seduction with a capital F. True to his word, Owen showed me to a room, delivered a chaste kiss good night at the door, and left me alone.

The room was suitable, if a little stuck in the eighties, done up in a Laura Ashley–inspired mix of stripes and flowers in pink, green, and white. Chiffon curtained double doors opened up to a balcony that let in the soothing sounds of surf. The bed was beyond comfortable, and even though I soundly believed that I wouldn't sleep a wink, I opened my eyes to filtered sunlight and a faint knocking at the door.

I peeked at the clock. Seven A.M. I'd slept a good seven hours. I felt refreshed, rested, and badly in need of mouthwash.

There was a sharp knock at the door, and then Owen's deep voice. "Good morning, Kate." He stood on the other side of my door. At seven A.M. Probably freshly showered and devastatingly handsome as ever.

And I? I was a disheveled mess, not to mention I'd slept in the nude for lack of nightwear.

"Hang on," I called, then scrambled out of bed in an attempt to gather my clothes. The door opened. I shrieked and pulled the bedspread around me.

"I said hang on."

"Mm. Did I catch you by surprise? I thought you said come in." He leaned casually against the doorframe, his gaze dropping up and down as his lips parted in a smile of lecherous approval.

I wrapped the covers more tightly around my middle. Instinctively, my hand shot up to my tangled hair. By contrast, he looked like he'd been up for hours. He was showered and fresh, and dressed like Indiana Jones about to lead an expedition through the heart of darkness. Safari jacket, khaki trousers tucked into boots. He lacked only the whip and signature fedora.

The thought of the whip brought a temporary flush to my cheeks. Kinky.

"Did you find everything you need?" A little late to present himself as a gentleman, he shifted his gaze to the corner of the room. "There are personal products in the bathroom. Spare toothbrush. Pajamas." His eyes flicked back to my bare shoulders, then to my legs, and his smile widened. "Not that I don't appreciate the alternative."

"Thanks," I said, wishing I could hide my flaming cheeks.

"Are you in a hurry to be anywhere today?" he asked, straightening and taking a step inside the room, shifting his head left and right as if he were trying to get a peak inside the bedspread.

"No hurry." Suddenly I considered dropping the spread.

"Good. Come down to breakfast. I have something for you." He winked, then slipped out of the room.

I showered and got dressed in yesterday's clothes, wishing he'd warned me to pack an overnight bag. But where was the fun in that? The island jaunt was a nice surprise, and I didn't regret it for a second. Especially if today proved any more productive toward sating my need for him than last night had been. Downstairs, the dining room table featured a spread not unlike one of my finer Curtain Call displays. Croissants, gourmet jams, whipped butter, and a variety of juices sat next to a steaming thermal carafe.

"Coffee." I headed straight for the java jolt, though I didn't really need it with the Owen buzz wreaking havoc with my system.

"Good morning to you, too." Owen stepped out of the sitting room and joined me at the table. "At least, it is now."

"Now that I've cleaned up and appear human again?" I asked.

He laughed. "For the record, I like you dirty."

My stomach did a flip, the good kind.

"I hope you like me eating, too, because I can't resist fresh croissants."

"Have at it." He pulled out a chair. "I'll join you just as soon as I fetch your gift."

Gifts were exciting, but they also made me nervous. It was too soon for extravagance. He'd already given me so much. Flowers, the crystal vase, *South Pacific,* Bali Ha'i. I liked jewelry, but it wouldn't feel right yet. I spooned blackberry preserves on my plate and tried not to worry.

When I saw the size of the box, my curiosity returned. It was about the size of a coat box, too big for jewelry.

"Open it. I can't wait to see what you think."

He handed it over and plopped down in the chair next to me.

I ripped into the paper. The box was plain with the word *Hunter* written across the top. Inside was a pair of red rubber boots. "Wellies!"

It was the perfect gift. Absolutely perfect. Nothing I needed or would ever buy for myself, but they made me so ridiculously happy. I kicked off my shoes, thrust my feet right into them, and got up to take a turn around the table.

"They look smashing," he said.

"They feel smashing. Quite comfortable. Just the right size. I had a pair just like them when—" My heart skipped a beat. I met his gaze. "When I was a child. They were my favorite."

My dad used to read me Paddington Bear books complete with a funny little bear voice. He'd even bought me a stuffed Paddington and red Wellies just like Paddington Bear's. I wore them everywhere. It drove my mother crazy. But Owen couldn't possibly have known that. Could he?

Somehow, he knew. He'd talked to Bennie, maybe. Or, he'd just guessed the right thing. Kismet, isn't that what they called it? Fate? I'd never believed in signs, but for once, I wanted to believe. A shallow, breathless feeling came over me, a tickle-in-the-belly sort of excitement I hadn't felt since childhood.

Owen grinned. "Let's finish breakfast. I'm taking you on an adventure and you're going to need those."

"I'm going to need Wellies? It's a beautiful day. Where are we going?"

"You'll see," he said, and bit into a croissant.

* * *

After breakfast, we drove up the coast in Owen's midnight blue BMW convertible. It was a scenic jaunt with the breeze rippling our hair and the sun on our backs. It was nice to ride along, just the two of us, to sit beside him and watch him in the driver's seat, his powerful grip on the stick shift reminding me of his skilled fingers doing other things. Considering the Wellies, I'd all but given up on the idea that he was taking me someplace to consummate our mutual desires. Unless he had a weird thing for women in rubber boots. But that just bordered on bizarre. Before I could stop myself, I laughed out loud at the thought of me seducing him wearing nothing but the boots.

"You're laughing." He cast a quick glance in my direction. "Care to share the joke?"

"No joke." I hoped my reddening cheeks didn't give away the fact that I'd been having outlandish private thoughts. "I'm just happy."

"Happy?"

"To be here." I put my hand over his on the stick. "With you."

"I like the sound of your laughter. Your sense of humor is one of the first things that drew me to you."

"At Bennie's? I don't recall being in top form that night."

He shrugged, his focus on the winding road. "You're witty. It's natural for you, to the point you probably don't even notice it all the time."

"Hm." He shifted gears again, and I stared out at the landscape, tall sea grass, the occasional scrub pine, and sand and rocks to the right. To the left, luxury hotels and houses, the occasional breathtaking view of the ocean apparent through breaks between buildings. "I remember you surprising me in the kitchen, as if you came from out of nowhere."

"I came through the back door. I hate to make an obvious arrival when I'm running late."

"Don't we all? I can't remember the last time I used Bennie's front door, like a regular guest."

Couldn't I? I used the front door the night she'd tried to fix me up with Rob the Garden Gnome, the same night I'd hit on the idea of starting Curtain Call Designs. The same night I'd joked about dating the devil. And now here I was, with the man who shared his name.

"Why Owen Glendower?" I asked, rekindling the conversation from the night before.

"Why not? As I said, it seemed to fit."

"But, the devil? Don't you ever worry it will give the wrong impression?"

"People form impressions all the time, often with very little fact for basis. Not many people are even properly aware of the history of the name."

"Or your history, for that matter," I added, hoping to prompt him to fill it in.

"I never set out to be a mystery. My entire history is out there for anyone who cares to look."

"I looked." I admitted, training my focus full, on him and his facial expressions in response to my words. "I barely found a thing."

He didn't even flinch. He did seem open, honest, ready to talk with nothing to hide. And yet, I didn't know what to think, or what to ask. Could Owen Glendower actually be everything he seemed? I wanted so badly for it to be true. I didn't realize how very much until he reached for my hand and placed it between the open collar of his shirt, right over his steady-beating heart.

"Perhaps you simply haven't been looking in the right place."

After twenty minutes, he pulled over into a remote area. "We're here."

"Where?" I looked around. We'd left golf courses, private residences, and grand hotels behind when we'd turned onto a dirt road some time ago, but I'd been too distracted to realize we'd driven into what seemed to be the middle of nowhere. Trees, rocks, the sound of waves crashing somewhere close. No signs of civilization.

"You'll see." He opened my door and took my hand.

My Owen tingle had become a hollow yearning. I hardly knew how to fill the growing ache inside me, but sex would have been a start. Strangely, Owen didn't seem quite as focused on sex as I was. Not that he didn't seem interested. I'd been with him enough to know that he had a healthy desire. But his attraction to me didn't hinge on sex alone, which was so different from the other men I'd dated, and it certainly fed my curiosity to see what else he had in mind.

I followed, willing, wondering. The stones crunched under my feet, and Owen's gaze held all the sharpness of the rocks on the path as he guided me along. We stepped into wet grass, and mud pulled at my boots as they sank into the soft marsh, threatening to hold me in place.

"I'm beginning to understand the Wellies," I said. With every step I took, I had the sense that I was getting closer to Owen.

The brush got thicker, the low branches obscuring the path and slapping at our backs and faces as we wedged our way through them. I hesitated, but Owen smiled and tightened his grip on my hand. "We're almost there."

Finally, we came to a clearing overlooking the beach. The sudden appearance of whitecaps took my breath away, and I stood stock-still, in awe of the rugged beauty. From behind, he wrapped his arms around my waist and held me to him. His breath heated my neck and stirred something deep inside me. I felt suddenly, achingly, overwhelmed with a need I'd never known. Beyond physical desire, I wanted to be part of him, to be woven straight into the fabric of his being, to know him as completely as he knew himself, and as he seemed to know me.

He took my hand again. "Down here," he said, leading me down the rocky embankment to the sandy shore that formed a narrow apron around a cliff. Up ahead, the shoreline tapered off. The ocean was a show of rugged beauty as it splashed against the stone, but Owen didn't seem interested in watching the wild display. He diverted my attention behind us to the rocks. In the base of the cliff, a crevice opened. We headed for it. From even the short distance, it looked barely large enough to house a small child. Getting closer, I could see that it was just large enough to accommodate us walking side by side. Owen stepped ahead, guiding us through the opening and into an enormous cave.

"Wow," I said. Stalactites dripped from a low ceiling, touching the ground in spots around us. Occasional rays of light filtered in from unseen cracks to reflect off puddles that lined the uneven floor. I guessed the ocean came in at high tide. In the cave's furthest reaches, the water looked deep enough to drown unsuspecting waders.

I walked around, keeping to the dry areas, and he watched me carefully.

"Perhaps it takes some getting used to," he said, his voice taut with anticipation. For what? I sensed he looked for my approval, but it surprised me that someone of Owen's caliber would need any sort of reassurance from me. The mystery shrouding him was a veil that had begun to lift, just at the corners, just enough for me to see. Enough to let me in. I trembled at the honor of his choosing to share his secrets with me, if only just a few of them, if only just for now.

"No. I like it." I reached up to stroke a cool, damp wall. "It's slightly unsettling, but fascinating at the same time."

He closed the distance between us. "It doesn't frighten you?"

"Sure it does, a little. It's dark. I'm not quite sure what I might find, but that's part of the appeal."

"The unknown?"

"It makes me want to explore."

He sighed, as if relieved.

"It could do with a little light," he said. It was a simple statement but I sensed that it meant much more than the obvious. It humbled me, to think that I could be that light in his life. Could I give him what he needed? In that second, I'd never wanted anything more than to try.

I slid my arms around his waist and leaned into him, resting my head on his chest.

He kissed my forehead. "You're cold."

"Not now, I'm not." My body heat had shot up a few points with his proximity. I looked up at him.

His gaze, knowing and intent, burned through me. I thought wicked thoughts about what I'd like to do to him in the cave, and I hoped he could tell what I was thinking. I reached up and stroked his cheek, already rough with afternoon stubble. My breath caught.

"You're beautiful," I said, my voice a velvet caress. "You're beautiful, rugged, sharp, and so deep I could get lost and wouldn't care. I wouldn't even care." My words echoed off of the dark walls and rang out all around us.

"You might care." He took my hand and seared the open palm with a kiss. "If I was all you had."

"You might be all I need." My heart raced with the gravity of the statement. My breath came in shallow rasps. All I need, standing right here in front of me? Could it be so simple?

I ran my hands through his thick silken hair, cupped them around his neck, and brought my mouth to his. I may have failed seduction the previous evening, but I'd learned a thing or two. *Less is more.* I barely touched my lips to his, then I turned on my heel and walked out of the cave without so much as a glance back.

Owen followed a moment later, his heavy-lidded eyes suggesting that perhaps getting me back to the bedroom had become an urgent priority. He put his arm around me as we walked back to the car. I felt the tingle spread from my toes to the base of my brain. At last! I could hardly wait.

Once we were back at the car, he turned to me.

"All I want to do is get you back to the house, but we have other plans."

"Other plans?" A stab of nearly physical pain went through me. How much longer would I have to wait for this man? I couldn't hide my disappointment, but I wasn't ready to give up. I slid over in the seat and ran a finger along the edge of his ear as I leaned seductively close to him. "Can't we perhaps put off the other plans?"

"No."

A cryptic one-word answer was all I got before he threw the car in gear and pulled back out to the road.

No. Just like that. Okay. I could deal with rejection, for now. Perhaps he had something else up his sleeve? A hot air balloon ride over the island? Or maybe he planned to drive me out to a picnic area on the road, another secluded spot all tricked out by the minions with a feast, flowers, candles, and a private cabana complete with bedding? I couldn't fault him for being romantic.

I could only speculate as we made the long drive in complete silence. My tension gave way to sheer excitement as I began to contemplate a relationship between us. Not just sex, but so much more.

A few minutes later, we pulled into the parking lot of one of the island's many posh hotels. My tingle spiked to new heights. This was it! We were going to check in and hit the sheets! He turned in his seat and took my hands, but his eyes had lost the heavy-lidded look that put me in a bedroom frame of mind in favor of a new gravity, as if he was about to get very serious.

"We have something in common," he said.

"Yes?"

"We both made due without fathers."

Fathers? I couldn't imagine where this was headed, but I was willing to go along. I gave his hands a light squeeze. "I had no idea you lost yours, too. I'm sorry."

He smiled warmly. "No need. I really didn't know what I was missing. I never met my parents. My brother raised me."

"Oh." Did he want me to meet his brother? Oh, God,

was this a meet the family kind of weekend? I had no idea. That was really not something to spring on an unsuspecting girlfriend. Girlfriend. I liked the sound of it, and the feeling of couplehood that went along with it. Perhaps I could handle a little family meeting. "So you have a brother?"

"Two. We're not close. I have a lot to learn about family. I'm getting some clues from watching yours. You were close to your father."

I looked down at my new Wellies. "Yes. Until he left us."

Just because I was ready to meet his family didn't mean I wanted to get into any detail about mine. I had some tender feelings for my father, this was true. He'd left my life so suddenly, and I'd often wondered about him. Where he had gone. What had become of him. If he ever thought of me. I missed him, more so at first but sometimes even now. But now was not the time to dredge up all that misery.

"Sometimes it's harder to know what you're missing."

"True enough," I said. "My dad used to tell the best stories. Every Sunday afternoon, we'd read together. It always ended with me laughing so hard my stomach ached. I miss those Sundays most of all. I didn't laugh for the longest time after he left." I blinked back the beginnings of tears. The last thing I wanted was to get maudlin about my family. I turned the focus back to him. "Do you wish you knew your dad, then?"

"No. I believe I'm better off without that particular knowledge. My father was reportedly quite wicked. Though I suppose I have him to thank for what I do."

"Glendower Enterprises?"

He shook his head. "It's rather complicated."

"If he holds any credit for the man you've become, I can't dislike him, wicked or not."

He smiled as if a weight was lifted. "I'm glad you refrain from passing judgment. I have enough of that in, er, *at* work."

"Passing judgments?"

He nodded. "You've no idea. Sometimes it seems that the fate of the world rides on my shoulders."

I treasured his confidence. His openness stirred something deep inside me. *Love?* "They're very capable shoulders. And hands. You have strong, capable hands. Nimble fingers. Dexterous. I would trust them with *my* life."

I smiled. He smiled back. In that second, our intimacy ran soul-deep. I held my breath, afraid that if I so much as sighed, I would lose that amazing feeling.

"You *are* a rare find, Kate Markham."

"That's probably a good thing." I sensed the need for some levity. "I'm not sure the world could handle two of me."

"Don't trouble yourself with worrying about the world." He reached up to brush the hair out of my eyes. "You leave that to me."

Usually, the big strong man act failed to impress me. With Owen, it took on a larger-than-life importance— as if he truly believed what he said, that he could handle the world and keep the more unsavory elements at bay. That he could shelter and protect me. And, instead of my usual need to insist I could take care of myself, I cherished the thought of being protected, of being held safe in his arms for all time.

"You're still wondering why we're here, I'm sure," he said, "when we could be back at the house, enjoy the day together? I would like that, too. But if things go according to plan, we'll have all the time in the world."

"According to plan?" My mouth went dry. He had plans. Long-term plans that included me. It was far more than I'd ever expected from him. Still, suddenly everything was moving much too quickly. I needed more time, more dates, more than just a few days away with him to know if this was truly for real.

"A weekend away *at least,* that's what you'd said," he said, and it was as if he'd just read my thoughts. But how could he know what I was thinking? "Perhaps I took you too literally. But, of course, it's not even the weekend, is it?"

"What are you going on about? It is Friday. That's almost the weekend."

"Never mind that." He shook his head as if to clear it and met my gaze with his most serious stare. "I want you, Kate. And I think you know by now that I don't just mean in my bed. I want more with you. More than I think I've ever wanted in all my time. It's unnerving, really."

Hardly a romantic thing to say. "Unnerving? I'm so glad to oblige."

"I mean it in the best way." Imploring, he placed his hand on my knee. "I have a lot of resources, a lot to offer you. I want to give you everything you've ever wanted, and more."

Suddenly I didn't know what I wanted, besides for the world to stop spinning and give me a chance to think.

At once, he seemed to understand. "Stop fretting. I'm not trying to pin you down or force any life-altering decisions. There's time for us. Plenty of time. All I wanted was to bring you here and give you back something you've been missing. Something you've wanted for a very long time."

"The boots are great. I love them."

"It's more than the boots," he said, keeping his eyes on the hotel lobby doors. "Look."

A random group of people lingered in front of the hotel. There was a woman in a too-tight dress and floppy hat who strolled out to the parking lot; some men in shorts, perhaps business travelers taking time out to play golf, who got into a car waiting at the door; and a man off to the side, leaning against the wall near a waste can as he puffed on a cigar.

"The one near the door." He gestured.

The smoker. An ordinary island tourist type in Bermuda shorts and a tropical shirt, ball cap pulled low over sandy blond surfer hair, taking time to enjoy a moment with his stogie.

"What about him?"

"For so long, you've wondered what became of your father. Now you can find out."

"What?" My eyes narrowed. "Dad?"

A slow, sick feeling came over me. A wave of recognition? No. I didn't know the man. Shock? Horror? I had no idea what I was feeling. I only knew it wasn't good.

"Michael Markham. Age fifty-five. Car salesman from Las Vegas, Nevada. Divorced, two children, long estranged." Owen rattled off the facts as if reading from a resume—or a rap sheet. "Care to rectify that?"

"What? No. I don't know." Dumbfounded, I stared off, watching the man. Did he know I was here? Was he waiting for me? The sick feeling rose up to my throat. I couldn't breathe. I leaned over, my face in my hands. "Oh, God."

Owen stroked my back, a soothing motion. "He

doesn't know you're here. He has no idea. What happens next is all up to you."

Once I was able to breathe again, I straightened up. "Up to me? If it was up to me, I would still be in the dark about my father. What are we doing here? How did you know?"

"I've had connections to your father for quite some time. Gambling can blacken a man's soul, get him in deep."

"In deep?" I shrank away. "What are you? Some kind of mob boss? Does he owe you money?" My mind went wild. I had no idea or what to think or what Owen was telling me.

"Nothing like that." Owen's voice was gentle, as if he was trying to be reassuring. "I simply have access to information that most people don't. I wanted to use my connections to help you, to give you something no one else could."

I struggled to stay calm, but I became angrier with every word. "Connections? So you're rich, powerful. You dug into my past and came out with my father? Did you think this could go well? That you were giving me some sort of special gift? Why stop at *there he is*? Why not put him in a big box and wrap him up with a bow. God! I can't *believe* you."

Owen seemed perplexed by my reaction. "Haven't you always wanted to know your father? I thought it would please you."

"Please me? You thought going behind my back, digging up personal information, and trotting out my father, all this would somehow please me? Impress me? You really have no idea."

And that, precisely, was what really bothered me about the whole ordeal. Owen's stunning move to win me over was impressive, but it was completely the wrong thing to do at the wrong time. I'd begun to think, to honestly believe, that Owen and I shared some cosmic kind of connection. That he knew me, really knew me, deep down and completely. That he could be my soul mate, something I'd yearned for practically all my life. Who doesn't?

But now, in the face of this strange situation, I began to doubt our deep connection. He was a man. Fallible. *Unable to see inside my soul.* I'd only just begun to believe that true love could exist for me—only over the past few days, in fact—and now . . . My faith was shaken.

Owen looked as shattered as I felt. Fragile, wounded.

"I'm sorry," I said. "It was a lovely thought. I'm just not ready for it."

"Are you sure? Take some time. Think." As if by just wanting me to want his gift, he could will it to happen. His eager-to-please attitude was a desirable trait. He played Jimmy Stewart's George Bailey to my Mary. All he wanted was to give me the moon. My anger evaporated. How could it not?

No doubt he was used to courting women properly, to delivering up exactly what they wanted and winning them over completely. But I just could not be won in ordinary ways. I didn't want the moon. I'd only wanted *him.* Now, once again, I had no idea if what I wanted even existed.

"All the thinking in the world won't change my mind. I'm not ready to face my father. I do want to know more about him, though. Did he remarry? Does he have other kids?"

It occurred to me then, for the first time, that my parents had never legally divorced.

"There are things you do need to know," Owen said.

"If you don't want to meet him now, let's go back to the house and I'll fill you in."

Back at his place, I sat quietly on the sitting room sofa and listened as Owen, standing in front of the fireplace, laid out the tale.

My father's history was neither long nor particularly sordid. He was simply a man who'd made mistakes and had gone to great, misguided lengths to seek redemption. When he left, he left behind a slew of debts, most in his own name that he never believed would fall to my mother to pay. In some cases, he was right. In others, not so much. At any rate, he trusted in my mother's deep connection to my grandparents to help her get on with her life and take care of two growing kids.

"In his heart," Owen said, "your father honestly believed that you were all better off without him."

"How do you know what was in his heart? You can't just make assumptions like that."

"He did. I know." Owen's voice held an edge of insistence that I didn't want to argue with, but I didn't automatically believe. "He thought that he would hit a big jackpot in Vegas and come back a hero, rich and ready to pay off his debts, win his wife back, and be a dad."

"But he never did." I got up and paced the room, filling in the blanks. "Did he? He stayed on and kept on gambling."

"He ended up in some dire situations. At one point, he was desperate enough to sell his soul to the devil for a win."

"For all that was worth." I scoffed. "I'm sure the devil himself wouldn't have jumped on the offer."

Owen narrowed his eyes and crossed his arms across his chest. "You don't know a thing about the devil."

"Ease up there, cowboy. It was only a comment."

"I know." He ran his hands through his hair as if to calm down. "I just don't understand why people are always so willing to offer their souls. The devil is thought to be such a bad guy, and eternal damnation is certainly as horrible as it sounds. But—never mind."

"And my dad?" I asked.

"Well, he still has his soul, to be certain." He appeared more relaxed as he leaned against the mantle. "He relied on friends, found jobs when he needed them, made ends meet; he even won a few times, not much but enough to help pay the bills. Your mother tracked him down years ago."

"Mother?" It was a bit of a shock. All these years, she'd played the wounded widow, as if Dad had disappeared and never resurfaced.

"She didn't see him, but she worked through legal channels to get him to sign divorce papers. She never pressed him for child support."

"Small wonder there. I would have thought her to be more vengeful."

"She just wanted to remarry."

"Hal, of course." It all made sense. "So that's how she was able to remarry. It's kind of annoying that she knew how to find Dad all this time and she never told me."

More than annoying, it made me angry with her, as if I needed more reasons to be mad at my mother.

"How old were you by then? Off on your own, certainly."

"True. The wedding was the summer before I moved to Manhattan, so . . . I was twenty-six."

"Old enough to be moving on, not interested in what

your parents were up to, or so she probably thought. No need to trouble you."

"Maybe." Owen was far more ready to give my parents credit than I, most likely because they weren't any relation to him. "But back to Dad."

"Not much else to tell. He worked, played, made friends, moved on. But he never stopped thinking about you and your sister. He carries your pictures in his wallet."

I looked at him, again wondering how he could possibly know such intimate details and deciding that I didn't want to know. Not now. My feelings about Owen were all up in the air, scattered like a flock of birds when a shot rings out in the distance. I didn't know how to get my emotions soothed enough to straighten up and fly back in formation.

"So he thinks about me. Big deal. It's not as if he couldn't have come back and tried to find me. I'm in the phone book. So is Bennie. My grandparents have lived in the same house for the past fifty years." I sounded like a little girl, petulant and whiny. But it was all my gut reaction and I couldn't force myself to rise above it.

"Perhaps he will." Owen shrugged. "He finally hit the big one, a two-point-five million dollar jackpot on a slot machine. That's why he's here this week. He brought his buddies out for a golf and beach vacation and then, who knows. Maybe he plans to look you up."

"Or maybe he'll head back to Vegas and blow it all. It doesn't matter." I drew in close to Owen, my eyes drawn to his hands. His large, skilled hands. How much I'd wanted to take his hands and let him lead me. "He's nothing to me now."

"And what about me?" He raised a brow. "Are you through with me as well?"

My heart skipped a beat when I looked at him. Sultry eyes, decadent smile, broad shoulders, and soccer-player thighs. Not to mention the trouble he'd gone to in an attempt to give me my heart's desire. Oh no. I most definitely was not through with him. But what I wanted with him, I didn't know.

I stepped into his arms, held him close, and raised up on my toes to kiss his cheek. "I'm not through with you yet. But I need some time to think."

He drew me even closer, his hands sliding down to rest on my bottom. "Fair enough. But I still think you should meet with your dad. Deep down, you really want to see him."

I rocked back on my heels. *Mental brake-screech.* "You know, Owen, that's part of my problem with you right now. You may not mean to be, but you are so darn arrogant. You say things you couldn't possibly know without even a question in your tone, as if you think you know exactly what other people are thinking. Well, news flash." I poked him right in the chest. "You don't know it all. I'm not ready to see my father. Right now, all I want is to go home."

"Now who's arrogant? You're so ready to point the finger at me without even considering that I may be right after all. That perhaps I know you even better than you know yourself."

He drew me up short. I had no angry retort, no witty comeback, no answer at all. Yesterday, I'd stood in this same room across from Owen. I'd been filled with hope, wonder, and excitement at where the night would lead. Today I felt drained, confused, and full of doubt. "I need to get home."

"I can have the plane ready in under an hour."

"No." I placed my hand on his arm and felt his heat again. The delicious heat he radiated. It was enough to make me melt all over again, if I let it. I didn't. "I need to be alone. If you can arrange for a ride to the airport, I'll book a flight."

"That's not necessary," he assured me. "I have some business that will keep me here. I'll have the plane ready to bring you home. Alone."

Chapter 9

On the plane, I had the chance to reflect on my father and to try to make sense of my feelings for Owen. At the time, fresh from the shock of seeing Dad again, I hadn't wanted to face him. As the minutes ticked away, bringing me further from Dad and closer to home, all I could think about was what I could have said to him, what I possibly needed to say.

My mind kept going back to the same ridiculous conclusion, that perhaps Owen had been right. I needed to see my father again. Maybe Owen really did know me better than I knew myself. I would sort out my feelings for Owen later, maybe once I could see him again under more stable circumstances—but I wasn't sure stable was in my future any more than it had been a part of my past.

I had the feeling of being frozen, emotionally crippled. For years, I'd blamed myself for Dad's leaving. I thought if I'd been a better daughter, more of an athlete, less of a girly-girl, he might not have gone. I'd imagined that he'd run off and made a new family, a family of big rugged boys. Would he have stayed if his firstborn had been a son? I went over the conversation in my mind, the one I would have had if I had been brave enough to face him.

There was nothing I could do about it now. I'd been too afraid of what I might say, of unleashing the kind of venom that used to spew forth from my mother's lips. I'd sworn I would never be her, but I could understand her feelings of betrayal and all the hurt left in their wake. I'd been left behind as well.

And so had Bennie. I couldn't wait to talk to her. So much had changed in the short time she'd been away. I'd fallen in love, almost. I'd seen Dad. The foundation of my entire world had been shaken.

Bennie returned the day after my solo flight from Hilton Head to Boston. She invited me to lunch, not dinner. She probably didn't want me to say no in fear of another fix-up. I wasn't about to refuse. I showed up with wine in hand as if I *had* been attending one of her parties. We had a lot to discuss, and I thought the wine might help take the edge off a bit.

"If I have to sit through pictures of the kids posed with every imaginable Disney character, I'm going to need this opened immediately," I said, handing her the Chardonnay as I walked in.

She took the bottle but shook her head disapprovingly. "Oh, please. My children are dolls. You love looking at them, no matter the scenery."

"I do love your kids."

"And did we get some great shots!" She set the wine aside and led me into the living room, where she was already hard at work putting together the Disney scrapbook.

"I'll say you did. What are there, a hundred pictures

there?" Before she could force me into a seat, I turned on my heel, headed back to the kitchen, and retrieved the Chardonnay.

"A hundred and eighty-five, but who's counting?"

"Right." I headed straight for the bar, opened the wine, poured out two glasses, and returned to curl up next to her on the couch, handing her a glass as I sat down. She took a healthy sip before she set it aside and went right back to trimming Mickey ears cut out of construction paper, a decorative backdrop for a page of Spencer, Sarah, and the Mouse. "So where are the troops, anyway?"

"The dogs are outside, and Patrick took the kids to enroll in a group swim hour at the Y. They had so much fun at the hotel pool that Patrick decided they could all take up swimming together over the winter. Isn't that great? I thought he would be eager to head straight back to work, but no calls from Glendower Enterprises."

I blushed, the knowledge of Owen's whereabouts and why he wasn't hounding Patrick still my own intimate secret. "Thank goodness for small favors. I bet Patrick's delighted to have more time with Spence and Sarah."

Bennie nodded, reached for her glass, and took another sip. "Yes, and so am I. Mr. All Business finally realizes he has a family, too. Vacation time was just what we needed."

"So, you're thinking a little more kindly toward Owen Glendower, perhaps?" I tried to raise a brow. No dice.

"Kindly? No. More appreciatively, perhaps. I don't know where this whole generous instinct came from, but it isn't in character for Owen Glendower to be kind and giving as far as I've seen."

"What do you mean?" In my experience, Owen was the complete opposite of the man Bennie described.

"I mean he's always calling with last minute demands. He buys houses like they are going out of style. What's he doing with all those houses, I ask you? And why is it always rush-rush, got to have it now? And the worst part is that he expects Patrick to just drop what he's doing and run out to check on all of the new properties."

"He is an investor," I reminded her, taking another sip of my own wine for courage. But I had to stay in top form. Getting a buzz on was all well and good, but the plan was to feed Bennie's buzz and keep my wits about me. "I imagine he's always after solid moneymakers. He probably holds on to them for the short term, then re-sells them for big bucks when the market heats up."

Bennie shook her head. "The man needs a good dose of reality, if you ask me. He's too rich. He forgets what it's like to struggle."

I couldn't even stifle a laugh. I looked around at Bennie's expensive furniture, pricey art accents, Lladró figurines scattered around the room, and the imported crystal chandelier hanging overhead. "You're hardly struggling here in suburbia."

She harrumphed and sipped again. "Compared to him I am. Plus, he's so selfish. He has no idea what it's like for people with families. As if Patrick should just make himself available at all hours to appease His Highness Owen Glendower. Get real."

"Maybe he's going to get a clue one day soon," I said, a flush of heat warming me straight to my toes. "Who knows, if the right woman comes along, he may begin to more fully understand family values."

"The right woman?" She downed her glass and held

it out for a refill. "I don't think Diana D-Cup quite makes the mark for future wife material."

"Diana D-Cup?" I took her glass, refilled, and returned.

"You know, that actress? With the—" she gestured at her chest, took the glass, and set it down.

"Big fake boobs, yeah. I know the one." Diana Di-Carlo was a former Playboy model turned movie actress, more popularly known as Diana D-Cup in the tabloids. "Was she one of Owen's former flames?"

"Former?" Bennie laughed. "Hardly. They've been on and off for some time now. I believe Owen plans to take her to the Bahamas this weekend."

"Oh? *This* weekend?" My chest tightened until my heart felt like it could explode. Could it be true? "How do you know?"

How easily I'd put aside the fact that he could be dating any number of women, even now. Why not? We'd hardly agreed to be exclusive. I had no reason to believe he wasn't pursuing half a dozen women as hotly as he pursued me. But I had believed. When I'd looked in his dark brown eyes, I had been convinced that I was the one and only. Up to now, my doubts were solely focused on if he could truly be the one for me. Now I had to wonder if I could truly be the one for him, and not just one of many.

"His secretary told Patrick that Owen was going away, then Diana kept calling with questions about what temperature it was in Nassau this time of year, if she needed to pack two or three bikinis, that kind of thing. Naturally, it's what we assumed."

"Naturally," I agreed. I carelessly downed the rest of my glass. Then I reached for Bennie's and downed hers, too. Sobriety be damned. "Time for a refill." I headed back to the bar.

Diana DiCarlo? I didn't want to get mad. I didn't even want to think about it. He hadn't really argued when I said I wanted to fly home alone. Perhaps it made it easier for him to get on with his plans for a weekend getaway? Shouldn't he have called to check if I had gotten home safely? Yet I hadn't heard a word. Maybe it was true.

I handed Bennie her freshly filled glass and plunked down on the sofa with enough force to slosh some Chardonnay out of mine. "Oops."

"Oh, don't worry about it." Bennie blotted the drops up with a paper towel she had handy to wipe up the extra glue from the edges of her scrapbook pages. "Now, enough about Owen Glendower. Let's dish the real dirt. What happened between you and Marc? Did he call?"

"No calls." And thank goodness for that. I had enough trouble with one man, let alone two.

"I'm surprised. I thought he would call. He said you were hot."

"That's quite the compliment." Actually, it was, but there was no point in getting Bennie all excited in thinking there was any hope for Marc and me. I wished I could ask her about Owen, but the Diana DiCarlo revelation made all talk of Owen off limits for now. I turned Bennie's attention back to her pictures of the kids until I could find a way to bring up our father. I picked up a snapshot. "What a great family photo. How'd you manage that?"

"Oh." She looked at the picture of the four of them in front of Cinderella Castle. "Yes, that's my favorite. One of the cast members took it for us."

"Cast members?"

She rolled her eyes as if I was so out of touch. "That's what Disney calls their staff. Cast members. Everyone plays a role in making the magic."

My turn for the eye-roll. "Listen to you, the big Disney convert. Didn't you use to make fun of people who vacationed there?"

I recalled the too-cool-for-school Bennie from back in the day, before Patrick and the kids. She was Miss Popularity at Newton High, the one who always wore the right clothes, had the right hair, and knew the right people and all the right places to go.

"Well, yeah, but that was only because Mom never had money to take us and the Mareks went all the time." Maura Marek, the other most popular girl, had been Bennie's best friend—and enemy—all through school.

"That's right." I laughed. "You couldn't stand it when Maura got something you wanted."

"Yes, but she really wanted Patrick." Bennie held up her left hand and wiggled her fingers, making her enormous diamond sparkle in the light of the chandelier. "And look who got him."

"Of course. How could he resist?" We laughed and went through more of her pictures. "I wonder if we ever would have gone to Disney World as a family if Dad had been around."

"Dad? Who knows. I used to imagine that he would come back and take us all around the world. Of course, we traveled by flying carpet. And he usually arrived dressed as a prince riding up on a white horse. He was the big hero of all my childhood fantasies."

"Hero? The man left us."

"Yeah, but he left us *with Mom*. Not that she was so

bad, but it was easy to cast her in the role of the evil witch to my virtuous Rapunzel." She smoothed her hair and batted her lashes.

"Virtuous? You *did* have a rich imagination." We laughed some more. "So, if you could see Dad again, would you want to talk to him or would you rather pass unnoticed?"

"Pass unnoticed? Are you kidding? I would be so happy if he came back."

"Even now? Even after all these years?"

She sighed and looked at me, suddenly serious. "You know, Kate, that's one way we're different. No offense, but you can afford to be selfish. I have a family to consider. What about the kids? I was robbed of my father's company, but why should they be denied a grandfather?"

"I guess." I'd never thought of it that way. Patrick's dad had passed away years ago, when Bennie's kids were too young to remember. If single motherhood ever panned out, my child would also lack a grandfather. Maybe I *was* selfish. I hadn't even been thinking a father was necessary, let alone a grandfather. "But they have Patrick and Pops."

"A father and a great-grandfather, sure. That's great. But having Pops never stopped me from missing Dad."

"After all these years?" I asked, but it was a pointless question. The years didn't matter. I knew how she felt. I still missed him, too, and now I had the power to bring him back into all of our lives. The problem was, I still wasn't sure I wanted to risk rekindling the relationship for fear of ending up disappointed all over again.

Chapter 10

A week passed without any word from Owen. Perhaps he was giving me time to think. Perhaps he was so busy with busty actresses he barely had time to think of me. I wasn't about to be that woman who sat by the phone. I put Owen to the back of my mind—as much as I could with the image of his wicked smile burned in my brain—and focused on my own work. Things were looking up. Much to my relief, Saturday's open house was scheduled to go on as planned.

The florist had just arrived to unload when I pulled into the drive.

"You can just leave them in the dining room," I told the deliveryman on my way in. He nodded.

As I was shrugging out of my coat, he placed three bouquets of lovely white roses accented with purple freesia on the table.

"Roses?" I said to the deliveryman. "I ordered peonies. And I didn't want them arranged."

He was checking his order form when there was a knock on the open front door.

"Yes?" I looked up to see a second man in the bright yellow delivery coveralls, worn by the Carey's Flowers delivery staff, my usual florist.

"Flower delivery. Do I have the right house?"

"Of course, yes. Bring them on in." So if *this* was my florist, who was the other one? In the meantime, the first florist had returned with arms full. Three more bouquets of roses, two white and one a dark crimson red.

Red roses. White roses. Roses? I was beginning to feel a bit like the Queen of Hearts in *Alice in Wonderland*. "I think there's been some mistake," I said. "I didn't order roses."

He sighed, placing the bouquets on the now over-crowded round oak podium table.

"No mistake. I have the right address. They're all yours." He handed me a card from the red bouquet. "Eight more in the truck."

"Eight more? You've got to be kidding." That's when I spotted the card. I read it, a tingle coursing through my veins.

ETERNALLY, O

Owen *hadn't* forgotten about me.

I'd never been sent more than a dozen roses, and that only once. He'd even gone through the trouble to find out where I would be today. He could have just sent them to my condo, but that would have been too ordinary. Ordinary wasn't his style, or so I was learning.

I was unsure of where this thing with Owen was headed, but the roses sent my spirit—and my ego—skyrocketing. Take that, Diana DiCarlo. Of course, she could be getting roses today too, but I had no idea and

I didn't care. Owen was thinking about me, and the automatic rush I got at the knowledge proved that I still wanted him as badly as ever. I could have danced around the room. I didn't, of course. The delivery men would think I'd gone nuts.

The open house would be starting soon. I checked my watch. I had an hour to figure out how to put fourteen bouquets of roses to good decorative use around the house.

Fortunately, Val arrived to help.

"What's with the roses?" she asked. "I thought you were going with peonies and mixed wildflower bouquets?"

"I am," I said. "The roses were an unexpected bonus."

She grabbed a cup from the counter and poured herself a coffee. "Like a lucky thousandth customer bonus or like a big spender of the month bonus?"

"Something like that," I said absently as I spied the card on the edge of the table where I'd carelessly put it down. I reached for it. Val must have followed my gaze because she reached at the same second, and she got it first.

"Eternally?" she said. "My ga-awwd. Who is this O?"

"No one," I said, trying to stay calm. My cheeks reddened instantly, giving more away than I intended. "Just a guy."

"Just a guy?" She put her hand on her hip. "Just a guy, with a card signed eternally? You've been holding out on me, Kate. How long have you been seeing this O?"

"It's no big deal." I tried to shrug it off but my racing heart made it hard to keep my voice steady. "I met him a few weeks ago at Bennie's."

"There's like a bazillion roses here. Who is he, Donald Trump? Or that guy everyone's calling the new

Donald Trump? What's his name, Owen something?"
She laughed.

I met her gaze. "Glendower." The Owen buzz raced
around inside me again, wreaking havoc with my nervous system.

"No shit!" Val did a little dance. "You're dating Owen
Glendower? I just read his profile in *People* magazine.
You're dating someone who has been in *People!*"

"Not dating." I corrected. "I mean, yes, we've gone out
but—" I was saying too much. "He's just showing off."

"Showing off? I'll say." Val counted bouquets.

As if on cue, the delivery guy reappeared laden with
even more roses. Val gasped.

"It's nothing," I said again.

"It ain't nothing. I used to get nothing from Jim on
our anniversaries. And trust me, it didn't look like this."

"Men like Owen Glendower can afford to make
grand gestures. You know how it is."

"No." Val snorted. "But apparently *you* do. I have no
idea except what I read in glitzy magazines."

"Exactly. Men like Owen don't do real life. They do
flash, glitz, whiz-bang, thank you, good-bye."

I played it down to keep myself from getting too excited. Owen and I hadn't settled anything between us.
If I decided to jump in and explore the affair, I wanted
it to be an exclusive relationship. I wasn't up for shar-
ing him and I would have to let him know before pro-
ceeding any further, even if it ended up chasing him
away.

"You already got to whiz-bang?"

My cheeks were growing hotter by the second.
"Absolutely not."

"Not yet." She affirmed. "Oh Kate! This is so exciting. You have to introduce me. Tell me all about him.

What is he like up close? Is he really short in person? Like Tom Cruise? What a letdown."

"He's tall," I said.

"Did he kiss you?"

The kissing. Oh, God. The Owen buzz strengthened until I swore I could feel it ringing in my ears. My physical reaction to this man, even in mere mention, was seriously weird. Appealing, but weird.

"Look, we have a lot of work ahead of us. Why don't you find places for the roses? I'll start making the peony arrangements."

"Fine." Val chugged the rest of her coffee. "Flowers for now. But later," she gestured with a chocolate glazed cruller, "you're going to tell me all about Owen Glendower."

"Later," I said, wondering how long I could stall her. I needed to talk to Owen and get a handle on my feelings before I let Val talk me into getting carried away with the romance of it all. I knew I was in too deep to settle for a wild, whirlwind affair, but Owen bringing me to my father had raised my emotional stakes.

With Owen, it was all or nothing for me now.

The open house was a hectic success. Hours later, as the crowds dwindled and the excitement started to fade, I began my usual sweep of the rooms to adjust misplaced room accents and start wrapping things up.

I'd leave the furniture for a few more days in case of private showings or a sale. If a couple buys the house, they may want some of the pieces to stay. If not, we'd bring in the movers and take it all back. But as long as my pieces were in the house, I wanted them to look as close to perfect as possible. I was in the nursery, carefully refolding a baby blue layette, when Val ducked her head in.

"Someone's making a bid on the house," she said. "Let's go see what's up."

Intrigued, I followed Val to the kitchen to see what kind of offer was on the table. Since the buyer expressed interest following the open house, I was due a commission out of the deal. Thank God for small favors. It was my first commission in weeks.

"Hello," I said, walking into the kitchen with Val on my heels.

"Kate, hi." Debby, the realtor, stood to greet me. "This is Zelda Fitzgerald. She's representing the buyer."

Zelda Fitzgerald? I stifled the urge to ask if the buyer was F. Scott. A good thing, too, because when Zelda stood to make my acquaintance, she snarled. I jumped back. Only then did I see that she held a teacup poodle—a small ball of well-groomed fluff in the exact peach shade of her fitted suit.

"I'm sorry," Zelda said, in distinct Southern belle. "She doesn't like women."

"Nice to know it isn't just me."

"Down," Zelda commanded the pooch. "Behave now, you hear?" The tiny dog snorted and settled deeper into her owner's arms.

"Shall we get back to the paperwork?" Debby asked, a little overeager. I wondered how large a bid the buyer had put in. Deb usually played it close to the vest, but now she was practically drooling.

"Of course darlin'," Zelda cooed, sweet as peaches canned in syrup. Gag. "I just want to compliment Miss Kate on her lovely decorating."

Miss Kate? How very *Gunsmoke* of her.

"Thank you," I said with a smile.

"I just love everything." She spun a little pirouette on her delicate dyed-to-match slingbacks. "Every little touch. I hope you can afford to part with your stock, because I aim to take it all. The buyer's a very discerning man and I know it will suit him. He's too busy to go out and shop on his own. You know men."

I tried not to bristle when she nudged me with her elbow, as if we were co-conspirators against men, an alien race. Also, her description of the buyer sounded incredibly familiar to me. *Too* familiar. Still, I tried to shrug it off.

"Everything?" I asked, trying to do a fast estimate in my head. The commission plus the sale of over half my inventory would make for a tidy sum, enough to make up for all my lost business earlier in the month. I felt a wave of euphoria that was better than sex. My mind called up the memory of being on the chaise lounge with Owen at the beach. Not better than sex. But pretty good.

"Why yes indeed," Zelda said. "It's done up perfect. Right down to the little doilies on the end tables. Irish lace adds a sweet touch to soften the hard masculine planes of the room. Nice choice. You know what they say." She met my gaze, her crystalline blue eyes direct and burning into mine. "The devil is in the details."

And just like that, I knew who the buyer was.

"Does the buyer intend to live here," I asked, unable to control my curiosity. "Or is it just another investment?" There was a fine line between caring about my well-being and cutting me a pity check, and I didn't need Owen Glendower's money. It was the second time he'd interfered in my personal affairs, and the second time I wasn't fond of the lengths to which he'd gone uninvited.

"He plans to move right in, of course," Zelda said.

I was only slightly relieved. Why this house? Why now? It all seemed a little too convenient, and from all of the roses, I knew it couldn't be just a coincidence. Sure, Owen was looking out for me, but I would feel so much better about it if only I could know his reasons behind the acquisition.

"I know a few things about Owen's personal preferences, too," I said to Zelda, testing her further. "Why don't you have him call me and I can make sure the house is done exactly to his specifications before he moves in?"

"Owen?" Val gasped and looked from me to Zelda and back again. "Owen Glendower's buying the house?"

"There's no need for you to bother Mister Glendower. I'm qualified to speak for his interests." Zelda's gaze swept over me as if she was assessing a new rival, and it prompted me to do the same.

Given her attitude, I couldn't help but wonder if she was more than just a business partner. Had he sent *her* roses? If he had, I was pretty sure they'd all been peach. Everything about her was peach-perfect. Peach-blossom skin, peach clothes, peach-toned highlights in her warm chestnut hair. Even her dog was peachy. I stifled the urge to ask if Zelda had been homegrown in Georgia, but I smiled as I pictured her dropping straight out of a tree to land on her perfect peach-curved bottom.

Val swooped in with coffee for everyone. I reached for a cup, though the last thing I needed was caffeine. I was jumpy enough without it.

"Mr. Glendower wants to take possession right away. Will that be a problem?" Zelda asked Debby.

"Er, I'll check to check," Debby said. "But I'm sure it won't present any difficulties."

"Delightful," Zelda twanged.

It would be just like him to take possession immediately. Take, take, take. Did he ever think about what he was taking, or just grab what he wanted and run with it? I took a deep breath to try to calm down. I really needed to talk to him. The sooner, the better. But I had no idea how to contact him or when I would see him again.

"There is one more thing," Zelda added. "The nursery. You can move the baby furniture out of there. That's one change I'm sure Mr. Glendower is sure to insist upon."

"No baby furniture?" Of course, it only made sense. He was a single man with a world of women at his fingertips. But I loved the nursery. I'd set it up with such loving care and everything fit so perfectly in the room. As silly as it seemed, part of me had hoped he would love it, too.

"Heavens no! Can you imagine Mr. Glendower with children?" Zelda laughed. "Get it all out. Bring in some office furniture instead. It's just the right size for an office. That will be so much better."

"Easily done," I said. But not so easy to accept. I took a deep breath in order to fight the tears that threatened. I had been ready to picture Owen with children. *Our* children. But now I was more confused than when I'd gotten on the plane to come home.

Chapter 11

By Sunday morning, I still hadn't heard from Owen. Fortunately, I had a family gathering to distract me from thoughts of him splashing in the surf with Diana DiCarlo. One Sunday a month we all got together at Bennie's. Normally, I dreaded it. I was no more immune to my grandmother's scrutiny at brunch than I was to Bennie's set-up attempts at her dinners. Today I welcomed the chance to reconnect with the people who knew me best.

I arrived late, as usual, and ran into my grandfather pilfering a butterscotch from the foyer candy dish.

"Hey Pops, be careful not to ruin your appetite," I said by way of greeting, placing my hand on my hip and waving my finger in an exaggerated imitation of my grandmother.

He laughed and gave me a brisk handshake, his trademark hello. My grandfather had his sweet tooth to get him through these occasional family ordeals, but my numbing agent of choice packed a little more potency. I headed straight for the living room, where

Patrick, on mimosa duty, already had an array of glasses poured and waiting on the bar.

"Bless you, my brother." I skipped the small talk, grabbed a glass, and headed for the kitchen to announce my arrival to Mom and Gran before they organized a formal search party. Despite my habitual lateness, they freaked out and assumed the worst if I didn't arrive their standard ten minutes early for family functions.

His voice reached me, nearly stopping me in my tracks before I even opened the kitchen door. "Ladies, no fighting. I'll sample both."

Owen. The usual buzz rushed over me. My head felt light. My knees shook with excitement.

Owen? In the kitchen? Laughing with Bennie, Mother, and Gran as if he'd always been part of the family. What?

Gran stood on one side of him with ham pinwheels, Mother on the other feeding him a deviled egg.

"Thanks, Susan." he said, devouring the entire egg in one bite. "Oh yes. I'm definitely in favor of the eggs."

"What about my pinwheels?" Gran pouted. "I thought they were your favorites."

"Now, Millie, don't get possessive. I'm a man of many tastes. I like both the pinwheels and the deviled eggs." He was already on a first-name basis with Gran, for God's sake. No one under the age of seventy managed that without a stiff lecture on respect for the elders.

"What are you doing here?" I asked, unsure if I was angry or thrilled. My body felt sure, all senses pulsing on the side of thrilled. My mind tried to wrap around the idea that he'd infiltrated my private life once again without my invitation.

"You've met Mr. Glendower?" Mom asked, looking up from shaking paprika over her eggs.

"We've met," Owen said, meeting my gaze at last. "Kate, so good to see you again. Patrick invited me to come by for the afternoon."

"He did, did he?" That rat! "He didn't tell me we had a guest."

"He doesn't know I've arrived. Susan and Millie have been so entertaining that I nearly forgot my manners. I should go say hello."

Without so much as a nod, he scooted by me out through the swinging door. With moony eyes, Mother followed after him, holding the tray of eggs as an excuse.

"I'll take those." I made the grab and followed Owen out.

I experienced some measure of relief that Owen showed no signs of intimacy, followed by some measure of concern that he showed no signs of intimacy. Was this a part of the courtship ritual? The suitor meets the family? Or was it simply a *boss dines with the family* kind of affair? In either event, I was instantly on edge, afraid of what might happen next. I hadn't told Bennie a thing about my dates with Owen. What if she didn't approve? What if my family hated him? And worse yet, what if he'd written me off in favor of Diana DiCarlo and his appearance here was strictly business after all? Why hadn't he called me?

I stood back trying to read the situation as Patrick greeted Owen, then introduced him to Pops.

"Very nice to meet you," Owen said, and then, as if they'd known one another for years, the two of them launched into an in-depth discussion on the televised golf tournament. Golf, the way to my grandfather's heart.

"Care for an egg, Pop?" My grandfather grabbed a few off the tray as I worked my way between them to see what kind of reaction I might receive. Friendly smile, lecherous wink, playful slap on the behind? I was up for anything but the indifference he offered, with a shrug and no thanks before he got right back to comparing the swing styles of Tiger Woods and Retief Goosen.

I put the eggs down on the side table and took a seat on the sofa closest to the bar and furthest from where the men gathered around the television. Even Patrick had become absorbed in the golf to the negligence of his normally superior hosting duties. After a few minutes, I got up, replaced my empty glass with a full one, and sat back down to find that Owen had disappeared entirely.

"Where's your guest?" I asked.

Patrick headed back to the bar. "He went upstairs to meet Hal and the kids." Hal, my stepdad, always felt more at home in the company of the kids. At least, in the company of their high-tech toys.

"On his own?"

"Yeah. He figured Spence could show him his new video games by way of introduction."

He seemed to know just the right way to charm the whole family, and video games were definitely Spencer's forte, and right up Hal's alley, too. Within seconds, my niece Sarah came tearing down the stairs and plunked down next to me on the couch. I set my mimosa down on the coffee table in time to avoid sloshing it all over at her exuberant greeting

"Aunt Kate!" After a bear hug, she settled by my side.

"Princess Sarah, I presume." With her abundant red hair, she looked more Little Mermaid than Cinderella, but she'd always had a thing for the Disney princesses.

"*Don't* call me that." She shuddered. Apparently the princess phase was over.

"Sorry."

"It's okay. I'm just in one of my moods." She rolled her big blue-green eyes.

I stifled the urge to laugh at her seven-going-on-forty routine, as well as the desire to ask if she was having a hot flash.

"I'm in a mood, too," I said. "We can be surly together."

"Surly?"

"Moody?" I said.

"Oh. Spence won't let me play *Rogue Squadron*. He says I suck."

"I'll bet he's just embarrassed at the thought of being beaten by a girl."

"No," she said. "I really suck. But it's not fair. I want to play."

"What about Hal?" I asked.

She rolled her eyes. "Hal hogs the game worse than Spencer. And now the new guy's getting a turn before me!"

"The new guy, hnh? He's trouble. Take it from me."

"Yeah but he said he's never played Nintendo before so he probably won't take long."

"Don't count on it. He's good at everything."

"No one's good at *everything*."

"Trust me, the new guy's good." Or bad to the bone. I still couldn't decide which. I only knew that his mere presence scattered my brain and made my body go haywire. Why was he here invading my home terrain?

"Wanna hear about my trip?"

"Sure," I said. "Your mom showed me pictures, but it's not the same as hearing all about it."

"It was so cool, Aunt Kate! We got to ride Space Mountain!"

"I love Space Mountain," Owen said, and I jumped at the sound of his voice. I hadn't even noticed him coming back down the stairs, and there he was behind us, getting a drink from Patrick at the bar.

"I bet you do," I said. "It's fast, cold, and so dark you can't see where you're going."

"I always know where I'm going," he said.

"Yeah, Aunt Kate. If you look hard enough, you can see the track."

I couldn't see the track. I had no idea where I was headed with Owen and it scared me a lot more than riding Space Mountain. Mimosa in hand, he took a seat on the other side of Sarah to compare notes on Disney World.

I enjoyed seeing him interact with a child. I hadn't quite had a chance to actually picture him as a dad, but he proved up to the task. He engaged Sarah without being patronizing. He'd clearly had some experience with the under-ten set and patience to spare, no matter what his representative Zelda had said to the contrary.

Sarah chattered a mile a minute, obviously as taken with Owen as Mom and Gran had been earlier. Was there a woman alive he could fail to win over?

I excused myself and headed to the backyard to get some air. It was cold, unusually so even for November in Massachusetts. The sky was a gunmetal gray, heavy with clouds bearing rain, or possibly snow. I was glad I'd worn my Cole Haan driving shoes, but even stiletto heels wouldn't sink into the frozen earth.

I wrapped my arms around my middle, an effort to keep warm in my thin cotton sweater. I wasn't about to head back inside for my coat. Not just yet. I felt fragile. Once again, Owen had invaded my turf. I wasn't ready, and it sent me for a tailspin. I blinked back tears.

A minute later, Patrick came out to join me.

"Hey now, come here." Without asking what was wrong, Patrick enfolded me in a warm embrace. I'd always known what Bennie had seen in Patrick. He was a sweet, caring man with terrific people instincts.

"Thanks." I took a deep breath and backed away. "I don't know what's wrong with me. I just suddenly felt overwhelmed."

He smiled. "With Bennie, I would guess it was a certain time of the month. In that case, the cure is inside. I make a mean chocolate martini."

"I remember. I think I had one too many of those last Valentine's Day."

He had a point with that, too. It was nearly that time of the month. Silly me. It wasn't just Owen. I was carried away on hormone overload.

"Ah yes, the famous *I don't need a man, I just need martinis* episode."

I laughed.

"So, what's Owen Glendower doing here?"

"Owen?" Patrick stared off at the woods. "Oh, just thought it would be nice to have him over. He has no family, you know. That's got to suck."

"Family's overrated," I said. "You've met Gran."

Gran had actually once suggested I take a side job as a waitress to attempt to catch the eye of Gus, a cook at her favorite diner who bore an uncanny resemblance to Gus, the mouse from the Disney version of *Cinderella*. No thanks.

I faced him full on, drawing his attention back away

from the trees. "So cut the crap. Tell me why you *really* invited Owen."

Patrick sighed. "He invited himself. I didn't have the balls to say no. Glendower's been a lucrative client, and not a bad friend to have in this business. He tells me he bought a house that you decorated."

"On Tuesday. It's an enormous colonial on Farnham Road in Newton."

"Right. Well, I guess you intrigued him. He said he wanted to get to know you a little, get some information on your design techniques. It could be good for you. If he took you on at Glendower Enterprises, you'd have good steady pay for years to come, no worries."

"No worries." I stifled a laugh. I'd gone a little beyond the worry stage concerning Owen. Patrick had no idea.

"Besides," Patrick said, his cheeks turning as red as his hair. "I think Bennie's matchmaking ways might be rubbing off on me. The man's a catch, right?"

"Oh no, not you, too." Apparently, he wasn't all that worried about Diana DiCarlo stealing Owen's heart for good. Maybe I *did* have a shot. I felt suddenly encouraged. And then on cue, Owen walked through the door holding my coat.

"Speak of the devil," Patrick said.

"You forgot this." He closed the distance and draped my coat over my shoulders. "If you're going to hide out here all day, you're going to need it."

"I'd better get back." Patrick gestured toward the door. "If we're lucky, we'll get Gran drunk and she'll pass out before dessert."

"Good luck with that." Gran, a diabetic, kept away from alcohol. It was more likely Patrick would get a buzz on to minimize Gran's effect on him.

"You have a lovely family," Owen said once Patrick had disappeared into the house.

I shrugged into the coat as he held it out for me and turned to face him.

"Sarcasm?"

"No. I mean it. They're a nice bunch." His eyes held genuine warmth, warmer than the coat. I almost melted on the spot, then I remembered that I was supposed to be angry at him for his interference in my private affairs. Or was I just jealous of Diana D-Cup? What *did* I want with him?

I narrowed my eyes. "Why are you here?"

"You're here. I miss you. Plus, I figured it was time I got to know your family better."

"Most men would wait for an invitation."

"I'm not conventional. Are you going to hold it against me?" With his rumpled hair and dark eyes, he tempted me to hold everything of mine against him. His casual white shirt, open at the neck and tucked into dark jeans, revealed his fine physique. But I was stronger than my hormones.

"That depends on your motives," I said honestly. "I have things going on in my life. Serious things. I don't plan to drop everything to indulge in some hedonistic affair. You said you wanted more with me, and then I heard about you running off with some cheesy actress. Are you seeing Diana DiCarlo?"

He laughed. Honestly laughed! As if the whole accusation was ridiculous. It filled me with hope. He gripped my hands. "Jealous? I think I like this side of you, Kate. It's so unabashedly wicked."

Feeling slightly foolish, I pulled my hands away and tucked them under my arms. I'd never been possessive over a man. "I'd like to think of it as petty, thank you very much."

"No," he drew in closer, not giving me a chance to walk away. "It's sweet, really. Not wicked or petty. I like that you want me all to yourself. It means you care as much as I had begun to hope."

I hazarded a glance at him. He met my gaze directly, the darkness of his eyes pulling me in. "My *assistant* is seeing Diana DiCarlo."

"Your assistant?"

He nodded. "Of course, Byron's also seeing half the women in my office. He's quite the cad. So if he gave anyone the impression that I was seeing Diana, it was probably to save himself. They're still in the Bahamas as we speak."

"They are?" I felt a rush at the news, but I didn't want to get too careless too soon. "This Byron must be quite the womanizer. What does he do, woo them with poetry?"

"In fact he does. *She walks in beauty, like the night.* One of his better lines, if you ask me. Except I've taken a preference for the day, light over dark. You make me feel as if I'm basking in the sun, Kate." He reached up, smoothed back the hair that had fallen over my face, then cupped my cheek in his large warm hand. All my cares fell away. Byron who? Diana DiCarlo was all but forgotten. "All I want to do is stretch out and let your warmth graze over me."

An image of him stretched out came to mind. Stretched out, naked, waiting, his body ready for my touch. My mouth went dry. I struggled to remember what else was bothering me. It was now or never to figure out where we were headed.

"What about finding my dad? Then buying the house?

And showing up here all of a sudden, no warning? Don't you think you could have consulted me first?"

"You've been thinking about your father, haven't you? My timing may have been off, and for that, I am so sorry. But I was only trying to give you something special to show you how much I cared."

He cared. His timing had been off, but he was dead on that I had been thinking about my father ever since that last day on Hilton Head. "I am glad to know what became of him, and I do want to see him, eventually, after I figure out what to say. So thank you. I can chalk that one up to good intentions. And the house?"

He shrugged. "I need a new place, what can I say? I like the idea of being surrounded by things that remind me of you. What better way than to buy a house that you decorated? I make no excuse for wanting you all around me."

Heat shot straight through me. Now *that* was romantic. Suddenly being upset with him for buying the house seemed equivalent to being angry at him for wanting me. "Good answer. Now how about just showing up here and then ignoring me?"

"I didn't know how you would feel about my being here. It was a risk to call and ask in case you said no. I figured just showing up was my best bet. And I have not been ignoring you."

"You haven't exactly been showering me with interest."

"What am I supposed to do? Make love to you in the living room? The way we'd left things between us, I wasn't sure how you felt. Plus, I wasn't about to charge in and say we were a couple. That's up to you. I thought you would like a chance to talk with your sister first."

Again, his instincts proved correct. He knew me as much as I'd wanted, more than I had dared to hope.

The knowledge fueled my own desire for him. I'd never wanted anything or anyone more than I wanted him now.

"You could make love to me in the yard." I slipped my arms around him. "No one's looking."

He laughed, but didn't pull away.

"I'm not asking for a fling, Kate. I want you. All of you. You have plans, hopes, dreams. So do I. Why not dream together?"

"You don't want children." It was a risky move to even ask it aloud, but I was in an all-out kind of mood. Perhaps I had been hoping he would deny it, say he would consider having a family, eventually, with the right person, *fill in the blank, with me.*

"It's more complicated than that."

Not a yes or a no, promising enough. "So uncomplicate it. Tell me."

"I plan to. After we eat. This isn't the place."

"Then what is?"

"I have a new acquisition. It's a surprise. We'll have some brunch with your family, then we'll go. Just the two of us. There are things about me you need to know, and I'm ready to share them with you."

I swallowed hard. The rush of my blood echoed in my ears.

"I would like that," I said, gaining confidence. So far, his surprises had knocked the wind out of me. It took me a minute to realize that I was ready. Finally, with Owen, I felt ready for anything. I flattened my hands against his chest, remembering how he had placed my hand to his heart in the car on our way around Hilton Head. "I want to know everything about you."

"Good," he said, with the hint of smile on his lips.

"Because there's something I've been meaning to ask you and I'm hoping you won't say no."

"Okay." I took a steadying breath. Something to ask me? There was a good chance the word no had slipped permanently from my vocabulary.

"Let's go back inside," he said. "They're probably starting to wonder."

"They're probably about to eat," I agreed, and followed him inside. The sooner we got the meal over with, the sooner we could get to the surprise.

The Four Horsemen of the Apocalypse could have joined us for brunch and I wouldn't have noticed. I ate in silence, lost in thoughts of Owen. Fortunately, Owen's charm kept most of the family distracted throughout brunch. It was only when I passed on a second helping of Bennie's cherry cobbler—I never passed on seconds of cobbler—that Bennie flashed a concerned glance and asked if I was feeling well. Patrick, my hero of the day, came to the rescue with a pat of Bennie's hand, an unspoken signal not to push.

Would Owen and I have unspoken signals? Meaningful glances? A secret language all our own? I had no idea. I only knew it was nearly time to go and I had a major case of nerves. Everything was going so fast. He had something he wanted to ask me. We'd had Hilton Head, the Wellies, my father. He'd bought a house. My house. Plenty of room for two. Part of his *grand plans*? If things go according to plan, he'd once said, we would have all the time in the world.

My mind drew the obvious conclusion, and this time it had to be true. What else could he possibly want to ask?

"Thank you for a wonderful time." Owen said his

good-byes at the door. His gaze was on Bennie but I fought the temptation to answer in her stead. My excuses would follow. I would meet up with him outside. All this I knew without asking. Still, I watched him walk down the drive and willed him to turn and look at me one more time. The sensible side of me knew it was too soon to give us away. The more romantic side of me wanted everyone to guess by just looking at us together.

He didn't look back. No one guessed.

He got into his car. We all stepped back inside. Bennie closed the door.

"Well, that was relatively painless," Bennie said.

Patrick looked at me as if judging my reaction. Perhaps Patrick had a suspicion? I tingled with the hope that someone had a clue.

"He was on his best behavior," Patrick said. "Maybe he wanted to make a good impression."

"How could he not?" My mother practically swooned. "That is one fine-looking man." Hal made a face. "And so are you, dear."

Gran laughed out loud. "Hal's got nothing on that Glendower man. Hubba."

Gran didn't worry about prefacing anything with "no offense."

Pops added that the fella sure knew his golf, a compliment of the highest order. So everyone approved. Good to know.

"I have to get going too," I said, reaching for my coat. "Work."

"You never stay for coffee," Gran lamented. "Your sister makes the most wonderful coffee." Of course. Bennie, good to the last drop.

"Kate helped with the dishes," Patrick offered. "That earned her an early parole."

Before Gran could even get started on Patrick for comparing a family brunch to serving jail time, I slipped into my coat, said a fast good-bye, and headed out the door.

Owen, now parked at the end of the driveway, waited by his car.

"I want you to ride with me," he said, meeting me halfway up the drive. "I'll send someone for your car later."

"Are you kidding? The grandparents may be old but they're very observant. If they see my abandoned car, they'll think aliens abducted me."

Owen raised a brow. "I'll just go back and explain that *I'm* abducting you. How's that?"

He came close enough to kiss me.

"Is that your big secret? You're an alien?"

"Confessions come later. Kiss me."

"Now?"

"Why not? I miss you."

"My breath smells like asparagus from the quiche."

"No problem. I ate it, too." He put his arms around me.

"Real men don't eat quiche."

"Ah, you are onto me. I'm an artificial man."

As if acting on a dare, he took me by the waist and kissed me hard on the mouth. Deep. Intoxicating. Suddenly, I didn't even care that we were standing almost right outside Bennie's parlor window.

"You taste like cobbler. Delicious." He took my hand and led me toward his car. "You're riding with me."

His voice held an intense edge. I didn't want to say no. "And my car?"

"I'll have someone here in minutes." He got on the phone and made the arrangements before I could protest.

I could hardly contain my excitement as he held the door for me to get in. He hadn't even asked me to marry him, but I felt like a heroine from a romance novel running off to Gretna Green.

"Alone at last," he said as he got in to the driver's seat.

"Alone at last," I echoed, eager to find out exactly what he had in mind for the rest of our afternoon, perhaps for the rest of our lives.

Chapter 12

Owen took the Mass Pike into the city, a twenty-minute ride made in nearly complete silence until the skyline came into view.

As we drew closer to the exit, my mouth dropped open in surprise. The Prudential Center was iconic Boston, nestled in the heart of Back Bay, and easily the tallest building around. But where it used to read "Prudential" in large capital letters across the tower's top, it now said *Glendower Tower*. Written in stone. Or was it gold? I was surprised it wasn't neon.

The change was monumental. There should have been protests, demands, a humungous statewide uproar. But I'd heard nothing.

"What do you think?" he asked, as if daring to face me only once we were safely parked in the garage.

"You really bought it? The whole building?"

"I'm setting up headquarters on some of the top floors." He shrugged. "I wanted my offices to be closer to Tremont Street."

"And why would that be?" Curled up on the seat, I

leaned closer. The answer was that I lived on Tremont Street, but I wanted to hear him say it.

"You know perfectly well why." He wasn't going to give me the satisfaction of verbal acknowledgement. Yet.

"But your current headquarters is closer to Newton, where you've just bought a house," I observed, reaching out to stroke the leather of his seats, wishing it were the bare skin of his steely chest. I could play coy as well as he.

"Fancy that," he said, reaching to pluck my hand off the seat, bring it to his lips, and sear my palm with a kiss. "I may have to keep both offices open—one in the city, one just outside it. Let's go inside. I'll show you the view from my office."

A true gentleman, he came around to get my door and help me from the car, yet he seemed anything but gentle when he took my hand in his. Tender, yes, but not gentle. Owen reminded me of wild things, his movements economical and marked with the fluid, feral grace that masks a core of boundless strength.

The sight of him at my side chased any trace of dank November chill straight from my bones. I tucked into the crook of his arm, a natural fit, as we walked through the dim garage toward the elevator bank. Rays of light broke in from the outer wall, stretching shadows that looked like puddles across the cement. Cobwebs dipped from steel beams above our heads, stalactites in an urban cave.

I remembered being with Owen in the cave by the sea, feeling as if he'd stripped down to his essence to give me a sense of his unexplored depths. I'd fallen in love with him then, I realized. The rugged beauty, so lonely and fierce, sad beyond belief. All that I had felt from him, but also so much more. There was hope. He held hope deep in his soul and chased contentment like the light he claimed to crave.

It was no small responsibility to be light to someone's dark. Could we balance each other out? I only knew I wanted to try.

I leaned against him as he pressed the elevator call button. There was something he wanted to ask me. I wondered how he meant to do it. With Owen, there would be no need for fanfare involving the rest of the world. No stadium halftime proposal or getting down on one knee in the middle of a crowded mall. No singing in front of fountains. When his arm wrapped around my waist and pulled me tighter against him, I jumped with the thought that perhaps he meant to ask me right there, in the garage. But no. The elevator came with a ding. It opened, empty, and we stepped right in.

Once the doors shut, he spun me around with an unexpected urgency. He crushed my body against him, his tongue sliding between my lips to plunge to the sweet, hot depths at the hollow of my throat.

"God, I've been wanting to do that all day," he said, finally stopping to breathe. He kept his forehead pressed against mine, his breath hot on my face, smelling of the kind of sweet buttermints that my favorite restaurant used to keep in a jar when I'd first moved back to the city. It made me want to taste him again. This time, I kissed him, sucking his tongue deep inside me, drawing on it, biting at his lush lower lip.

The elevator door dinged open. His hand at the small of my back, he guided me from the elevator and down the hall. His clean, spicy scent wafted over me, a surprisingly calming influence for my overtaxed nerves. He didn't have to ask me to marry him. I would settle for shacking up. At this point, I would settle for a slow hard fuck with the promise of many more. I was beyond wanting him. My every nerve quivered for his touch.

I hadn't even thought to look at what floor we'd stopped on, but we seemed to be high up. A window at the end of the long, carpeted hall showed nothing but a glimpse of cold gray sky. Potted mini-trees in ceramic planters stood every few feet to break up the monotony of the hall.

He stopped almost at the end, at a pair of plain wooden double doors.

"This is it," he said, bowing slightly. "The suite of rooms I plan to take over for my executive offices. Come in, please."

He scanned a key card, pushed open the door, and reached for my hand to lead me across the empty room. The same blue carpet that lined the hall stretched out over the floor. Bare walls. No furniture. It waited for a designer's touch, but nothing anyone put in the room could hold a candle to the view. We walked to the window that wrapped around the corner.

Boston spread out around us, and she was a beauty. Fenway Park, empty this time of year. The Charles River, with all of the buildings standing sentinel along its icy edge. We were high up, probably right under the Skywalk Observatory. People crawled, busy as ants on the street below; cars were the size of toys. Traffic was backed up along Storrow Drive, even on a Sunday. If the sky had been clear, I probably could have seen New Hampshire's mountaintops dotting the horizon. But even with a cloudy sky, the view was beyond compare.

"You like?" He turned to gesture back at the space behind us, but my eyes were still drawn to the view.

Only one word came to mind, the often-used Boston favorite. "Awesome."

I meant it in the truest sense of the word.

"Perhaps you'll be up to helping me decorate."

"Perhaps." I looked around, a mental picture forming. A minimalist approach would make the most of the windows. Maybe we could tear up the carpet and do something with the floors.

"So you will, then?"

Mental brake-screech. His question took me by surprise. My stomach flipped. "Is that what you wanted to ask me? If I want to help you decorate?"

He laughed, took me in his arms, and swung me around. But his eyes held a gravity that belied his carefree actions. "Have you gotten your hopes up, then? You're expecting the moon?"

"No moon." I shook my head. "Only you."

He released me with a sigh, but I couldn't tell what kind of sigh. Relieved, happy, frustrated? "We'll see what we can do. Let's go next door."

My heart beat a rapid staccato. Was this it? Was he going to ask me to marry him? Or did he like to play with me? To build my hopes, only to dash them and build them up again? No. I knew he didn't mean to play. He simply had the kind of personality that would always keep me on edge, wondering what might happen next. In the long term, that might be a good thing. The unexpected would keep the relationship from going stale.

On the other hand, I craved stability. If he asked me, I still didn't know what I would say. No was out of the question, but I wavered between yes and maybe, knowing even now that the maybe was far-fetched. I had been at all-or-nothing for days now, and we finally hovered on all. Mentally, I practiced my reaction of surprise. *But this is all so sudden . . .*

He showed me into the next office in the suite.

At the edge of the large, empty space, he had spread a plaid flannel blanket out over the flat blue industrial carpet. An old-fashioned covered picnic basket sat in the center.

"Just a few nibbles," he said.

We walked to the blanket and I sat, cross-legged and grateful I'd worn my loose jeans, across from him and took in his glorious view. It was as if we hovered on a magic carpet above the city, only a pane of floor-to-ceiling glass separating us from the outside.

He opened the basket and pulled out cannoli and chocolate dipped strawberries, a few of my favorite North End treats. Next he produced crystal flutes and a bottle, Perrier Jouët Belle Epoque 1990. He popped the cork clean into his hand, producing a lovely white haze.

"Wow." Once again, he'd surprised me with all of my favorite things. How could he have known? I didn't have to ask him the question to know the answer. He knew everything.

I trembled, accepting the glass from his hands. It was all so perfect. Just the right setting. The two of us, the world at our feet.

"To us," he toasted. We drank.

He reached for my hand, his eyes darkening to an otherwordly black. An eerie coldness swept through the room, invading my very soul. There was a symphonic ringing at the base of my brain. My endorphins went crazy. What was happening? I suddenly knew that something was very wrong. Owen wasn't real. Or at least he wasn't human. I didn't want to look away, but I had to rest my head in my hands to catch my breath, as if the room were suddenly spinning.

"Who are you?" I asked, fighting back the wave of dizziness to look up again. I barely recognized my own voice.

His voice rang with genuine sympathy. "I think you've always known."

He reached out and tilted my chin up to face him.

"I need to hear you say it." The heat of his fingers warmed me, chasing the cold from the room, from my soul. Part of me just wanted to give in to the heat and forget the rest. But now I knew. I had to face it. My breath came in shallow rasps. I couldn't get enough air.

"I'm a god, Kate. Hades. Lord of the underworld, keeper of the damned."

"The devil," I said, quite clearly, before my vision fuzzed and I tipped forward, unable to steady myself, straight into his arms.

Chapter 13

I woke in a fog. Owen hovered, his eyes back to normal.

"Drink this." He handed me a glass of water. I think it was water. Maybe it was devil juice. I glanced up, suspicious.

"It's *water*," he said, concern, not annoyance, in his tone. "From the bubbler across the hall."

I sipped without tasting. My senses had all gone numb.

My vision seemed to be clearing. I let my gaze roam. Thick hair, chiseled face, dark bedroom eyes, hint of a beard, full soft lips. Lips that had kissed me. The devil.

Still, he looked like an average, everyday man. Strike that. Nothing about him was average. Was he even really a man?

How could I believe the alternative? The devil? I'd had suspicions about his mysterious ways, but seriously? Was it even possible? A sudden thought jolted me to my feet. I stood up, dropped the paper cup, and looked around.

"What show am I on?" I asked, frantically looking around for secret cameras.

"Show?" He looked confused.

They must have come in and rigged the place up before I got here. Maybe there were cameras at Bennie's too. In my apartment? How many weeks had this been going on?

"Kate, there are no cameras," he said.

"No? Okay, so you're the devil. I don't buy it. There has to be a catch." I paced to avoid the urge to reach out and feel him in my arms again, to assure myself that he was real, that what we'd had was no illusion. "What do you want? My soul?"

"I don't do that sort of thing." He shrugged out of his jacket and rolled up his sleeves. Human style, one arm at a time. Devil my ass.

"Oh? So what's your specialty?" I picked up the cup. "Turning water into wine?" I tapped my foot, impatient.

He wasn't intimidated by my sarcasm. He got up, meeting my glare with one of his own.

"How about turning wine into better wine? You didn't seem to mind the first night, at your sister's."

"The wine? I should have known."

"It beat the hell out of the bland little Shiraz." He smiled, his arrogance returning.

"Why me?"

"You caught my attention at one of your sister's dinner parties," he said. "But not the one you think."

"No? Which one?" My knees shook. I sat back down on the blanket. My body readily accepted what my mind would not. *The devil?* In my heart, I knew. In my mind, I struggled to reason it out. "I'm pretty sure I would have remembered meeting you."

"I wasn't there. I simply observed. It was over a year ago. You were with the little troll of a date."

"Troll?" It rang a bell somehow. I mentally scanned the dinner party fix-ups of the past year. "Gnome? What was his name? Rich?"

"Rob," he said. My skin prickled with alarm. "This is about *us*, Kate. You and me. We belong together."

As frightened as I was, I still I liked the sound of *us*. I'd been getting to know him. I'd actually been falling in love with him. What did that say about *me*? I finally fell in love, and the object of my affection was the devil himself. But it had all felt so right. He hardly seemed to be the ultimate evil.

"So you watched me? Why?"

"Besides the witty commentary?" He smiled fondly. "Your clever response to whom you would most like to meet?"

"The devil." I stilled my trembling hands by clasping them in my lap. "My soul would go for more than dinner and a movie."

"Three dates, at least. Maybe a weekend away."

"So this is our third date?" I tried to smile but couldn't bring myself to laugh.

He nodded. "We never had an actual weekend away. More like a midweek adventure. But that's where it happened, Kate. That's where I realized I was in deeper than I'd ever expected. I'd been looking for companionship, something to break up the monotony."

"In hell?"

He nodded. "And then I found you."

"You found me," I repeated. It all seemed so impossible. Me? From out of millions, the devil's focus centered on me as a chosen one. As a mate?

"You're alarmed." He sat next to me, placing his arm

around my shoulders. "I understand. Learning who I really am must come as a shock. But I suspect you've known all along, haven't you? Think about it."

"You're the devil?" My heart began to pound, fiercely enough that the sound of the beat filled my ears.

"Hades," he clarified. "But you'll think of me in whichever form you choose. It's all up to the believer."

"But I don't believe." But in my heart of hearts, I wondered if that was true.

"You don't *want* to believe, perhaps. But deep down, you can't fight what you instinctively hold to be true."

"Maybe I should call someone," I said gently. "I know a good therapist. She can help you."

He snorted.

"Or I could phone the police. A friend of mine's on the force. He can be here in five minutes."

"Go ahead." He called my bluff. "I know a few officers. And senators. The mayor. The governor. I've been to parties at the White House."

He was right. So what if he was insane? At the end of the day, he was Owen Glendower from the land of the fabulously rich and famous. And I was? No one special.

"You are special, Kate. You must never think otherwise."

"Ugh!" I grabbed my head. "Stop doing that. Stop reading my mind."

"Done. All you have to do is ask." He crossed his arms as if he'd proven some fantastic point.

"How about if I *ask* you to leave me alone?"

"If that's what you really want, but I don't think it is. Does it matter to you what *I* want?"

"It does." It did. I hated to admit it. Why was he here, making me fall for him? Is this what happened with Eve and the apple? Did she get a tingle?

"I never wanted to frighten you. I think you know by now that hurting you isn't my intention. For my part, I've been overwhelmed. I never knew I could feel so strongly. I never knew I could feel."

"Feel? You mean, at all? Weren't you married once? Persephone?" I vaguely remembered my Greek myths, the tale of the mortal who fell for Hades but couldn't stand living in hell.

"I've had plenty of physical responses to women, but I've never felt quite like this. Not for anyone else, and with nowhere near this intensity. I'm frozen without you, Kate."

I hesitated a moment, holding his gaze, trying to believe anything but what he presented as the truth. The devil. Hades. *Owen*. Could any other name change the fact of who he was? My heart raced. I reached out to touch him, my fingers grazing his fever-warm skin. "You don't feel frozen."

"Not now. Not with you. We're so right together. Please, try to understand how I need you. Always."

Always. On the way over, I'd imagined a proposal. I'd never pictured it going like this. "But how do I know it's real?"

I pulled my hand away. Suddenly, I was the one overwhelmed. "I'm real, Kate." He reached for my hand, drew it back to his chest, and met my gaze. "Feel my heart, how it beats for you."

Violently, tangibly, real. I shook my head. "But what about free will? You could be playing games with me. You have a history of temptation, a need for control."

"You've always been free to judge for yourself. You're free to choose now. Come away with me."

"Away?" This time, I knew he didn't mean Hilton Head. My breath caught. "To hell?"

"The underworld. It's not so bad. It can be, yes. I won't lie. But for the two of us, together? We can make it a paradise."

"But it won't be paradise. It'll be the opposite of paradise." *Hell.*

He stroked my face. "It will be what we make it. Together."

I caught his gaze. Temptation flared in licks of flame curling over my skin. How I wanted to let go. To give in. With Owen. But he wasn't even Owen. Not anymore. Now I knew. Or did I? How could I believe what he was telling me?

"Sure. What shall I pack?"

"I'm serious."

"It can't be real."

"Reality is all in your perception. So many religions, so many beliefs, all of them are real. All of them hold truth for the believer. You believe in me."

"And that makes you real?"

"It makes me true to your perception. To some, I'm the evil that lies in all men, dormant and waiting to be released. You've always been more pragmatic. You see me as I prefer to be seen, as a necessary force in a crowded world. Where there is life, death must follow. There can be no creation without destruction."

"Is that what you want? To destroy me?"

"On the contrary. I want to watch you live. You're a source of light where I have only darkness. Your life is what I treasure most. Come with me and it will never end."

"Immortality?" It might have tempted some. The thought of living forever always frightened me. To watch everyone dear to you die? But I would have to be dead myself, wouldn't I? I would give up my life as I knew it. No turning back. My mouth went dry. I couldn't force the thought into words to ask the question. Would I be dead?

"It will take some adjustment, but we can make it work. You may actually like it."

"The cave. It's why you brought me there. Is that what hell's like?"

He nodded. "A little."

"What if I don't like it? I seem to recall it wasn't so easy for Persephone to walk away."

"True enough. There is a rule about such things."

"But you're the boss, right? You can get around rules?"

"Not so easily. It's Zeus who holds the real power."

"Your brother?" What was I saying? Talking about mythical gods as if they were real and human? What was in the champagne?

Buoyed by nervous energy, I sprung to my feet and paced the room, my mind still frantic to make sense of it all.

Owen watched me, reclining in a casual pose, as if he hadn't a care in the world. "On the surface, this is all so much for you to take in. Deep down, you're not so shocked. You're strong and bright. Not only can you handle it, you were made for it."

"Made? To rule hell as the devil's consort?"

"Made for tremendous understanding. You're deeply intuitive. It's one of the many qualities that make you so qualified."

"Qualified." It sounded so detached, as if I was being considered for a job.

"So perfect. I want you with me. You make everything brighter for me. Don't you understand? You're my sun."

It sounded beautiful and sinister at once. The heavy responsibility of being the sole bearer of light and warmth to the devil overwhelmed me. Even if he was Owen. Hades. *The devil.*

Oh. God.

Reality hit in full force. I was face-to-face with the age-old representative of all things evil. The tears came unbidden, and I started trembling all over again.

"Oh Kate, no. I thought you were getting to know me. To see me, beyond the superficial. Please. Don't lose faith." He shot to his feet and closed the distance between us.

"Faith? Is that all it takes? If I believe in devils, clap my hands?" I took a deep breath, closed my eyes tight, and opened them again. Nope, not dreaming. I had to deal with my current reality, whatever that was. "I'm sorry. I don't know what to do. I've spent my life in denial of organized religion and now you're asking me to have faith."

"You've never embraced religion, so what?" He forced me to face him, placing his fingers under my chin, so warm. "You're very spiritual, Kate. You've always believed in something. In good, in evil, in right, and in wrong. In some deep-centered order of the universe. You studied Classics in college because you liked the idea of multiple gods to help in a variety of circumstances."

"More gods to share the blame."

"More gods to help you find your truth. I am truth. I'm standing here before you telling you things you feel so ill-prepared to hear, and yet you are. You're accepting me. You know what's real."

"I don't know anything. Not now."

"Yes, you do." He placed his hand to mine, palm to palm. "You know *me.*"

I felt him coursing through my veins. I knew him. I cherished the feel of him inside me, the power of our connection, the simple raw need binding us in a fabric of eternity. Two souls coming together. Could it be so easy?

No. It was a fantasy. A mind trick. I dropped my hand. "You're nothing I could ever know. I can't begin to fathom what you are. A god? A myth? All I want is for you to be a man."

"I wish it were that easy. I can't walk away from my responsibilities to indulge my own interests. The world would never be the same."

"But you're here now?" Even as I struggled to believe in everything that had happened, I harbored some insane hope that it all could be put to rights again, that somehow things would work out for us to have a normal life.

"I can manage to be away for short periods of time, nothing long term."

"I see," I said, but I didn't want to see. In my mind, I had planned a future. It hardly seemed as if I had known him for only a short period of time. I'd spun so many fantasies of life with him. Weekends at Hilton Head. Workdays at our Beacon Hill townhouse. A wedding. *Children.*

Family.

"I can't just walk away," I said. "I have family. I had other plans." The ache rose up unbidden. *The baby.*

"The baby. I know. The insemination didn't work but you'd planned to give it another try."

"You said you would stop reading my mind."

"I didn't," he said. "I already knew."

"You know everything." I hugged my arms against a wave of cold that ran straight through me.

He placed a hand on my arm and chased the chill, flooding me with instant heat. "I anticipated your concern."

All he had to do was touch me and I was ready to consider following him anywhere, even to the depths of hell. Owen wasn't the only one in deeper than he'd thought possible. It suddenly occurred to me how very much alike we were. And now?

"I want to have a baby." Saying my most earnest desire aloud slammed me back to tangible fact. I couldn't give birth in hell, even if I could somehow wrap my mind around going there. "But you can't give me that, can you?"

"I can give you so much more."

"But we couldn't have a baby together. Could we? Even if I went to hell. Even if I gave up everything to be with you, I couldn't have what I want most." Especially if I was no longer alive myself. A cold wave of fear washed over me. What would it be like? Before I even realized it, I reached out to grip his hands. Even knowing what he was now, I instinctively leaned toward him for support. *For love.*

"What about love?" he asked, as if still reading my mind, but I knew deep down that he wasn't. "The kind you could only get from one who *knows* you."

"Is love enough?" What if I began to resent him? What if the ache down inside me didn't go away after I chose him over a child?

"It can be. If you're ready to accept me."

"Accept you over my life now, over my family, over all my plans?" It was a tremendous leap, a lot to ask. "Couldn't you just come and go? Separations might be hard, but—"

I stopped myself. Was I honestly contemplating a

long-distance relationship with the devil? And yet, what option did I have? That, or turn and walk away. I pulled back from him, went to the window, pressed my head against the cool glass, with the glittering sparkle of Boston spread out below, and tried to decide. I felt as if I stood on the edge, a fine line between now and forever. I couldn't make the jump.

After a few moments, I faced him again. "I'm sorry. This is too much to take in."

Meeting his gaze, seeing the tenderness there, I felt the familiar tingle deep inside me. I walked back to him. "What if you're the one being influenced?"

He laughed, a telltale sign that he wasn't used to being out of control in any way. "By whom?"

"By me." I placed my palm flat over his heart. "I know it sounds odd, but the whole courtship, the way you've presented yourself to me, hasn't it all been shaped around what you think I want, who I am?"

"Yes, but—"

I put a finger to his lips. "You're presenting an image that you know I'll find acceptable. It's what we all do when we date, isn't it? Even Hades. You're presenting yourself in the best possible light to appeal to me. But what if you were just you? If I'd known from the start who you really are? Who are you?"

Looking deep into his eyes, I saw the truth. I didn't know him. Not really. As much as I felt I did, I knew he had facets that I'd barely even uncovered. Just as I hadn't shown him all of me. Yet. It really was too soon.

"You don't know?" His voice held a note of disbelief.

"Do you know me? As completely as you think? Even with all your gifts and insights?"

He shook his head, but not out of disagreement as much as from apparent disbelief. "I know you, Kate.

Who you are. What you want. You have it all wrong. I'm not simply who you want me to be or we would never have come to this. What you want is a fallacy. You'll never find it. Without me, you'll never have the happiness you seek."

I recoiled. Something in him had grown dark, almost sinister, as if a cloud passed over him, storms on the horizon. Was this the real Hades? The moment passed as quickly as it had come when he slid his arms around my waist to draw me back to him.

"Is that a threat?" I asked.

"Oh, no, sweetheart. No." I ached inside. For him, for me. My heart felt as if it was being squeezed dry, along with my lungs, my stomach. I'd never felt so bad. I let him hold me, hoping he could be the balm to ease my pain. "I would never threaten you. I just know. I know what happens. I know you'll never be complete. You'll always feel a little empty inside. Just like me."

"This is how it feels to be you?" The devil's pain, his loneliness, the startling ache. I felt it. I'd never understood before, never even thought about what it would be like to be him. Now I knew.

"Together, we could find our peace."

"In hell?" As much as he claimed to know how I felt, how I would always feel, I knew I couldn't find peace in hell. "I would have to give up everything else, my whole life."

Owen shook his head. "But you love me. Love is sacrifice."

I took a deep breath. He was right. Love was sacrifice, and I wasn't ready to make that kind of leap. Maybe I'd been wrong. Maybe I *didn't* love him. Or if I did, I didn't love him enough. I had dreams. I had a family. I wasn't ready to walk away from everything I wanted and everything I'd ever known for him.

"I don't know what to say. I need time to think. This isn't quite what I expected." Even though it was difficult to leave the safety of his arms, I withdrew and made my way to the door. I had to force my feet to keep moving before I ended up abandoning all sense of reason in favor of making it with the man I'd thought I loved. The incredibly sexy man standing right in front of me with tousled hair, heavy-lidded bedroom eyes, and a body to die for. Almost.

"I can give you time," Owen said. "But there's one more thing I'd like to tell you before you go."

"Yes?" I spun back around to face him but I had trouble meeting his gaze.

"Don't confuse a sense of duty for your real desire." He stood his ground. His stance told me he wouldn't come after me, which made me want to crawl back and beg him to touch me where I burned for him, even now, even after all I'd learned. But I wouldn't break down.

"What do you mean?" I finally looked into his eyes.

"Your family means a lot to you. I'm only beginning to understand the intricacies of the family relationship. But please don't use them as your excuse to throw away what we could have together. I'm not sure they would make the same sort of sacrifice for you."

Shadows spread out around him, a wave of darkness stretching across the room right before my eyes. I stared, shocked. Could my light really mean so much to him? I'd been thinking in terms of metaphor, when perhaps he'd been deadly serious. I fought to stand firm when I wanted to run back and hold him. I couldn't be everything illuminating to him. He had to have some light of his own. And if he didn't? It might only be a matter of time before my light became extinguished from having to burn too brightly for us both.

"If I'm sacrificing anything," I said, "perhaps it is simply to save a part of myself and not for anyone else."

The shadows passed through his eyes, black as a moonless night. "Perhaps it's just as well. The kind of love I want from you should be worth any risk. Think of me, Kate. Think of me and make up your mind."

Before it's too late. He didn't even have to say it aloud. The blackness of his gaze left me torn between returning to him and running away. Had I already crossed the line? I knew the right thing to do, what I had to do to save myself and all my plans. If I said one more word, if I stayed for one more second, I couldn't tell what I might sacrifice just to be with him.

I broke his dark gaze and ran from the room, leaving him standing there, alone, in the empty empire of Glendower Enterprises.

I let the elevator doors close before I slipped to the floor and sobbed. What had I done? I wrapped my arms around myself as the elevator descended in an attempt to quell the pain.

I made no attempt to hold back my hot tears, even as the elevator bell rang out and the doors opened to street level, a sickle of light slicing through the garage and across my face. I peeled myself off of the floor, squinting through the brightness, and walked out. Earlier, the day had been cloudy, but now, a mere hour before dusk, the sun shone with a vengeance and I hated to go out in it, as if it somehow marked my betrayal. My own scarlet A, the sun. But I hadn't been unfaithful. I simply needed the time to think.

But even as I walked toward home, my own thoughts rang hollow in my mind. Maybe Owen was right. If it had been real love, what sacrifice would have been too great?

I barely noticed the crowds of shoppers as I walked along. I welcomed the chill of the wind. I hadn't even stopped to get my coat. I'd been so afraid, but not of him. Of myself.

I knew exactly what he meant when he described how he felt without me, because I felt the same way without him. The chill I felt in the air had nothing to do with the frigid weather. Without him, I felt frozen. I prayed it was a temporary condition and walked faster, determined to get home, get warm, and get out of the harsh rays of the setting November sun.

Hours later, I lay curled in my bed, under my heavy down comforter, duvet, and extra blankets, still frozen. I couldn't get warm. Owen's words resonated. It was true that I wasn't ready to leave my family, but they were hardly the only thing holding me back. I had a lot of life left in me. Even if I accepted Owen's offer, I still couldn't think what it would be like, if it was a death or simply moving on, moving in with him. In hell.

Unfathomable.

And yet I missed him. I missed him already and it had only been a few hours since I'd left him, a few hours since my world had been turned upside down with the knowledge of who, or what, he was.

Restless, I got out of bed and went to the window. My car was parked out front. Tricky minions. A shiver traveled my spine. Suddenly, I was glad I'd never caught a glimpse of his minions.

It was only a little past seven but the sun had been down for hours. Somehow the dark felt reassuring. I had a sudden urge to see my mother.

I knew from past experience that my keys would be in my mailbox. I shook off the chills, got dressed, and headed over to Mother's, keeping watch for minions in my rearview as I drove, but there was no sign of them. Traffic was light, even for a Sunday evening, and pulling in to Mother's driveway provided some degree of relief. Not that the minions would hurt me, but it all seemed so odd. For the first time in as long as I could remember, I felt a familiar tug of comfort getting out of the car and walking up the drive to my mother's door. It was the house she shared with her new husband, and though I'd stayed there briefly at times, it was never my real home. But after the day I'd had, just the sight of it was comforting to me.

The door opened before I reached it, and my mother stood blinking in surprise on the other side. I lived less than a thirty-minute drive away, in weekend traffic, and I seldom visited, let alone popped in on her without warning. We didn't have that kind of relationship. For the first time in ages, I wondered what kind of relationship we did have, then. She was my *mother.* Why the emotional distance?

"Hi, Mom," I said, hoping I sounded sufficiently cheerful.

"Katherine, what are you doing here? I thought I heard a car." She opened the door wide. "Well come in."

"I should have called ahead," I said, stepping inside and taking off my coat.

"Nonsense," she said, and I followed her into the kitchen.

I smiled when I noticed the large wooden fork and

spoon hung in her sunny yellow kitchen, just as they had hung on the sunny yellow walls of my childhood home, the tiny ranch in Newton that she'd long since sold. It helped the new place to feel more like home, more like Mom from before Dad left and Mom changed into Mother, the woman who stood before me with her perfect coif and pleated jeans, her stockinged feet tucked into stiff leather loafers even though she was sitting in the comfort of her own house on a Sunday evening.

She hadn't always been such a stickler for perfection, I remembered now. It had been so long since I'd had a glimpse of the woman she used to be, the round-faced lass who hardly wore any makeup and let her long hair trail down around her shoulders after she changed into her favored flannel nightshirts.

Lass, that's what Dad had called her. *Come here, lass,* he'd say, right before he grabbed her and smothered her with kisses as Bennie and I watched, giggling. Then he'd call us his wee bonnie bairns and chase us around the living room.

What happened to those girls? To that woman? Perhaps Bennie and I had simply taken our cues from Mother. Or maybe Dad had taken them all away with him when he left. We weren't the same afterwards.

"Are you crying, dear? Your eyes are puffy. What's wrong?"

I swiped at my eyes. Tears. "Yes. I guess I'm having a little crisis."

The tears fell harder and faster, as if acknowledging them gave them permission to flow. I couldn't stop myself from sobbing in front of Mother, a luxury I hadn't afforded myself in years. Unlike Bennie, I hadn't thought of my mother as the enemy. I'd considered her more of a child in need of protection, fragile as the delicate porcelain dolls she tried to get us interested in collecting years ago.

"Oh dear." She put her arm around my shoulder. For a second, it felt so right, and I wanted to let her support me again, to lean into her arms and cry it all out just as I had when I was a little girl. "I have some new makeup in the powder room. Just your shade. It will brighten you right up."

Aha. That was the mother I'd come to know. Problem? Hide it under makeup and move on. I backed away, the frozen feeling seeping back into my bones again. As much as I wanted to, I would find no comfort here.

I took a breath. "No. It's okay. I don't need any makeup. I'm going straight home again from here."

"Still." She frowned, taking note of my rumpled blouse, faded jeans, and disheveled hair, a striking contrast to her trim, tidy package, hair cut to frame a face made up to hide all flaws. "You never know whom you might run into. It wouldn't hurt to look nice."

I sighed. "Right, Mom. Sorry. I may have blown a chance at that lucrative Ford model contract by leaving the house without eyeliner."

"You're always such a smarty pants. A little lipstick never hurts, you know. But let's not fight. Have a seat and tell me what's wrong."

I'd lost my desire to talk about it. Still, I took a seat on a vinyl-cushioned chair at her formica table. "It's nothing really. Just feeling lonely, I guess."

"Aw." She sat beside me, close enough to pat my leg. "I felt that way before I met Hal. It's hard to be alone. Don't I know it."

"It's not that bad. Maybe I'm just running on a serious cocoa deficiency."

"Oh, now don't play it down. Women need men. It's how we're wired."

I'd never bought into her "women need men" theory. "No, really, I think I need chocolate. How about we go get some sundaes or something? My treat."

"Hal's always up for a good sundae. He got called in to work at the shop, but he'll be home any minute if you don't mind waiting."

"No. Not at all," I said, forcing a smile. In truth, I minded very much. Hal was a good guy, but I just wanted to be alone with my mother.

"Thank goodness for Bernadette that she met Patrick straight out of high school. She'll never know what it was like for me before Hal. Or what it's like for you." She gestured to me, a sweeping hand motion from top to bottom as if presenting the booby prize on *Let's Make a Deal*.

"Thank goodness." Her mention of my sister called to mind other things, things I hadn't thought of in years. "Mom, can I ask you something?"

"Anything dear. What's on your mind?"

"Why didn't you ever let Dad do his share of the parenting?"

Gape-mouthed, she stared a few seconds before jumping to the defensive. "I was always after your father to take more of an interest in you girls, to do more for you."

"But when he did, you would take him to task. He was always too rough or too loud or too rambunctious. You wouldn't even let us go fishing with him."

"Out on a boat? Alone with your father? What if you had to go to the bathroom?"

I rolled my eyes. "I'm sure we could have managed."

"You don't remember how he was." She shook her head, indignant. "He was never careful enough with you. He would jump in first and think later. He might have let you swim in rough water. You were a terrible swimmer."

"But it would have been nice to try." To have some memories of the man that didn't involve Mother's constant hovering and intervention. "To let him try to take us to do things that interested him for a change."

"So you blame me, is that it?" She pursed her lips. "You think my not letting him parent chased him away?"

"I didn't say that." I thought for a minute before speaking again. It was obviously a sore subject for Mother, undoubtedly one she'd gone over in her own mind through the years. "I'm sure there were lots of things between you that just didn't work but—"

"And parenting was one of them." She agreed. "Oh, yes, it was a big issue. He never took responsibility."

"And you didn't want him to," I added, more certain of myself now. "Not really. I remember one night I woke up from a bad dream and called out for help. No one came, so I got out of bed to look for you. I must have been about eight years old. Dad was still up, sitting in the family room watching the Red Sox game on TV. He made room for me in his chair, pulled me up to sit with him, and asked me what was wrong."

"I'm surprised he was home," Mother interrupted. "It must have been an away game."

I sighed and went on. "He was home. And it felt great to have Dad there to comfort me for a change. His big strong arms, his scratchy beard. He smelled like

Old Spice and the soap-on-a-rope we used to give him every Christmas."

"I liked the Old Spice," Mom said, a wistful smile playing at her lips. "I haven't smelled that in years."

So they weren't all bad memories. This comforted me. "Mm. But it didn't last for more than a minute, my time with Dad. You came out from your bedroom and yelled at me for bothering Dad and not coming straight in to see you. He yelled back that he had a right to comfort his own daughter. You both got into it and I went back to bed on my own. I don't think either one of you noticed."

"Of course we must have noticed. We were fighting about taking care of you."

"You didn't notice. You started fighting about something else. There was always something else. But I still remember crying myself to sleep while you two argued. I wasn't crying about the nightmare by then. I cried about getting in trouble for going to my own father for comfort."

She shrugged. "You were just a little girl. You said so yourself. You're probably remembering it wrong."

"I'm not." I wasn't going to back off of the topic. "There were times, maybe not all the times, but there were times that Dad just wanted to be our father and you wouldn't let him. I begin to wonder if there were other times, after he went, that you kept him away on purpose."

Her eyes widened. "Now why would you suggest such a thing?"

"You didn't tell us about the divorce. Perhaps there were other things you didn't tell us. Did he ask about us? Did you tell him what we were doing without him? Proms, graduations, marriage, grandkids. I know Dad left us, but I find it hard to believe he fully intended to not be there for any of it."

She didn't say a word, and her silence was the most telling. I'd been chasing an instinct, and I was right. He might have been there for some of it if he had known. The blame didn't fall all on Mother. "He left without a word. Maybe he didn't deserve any other notice of events in our lives. But maybe he would have been there for some of it if he *had* known. Maybe an invitation could have served as a reminder that we were here, growing up, and maybe he would have come back."

"So now you want me to send him invitations?"

"No. Not now. But maybe I'll send him a few of my own someday."

"You know where he is?"

"I have connections. I can find out."

Mom looked shocked. I guessed the whole conversation had come as a shock. I'd been the one who'd come over crying, but now she was the one with a tear running down her cheek.

She wiped it away almost immediately. "Oh shoot. Don't want to smear my mascara."

I put an arm around her. "Wash it off, Mom. You don't need that stuff at home."

"Easy for you to say," she laughed. "You have youth on your side."

"I have great skin without makeup. It's genetic. I get it from you."

She looked down, as if caught off guard. "I didn't mean to keep him from you, sweetie. I hope you can forgive me. I didn't know where he'd gone for the longest time. You were in college by the time he called. Your freshman year. It was all I could do not to ask him to fork over some help in paying your tuition bills."

"You showed surprising restraint."

"Believe you me. But by then it was too late for proms and graduations. I figured it was too late for a lot of things, except for a formal divorce. We decided not to complicate things for you girls by even mentioning him again."

"We? Meaning you, Gran, and Pops?" She did everything with my grandparents since my father left, parenting by committee.

"We, meaning your Dad and I. I told him what you girls were up to and sent pictures."

"And he still didn't come home? Or even write?"

"No. He said he wanted to tie up a few loose ends before getting in touch, and then I didn't hear from him again."

A few loose ends. More like a few more twenty-ones at the blackjack table. It was disappointing to learn that Dad had passed up the opportunity to get back in touch, but not as devastating as I'd thought it would be. Talking to my mother had helped me feel better. I could see now that it wasn't just Dad at fault, it was her reaction to Dad. And it wasn't simply her chasing him away. It was him staying away, too.

I wondered about Owen. About taking a chance, making a tremendous leap of faith. Had I been harboring a fear of leaping only to push him away? Or was I more afraid that he would eventually tire of being in a relationship and I would be left with nothing? Mom had Gran and Pops. What would I have if I sacrificed for him alone? Maybe I wasn't as afraid of the idea of being in love with an otherworldly being as I was of giving up everything and having literally nowhere else to go in the event of failure. After hell, what else was there? I didn't know.

I only knew that without him, I might never be the same. Talking to my mother had helped, but deep down, I still felt frozen and so alone. I needed more time to think. And, as cold as I was inside, I certainly didn't need ice cream.

I patted my mother's hand. "I have to go, Mom. I need to make a few calls. Business stuff. I just remembered. Can we take a rain check on that sundae?"

"Oh," her face did not reveal her dismay, but her voice did. "Sure, dear. Hal will be so disappointed."

"What he doesn't know won't hurt him." I leaned over to kiss her on the cheek. "I'll call you later."

She walked me to the door. I felt like some of the balance had been restored to the mother-daughter relationship, as if I'd backed off on protecting her for a change and let her be a mother again. It must have felt right to us both because she gave me a big hug at the door, a genuine squeeze instead of the timid embrace I'd gotten used to through the years.

By the time I left my mother's house, it was late in the evening. I dreaded the thought of heading back to my empty apartment in the city, so I took a side trip to my old house, the one I'd grown up in. The small raised ranch stood at the end of a quiet cul-de-sac, making it hard to linger long without drawing notice. I parked outside with the motor running.

The yard was fenced now, a short chain-link boundary that might have helped contain children or a small dog, like the basset hound I'd always wanted but was told, repeatedly, that I couldn't have. Mother wasn't a pet person.

Toys in the yard, a bike with a flowered basket, and a Little Tikes picnic table, indicated the presence of children. It made me glad to see that there were still children in the house and it hadn't become the domain of a grouchy old lady, like Mrs. Cauley, our next door neighbor. But it looked as though Mrs. Cauley had passed on as well, because even her dreary old house looked cheerful. There were flowers dotting the driveway and a Dora the Explorer shade on the back window of a car parked outside the garage.

A light came on in the kitchen of my old house, and I decided it was time to move on before I drew unwanted attention. I put the car in gear and headed home, almost on autopilot. I watched the road, but my thoughts were too engaged with the past to focus beyond what was required of my present.

I remembered Bennie at two years old, how I'd dressed her up in my mother's cashmere sweater and my old red rubber Wellington boots wrapped in Christmas tree lights. The boots went up to her diaper. I'd meant to plug her in. Even then, I'd been all about the visual, designing displays. Before she was old enough to become a willing partner in crime, Bennie had started out as a perfect prop.

Mother had caught me before I could plug Bennie in. She got so mad at me that she'd screamed herself hoarse. She'd told me I was a wicked girl, and I'd believed her. It felt awful. I'd never meant to hurt Bennie, of course. She'd laughed the whole time I dressed her up.

My father had tried to calm Mother down but she ended up yelling at him. Dad went out and I don't even remember being awake when he came home. I'd been about six years old. My father could have stayed and fought for me, but it was easier for him to walk away. In retrospect, it was the beginning of a pattern for him. Back then, I just felt heartbroken that no one noticed how pretty Bennie could have been all lit up like the Christmas tree. Perhaps it was a harbinger of the women Bennie and I would become. She adored the spotlight. I preferred to take the focus off myself and place it elsewhere, on creative displays.

When it came to personal relationships, Bennie drew people around her, craving interaction and notice on a grand scale. I pushed people away, preferring to be left alone to seek the company of few and select individuals, people I admired and trusted not to run off and leave me when I needed them most. My family I could always count on, save for the one who ran away. Outside the family, I had few close friendships and even fewer romantic relations.

Somehow I'd always known the day would come when a man, or something like one, would expect my complete faith and I wouldn't know how to give it. Having to depend on a partner, on a man, was my own personal worst-case scenario, and yet it was exactly what running off with Hades required. Not only was I used to controlling my own environment, it had become necessary for my own emotional survival. If loving someone meant giving up that control, I wasn't sure I could do it.

In my career, I could afford to take risks because I knew, in the end, I could always rely on myself. In my personal life? I'd made it a habit to travel the safe roads. I couldn't imagine a temptation great enough to change all that until the devil walked into my life wearing his wicked smile. *Damned if you do, and damned if you don't* had taken on a whole new meaning, and I was no longer sure if safety or risk was the greater evil.

By the time I pulled into my own parking space and walked up the steps to my front door, I'd forgotten about looking around for minions. I was beyond tired and ready to fall right into bed.

Chapter 14

For the fifth night in a row, I came home from work so bone-weary and exhausted that I could barely make it to the couch before collapsing. Thank goodness it was Friday. I had no plans for the weekend but to catch up on my sleep, something that had eluded me since Sunday's revelation at Glendower Tower, AKA the Prudential Center. I wondered if it had all even happened or if I'd dreamed it. As of Monday, the Pru was back to being the Pru, no trace of Glendower remaining. How could it be?

Owen hadn't called. I double-checked the phone as I walked by just to be sure. Dial tone. Phone worked. No calls. I dragged myself to my room, undressed, and pulled on sweats, my weekend uniform. Still cold, I thought about adding a second layer, then decided against it. No amount of layers could warm me. My apartment thermostat was cranked up to eighty, but the cold came from inside and there was no chasing it, at least not with human methods.

As I made my way back to the couch, I wondered

what methods the devil might employ to thaw me out. I thought of his hands, his long fingers stroking the insides of my thighs, opening me to him. I must have fallen asleep at last because the next thing I knew, I rolled over and mashed my cheek into a small puddle of drool on the cushion. I wiped it off, sat up, and squinted at the cable box on the TV stand. It was eleven forty-five P.M.

The darkness made me feel more alone. I searched for the remote, clicked on the television, and got up to check the phone again. Still no calls. Why was I worried? I'd asked for time, I still *needed* the time, and he was giving me time. I hadn't made any life-altering decisions yet. Give up my life? It seemed more impossible than ever. Give up on what could be my one chance at love? I wasn't ready for that, either.

Instead of feeling like I'd been given my space, I'd begun to feel rejected. Not knowing what to do with my rejected self, I took a page from the *Hollywood Handbook for Jilted Lovers*. I recalled that step one of any movie breakup involved consuming an entire pint of ice cream straight out of the container, so I headed for the freezer and pulled out a tub of vanilla. I wasn't getting any warmer, why not embrace the cold? I returned to the couch, container in hand, and commenced channel-surfing and pigging out with my good friends Ben and Jerry.

I discovered I was frighteningly good at breakups. I finished the ice cream in no time flat and settled in. I barely moved off the couch for the rest of the night and the majority of the next day, except for the occasional bathroom trip.

When the batteries went on the TV remote, I switched to watching DVDs. I figured out that if you put one DVD in and didn't touch the machine, it just kept replaying that same DVD—perfect for those who would rather watch the same movie over and over than get up and take action. I'd had enough of Bali Ha'i, so I avoided *South Pacific* in favor of *Dangerous Liaisons*.

If I learned anything from three consecutive viewings of the same movie, it wasn't that John Malkovich was sexy in a deranged way. Or that maternity and corsets did wonders for Glenn Close's bustline.

I learned that dangerous liaisons were to be avoided. Look what happened to the pure and gentle Michelle Pfeiffer, all for losing her heart to Malkovich's Valmont. Trouble, with a capital dead. Not good. I had to shape up before it was *beyond my control*.

By Saturday night, I'd managed to ease into a slight change, from ice cream and DVDs to chocolate bars and reality shows, even though I had to get up to change channels now and then. I thought about showering and putting on some real clothing, but unfortunately, my recovery stopped at sweats. I couldn't bear to change into something less comfortable. Small steps, I assured myself. Small steps.

Sunday night, I tried a soak in the tub. Not because I felt I needed to bathe, but because too much time on the couch had put a knot in my lower back.

A long soak gave me time to reflect. I tried to picture myself in hell. What would it be like? What would I do there? I couldn't even fully imagine Owen as the devil. I'd had a small glimpse of what he might be like when the darkness came over him, but still, I couldn't chase the picture of Owen, the man, from my mind. Perhaps it was just as well. How terrifying could he become? How dark? What would we even have to talk about in quiet moments?

The age difference was nearly insurmountable. Yet conversation had never been a problem. We'd invented a language of our own. A very physical language. My pulse throbbed. I splashed water over my arms, smoothed it down my breasts, and imagined his hands on me, that supernatural heat radiating down straight to my bones, chasing the ice from my soul.

Tempting.

But as much as I wanted Owen, I also wanted to have a baby, to give birth, to know the bond between mother and child. From watching Bennie with her children, I knew there was nothing quite like it in the world. And though it didn't always turn out as expected, as I could imagine from having a mother of my own, it was something I wanted to experience for myself. To see the world again from the beautiful, wide eyes of a child. To touch the tiny toes and fingers and know that of all things, I'd created something pure and amazing. I knew I couldn't make a baby with Owen, but I'd always planned on doing it myself anyway, so why not?

Yes! I sat up in the tub so suddenly that water sloshed over the sides and all over my ceramic tile floor. I had the power to pursue both options, Owen and a baby. Why give up now? I could go back to my gynecologist, look over the profiles of donors, and make another attempt at fertilization. If I got pregnant, I would have every reason to stay here and not run off to hell. If he still wanted me, he would find a way to see me, to make it work.

I'd never been much of a fatalist, but I needed help. I liked the idea of taking a risk. Perhaps I was a bit of my father's daughter after all. It was quite a gamble, putting my decision in the hands of fate.

I was ready to roll the dice.

Monday morning, I got up bright and early and headed to my doctor's office. I couldn't get an appointment with such short notice, but I held out hope that they still had the profiles I'd requested from the cryogenics bank in my records. Feeling fresh and rejuvenated, despite the coldness inside that I just couldn't thaw, I dressed up my basic black pants ensemble with red shoes, a pair of platform pumps that would have done Bennie, who had a thing for shoes, proud. The sound of my heels clicking down the long hall leading to the office made me lighthearted, a feeling that lasted even after I entered the carpeted reception room. "Kate?" The receptionist, Mandy, knew me from high school. "Your appointment's not for another week."

"I know," I said, leaning forward in an attempt to be discreet even though the office was empty. "But I was hoping we could speed things up a little. Maybe I could go over the profiles again now, select a donor, and next week's appointment could be a little more productive, so to speak?"

"Why the hurry?"

"Why not?"

She exhaled loudly. "I'm sorry. I shouldn't have said that. I just mean—okay, I have three kids at home, Kate, and let me tell you, what a morning. Getting them up and off to school sometimes—well, to do it again, I wouldn't be in such a rush."

"You say that now." I smiled. "But I remember a time when all you wanted was to marry Brian Hadley and have his babies."

"Back in the day," she rolled her eyes. "I was so naïve. You think I would have at least had the good sense to go for Matt LeBlanc, huh?"

The *Friends* star had gone to our school, but he was a few years ahead of us.

"Yeah, but he had that perm then." I made a face. "Who knew?"

"You're right. I'm better off. Hey, want to see the new pictures of the twins?"

"Sure." I knew from being an aunt that there was no graceful way to say no when offered a look at pictures.

As I oohed and ahhed and Mandy beamed with pride, I knew I was doing the right thing. A baby would rely on me and love me without asking me to give up my independence, not that it would be easy. I would have to adapt my schedule and make some lifestyle changes but, before long, the frozen feeling might be replaced by the warmth of my own baby's smile.

"They're beautiful, Mandy," I said, and I meant it.

"Thanks. Let me run and get that file and I'll be right back."

She returned in a minute, thick booklet of donor profiles in hand.

"It will be the same as last time," Mandy explained. "You choose your donor and get the papers out. They'll deliver the tank here. We'll take it from there next Tuesday."

"Right." I nodded. "So we're all clear? Doctor Reyes didn't mind changing the appointment from checkup and consultation to insemination?"

"Not a problem. I'll just make a note on the schedule that your appointment will run long and you're good to go. Fingers crossed that the next time's the charm." She made the fingers-crossed gesture and winked.

"Fingers crossed," I agreed, taking my booklet and

heading out. I paused at the door. "Thanks, Mandy. See you next Tuesday."

Back at my office, I checked my mail first thing. Nothing. I checked my voicemail. I had a message, but as I punched in my code, I tried not to get my hopes up. "Kate, hi. It's Marc." A pause. "Ramirez? From a few weeks ago? I'm still thinking about your amazing green eyes." Score one for Marc. He'd noticed. "Well, I'm sorry I missed you. Maybe, I was hoping, you would like to go out sometime? Dinner? Coffee? Your call."

I chewed the end of a pen and stared out the window, trying to figure out what to do. Marc was a perfectly nice guy, but I hadn't felt any spark. Still, I hadn't heard from Owen in over a week. He was giving me time, all right, but maybe just a little too much time. In desperation, I'd finally called his office over the weekend and left a voicemail, but it hadn't come to anything. No calls back. Why hadn't I ever thought to ask for his cell phone number?

Maybe going out with Marc would send a message. Certainly, Owen would find out. He knew everything. It might convince him to pick up the phone and get back to me. At any rate, what was the harm? It wouldn't be bad for me to go out and remember what it was like to be among mortals. A nice normal dinner with a normal man who had no intention of whisking me off to the underworld could be just the thing to cure my Owen blues, but I still wasn't sure. The jealousy tactic had a way of backfiring on sitcoms and in movie plots. Perhaps Owen would decide I had made my choice and I wouldn't hear from him again. I wasn't ready to take the chance.

Instead of picking up the phone to return Marc's call, I turned to the one thing I could be sure of in any event: doughnuts, the ultimate comfort food. I'd skipped breakfast and planned on working through lunch. I deserved an indulgence.

After scarfing down a chocolate glazed and a vanilla crème, I couldn't justify sitting down at my desk any longer. I took a stroll to the warehouse to see what I could pull together for that weekend's open house, an enormous Garrison colonial in Natick.

I didn't get far. I got stuck at the nursery ensemble I'd moved through three separate open houses now. The whitewashed crib, beautifully handcrafted to radiate antique charm despite modern safety standards, had long been a favorite of mine. Each time I set it up in a house, I paused over it, unable to imagine it actually belonging to anyone else. Every time it didn't sell with the house, I breathed a sigh of relief.

I was stalling, I realized, putting off going over the donor lists in hopes that Owen would call and change all my plans with some stunning move I couldn't resist. Seduction, for example. I closed my eyes and imagined turning to find him draped across the queen bed in the display behind me. Naked, with a rose in his teeth. I turned. Nothing.

Oh, come on. The man had supernatural powers at his command and he couldn't detect that I was currently needy and ripe for the picking? Maybe he had other things to do, I realized, more important things. Perhaps he was in the underworld right now conducting crucial affairs? I tried to imagine him there reigning over his minions, a larger-than-life figure all in black with dark shadows falling over him, lending a sinister air to his perfect, chiseled features. I shivered, remembering the darkness in his eyes the last time I saw him. It should have scared me, but it only made me want him more now.

I pictured myself at his side, light to his dark. I would take him in my arms and kiss the pained look from his gaze. I could practically feel his lips, the growing urgency of his need as he pulled me closer, pressing me to him, and let his hands roam down my backside. Something rustled behind me. My heart raced, frantic. I turned.

"Everything okay in here?" Val stood, framed by the harsh rays of streaming sunlight in the doorway that led to the garage. "You want me to turn some lights on?"

I hadn't even realized I was sitting in darkness until Val came in. What was wrong with me? "I'm fine. Just checking on a few things."

"Okay," Val said. "I just got back from picking up lunch. There's some General Tso's on your desk calling your name."

"Thanks." It was a sweet gesture. Val knew I loved General Tso's chicken. I didn't have the heart to tell her I wasn't hungry. "I'll be right up."

By the time Val had gone back to her desk, my breathing had returned to normal. The frozen feeling returned, reminding me that for a few moments, those brief moments when I'd pictured myself in his arms, the freeze had melted away. I'd been fever warm. Even when he wasn't with me, he managed to have an effect.

I joined Val in the office and picked at the chicken and rice as I went over the donor forms in search of a dark haired, dark eyed donor. If I was going to have a baby, I wanted one as much like the one Owen and I might have made as I could possibly design. After a few minutes of reading, I found a match. A Harvard law grad, as far as the man claimed on his forms, with raven hair and dark brown eyes. Perfect. Or as close as I could get. I filled out my request and sealed the form in the envelope.

"Hey, Val," I said. "I've got to run out for a sec."

From here to maternity, I thought, smiling all the way to the FedEx box on the corner.

Chapter 15

Thanksgiving came, and still no word from Owen. I'd chanced another call to his office, but I couldn't get beyond the voicemail.

I had plenty to be thankful for, even if my love life was suffering. My family was happy and thriving. Business had picked up. I scored one more listing for an open house presentation on the week before Christmas. Financially, it was shaping up to be another good year despite the setbacks of the past few weeks.

The cryogenics tank containing my donor's sperm was due to arrive Tuesday morning, and my doctor's appointment for the insemination was scheduled for later the same day. I sipped at a mug of coffee as I stood in the door of my spare room and made a mental plan of how I would set up the nursery. The crib would look best in the corner, but where to fit a changing table and the rocking chair? There was plenty of time to work it out.

I went back to my room to dress for Thanksgiving dinner with the family and immediately thought how nice a wicker bassinet would look right next to my own bed. Perfect for the first few months. Perhaps something in blue. I tried to hum *Brahms' Lullaby,* but I couldn't get the tune right. It came out more like the Stones' *Sympathy for the Devil,* which made me think, again, of Owen.

I paused at my closet to pick out something to wear to Bennie's for dinner. I wanted to look my best in case Owen decided to show up, but deep down, I knew I only courted more heartbreak. The frozen feeling persisted and I spent more and more time sitting in the dark, alone, wondering where he was. It was silly, but I was glad for the holiday to have someplace to go and people around me, people who loved me and would always be there for me. People who insisted on turning on the lights when they entered a room. I shook my head, surprised to see that I'd been walking around with the lights off all morning, again.

True to suspicion, Owen had been a no-show at Bennie's, and there was no message waiting on my machine when I got home. Thanksgiving had been entirely uneventful, and even stuffing myself with turkey and pumpkin pie hadn't chased the frozen feeling from deep down inside me. If my family noticed my sullen mood, they didn't mention it. I longed to feel normal again, but I started to fear that normal was something I might never again know.

Why wouldn't Owen call?

At home in the dark, I was about to crawl under the covers for yet another session of trying to get warm, but I stopped myself. I'd been worried that being with Owen might overpower me and make my light go out, but instead, it seemed that being without him was doing more damage. I craved the dark. I always felt cold. It was as if I was making my own light go out—or was it the isolation of being without him? I only knew it was unhealthy. I may not be able to chase the chill from my veins, but I could certainly seek out some light in my life. Forget bed.

Despite the late hour, I picked up the phone and called Val.

"Val, hey. What's up?"

"What's up? Is it Kate or Bugs Bunny on the line?" Val cracked. "I need to know because I haven't had a date in a while and Bugs is looking pretty good. I always wondered about the size of that carrot."

Eww. "It's Kate. Sorry."

"Drat. Never a man around when you need one."

"Eh, who needs men? I know it's late, but how about a girls' night out."

"Really? We haven't done that in a while." She didn't say it to make me feel bad, but I realized I had been neglecting Val socially. I couldn't afford to alienate one of my few friends. It made me glad I'd called. "Sounds like fun."

"Great," I said. "I was thinking of seeing the new Reese Witherspoon flick, *Miss Fortune.*"

"The romantic comedy?" A pause. "Kate, you feeling okay?"

"Yeah, why?"

"You hate romantic comedies. You hate romantic anything."

"That's not true." Well, okay, it *had* been true, but the new Kate, Optimist Kate, planned to start enjoying a little romance now and then. And hell—er heck—she could use a little comedy. "It looks cute."

"'When kooky astrology buff Rachel Lear falls head over heels for a staid insurance investigator, good karma-dy ensues'?" She read from the ad. "*This* sounds good. To *you.*"

"Yes, Val. I'm telling you, I want to see it. I'm in the mood. I just want to forget my troubles and giggle like a schoolgirl again, Val. Is that so bad?"

"Normally, no. When it's you, I worry. Like it's a sign of the apocalypse or something." Val laughed.

"God, Val, shh. Don't say things like that." I gnawed my lip, then lightened up. I doubted any end-of-the-world activities were in order. Surely Owen would have warned me about an impending apocalypse.

"It was a joke, Kate. Sheesh. I'd tell you to lighten up but I'm already worried here. You lighten up any more and the world might explode from the force."

"When's the next showing?" I asked, ignoring her jibes. I knew she had a paper handy. Val always has a paper handy, plus she'd just read the blurb, proving my instinct correct.

"Eight-fifteen."

"Good. I'll pick you up in half an hour."

Chapter 16

*True to his word, he'd shut out her thoughts. He'd gone
back to the underworld to take care of business, and in the off
hours he remained sequestered in his haven all alone, no minions, no company to soothe his nerves. This morning he'd returned to the mortal world, but he still hadn't made contact
with her. He kept to the confines of his office. No longer could
he hear what she was thinking, soaking up every last idea as
if he'd thought it himself. But he hadn't cut off his ability to
feel what she was feeling, a fact that made him infinitely sorry
as her laughter fell all around him, cut glass on open wounds.*

*She could be happy without him. The knowledge stabbed
deeper than Artemis's deadly arrows. He didn't begrudge her
some happiness; he simply regretted not being the one responsible for her joy.*

*He'd nearly failed to win her over. In his wildest dreams, he
hadn't imagined that she would be able to move on without
him. He'd hoped a prolonged absence would allow her to realize the depth of her need for him, but what if that need just
wasn't truly there? Up until a day ago, he'd been making sig-
nificant progress. Something had changed in the last few*

hours. Her mood had lifted. She'd begun to find a way to shut out the darkness, the same bleakness that he felt without her. What more could he do?

In an instant, any trace of remaining warmth seeped from his bones. The office windows frosted over with the sudden change in temperature, blocking his view of the world outside. He sat, frigid and alone. Storms brewed outside to match his mood, and he hoped she could hear him in every boom of thunder, feel him with every crack of lightning. It was almost time for his return.

For nearly too long, he'd chanced to keep his distance from her. Instead of pining for him, she'd almost given up, decided she didn't need him, dared to think she would be better off alone.

He needed to do something drastic, to step up his game, or risk losing her forever. He wanted it all from her. Halfway would never do.

There could be nothing to keep her from him. He simply would not accept her turning her back on love for the sake of friends, family, or petty distractions.

He was prepared to do whatever it might take to win her over and keep her all to himself. Forevermore.

Chapter 17

Feet firmly planted in the stirrups, I stared at the blank white ceiling and tried to similarly clear my brain. No use. Even with my knees pressed together, I felt wide open to the world. Hello, world. Here I am, vulnerable and exposed.

My paper robe or the paper under my bare bottom crinkled with my every movement, destroying any ounce of calm I managed to build up between the booms of thunder from a storm raging outside. It had started raining Thursday when I was coming home from the theater, and it had kept on over the weekend right through to today. I wondered if Owen had anything to do with the weather, then tossed it off as ridiculous. There'd been no sign of him, no word. If he had any intention of seeing me again, he could have called. Right now, I had more on my mind, like hoping the speculum would be suitably warmed.

I breathed deeply. No need for panic. I was in a perfectly safe, albeit uncomfortable, environment. Sterile. Silver instruments still in packages, plastic table, paper robes. I had faith in my gynecologist. I even liked her. She had lovely eyes and a gentle hand. What more could a woman want?

Deep in my heart, I knew I wanted a baby. But despite my longing for a child, I didn't exactly want to make a baby in a sterile environment. I should have been making a baby with the man I loved.

No matter how much I tried to convince myself otherwise, Owen was the one I imagined when I thought of permanence, of forever. If only he'd been a real man and not a mythical god—a mythical god in charge of the underworld.

Doctor Reyes breezed into the room, taking a seat beside me. "Good morning, Kate," she said. "How are you feeling today?"

"All right," I said with a sigh.

"Just all right? That's not good enough. We're going to make a baby." She conjured a cheerleader's enthusiasm. Give me a B!

"God willing," I said, but I didn't say which god. I didn't want to know.

"Just relax," she said. "You've been through it before. It's not going to hurt at all."

"I know." But it wasn't going to feel good, either. It was going to be clinical and quick, a chance for egg and sperm to meet and do the deed. No foreplay, no cuddling.

No love.

I was about to embark on a joyous experience, but I'd never felt more alone. I *was* alone in this. No one even knew what I was about to take on. I hadn't even told Bennie.

"Ready, Kate?" the doctor asked, covering her mouth

with a surgical mask and taking her position between my knees.

"Ready," I said, before inhaling deeply.

She stopped and looked at me, worried. "You know, you could still do this at home. I can give you the syringe and the equipment. Some women feel more comfortable doing it themselves. Or with someone special."

Someone special? If I had someone special, I wouldn't be here using some other man's sperm.

"No," I said. I tried to think of Donor 567. On paper, he sounded ideal. Dark hair, brown eyes. A runner. Harvard law, top of his class. One day, he hoped to be a judge. But the only person I could picture was Owen.

"Let's go ahead. I'm eager to have it done."

Outside, the sky erupted with thunder, causing me to jump again. I tried not to think of it as some sort of omen.

"It would help if you lowered the lights," I joked. "Turned on some soft music. Maybe lit a few candles."

She smiled. I could tell by the crinkles at the corners of her eyes. "Whatever happened to romance?" I wisecracked, then I let out my breath. It was happening.

"Relax," she said again, easing in. I closed my eyes and saw him standing over me, that familiar wicked smile on his face. The hard table under my back was a desk, the one in his office. The paper under me, his contracts.

His large hands slid up my thighs, easing my skirt up, opening me up to him. I wrapped my legs around him, pulling him into me, tighter, deeper. My body pulsed around him. I could feel him moving, all of him. I could feel him breathe, slow and erotic.

I slid my bottom to the edge of the desk, urging him

deeper, as far as he could go. I wanted him all the way inside me, so deep he'd never leave. I shuddered.

"That's it," the doctor said. "We're done."

My eyes flew open. I wasn't in Owen's office, making a baby with him. I was on an exam table, alone, with a winter storm raging outside.

"That's it," I said, my voice heavy with disappointment. *It shouldn't be this way.* But this was how it had to be.

"Keep your feet up," Dr. Reyes ordered. "I'll be back to check on you soon."

She turned out the lights before she left. Alone in the dark, I cried.

I returned home to an empty apartment, slowly navigating the snowy streets. I'd planned on going straight to bed. The doctor didn't say I had to lie down, but I assumed it probably wouldn't hurt. Besides, I was so cold.

Without even turning on the lights, I dropped my keys on the hall table and proceeded toward the bedroom. Halfway there, a red light cut through the darkness. The answering machine. While I was out, someone had called.

I willed myself to ignore it. It was probably Bennie or Mother, or maybe Val. But I couldn't fight the voice inside that said it could be Owen. What if it was? What if he called to say that it was all a joke, a hideous mistake, and that he wasn't the devil after all?

I went to the machine. Pressed the button. Waited, stock-still, not even daring to breathe.

"Kate, hi. It's Marc."

Oh. Marc. Unexpected, but not entirely unwelcome. "I'd love to see you. Coffee? Or whatever. I was hoping it could be dinner. Tonight? Tomorrow I leave town for a game. If you're free, give me a call at—"

I picked up the phone and dialed before the message even played out. It felt like a respite, a midweek furlough. I didn't really want to give in to the cold, to lie in the dark alone. Marc had called a few times now, why not give him a chance? If I was going to be a single mother, I could use a few more friends. No one said it had to be anything more than a friendly dinner. Who knew when, or if, Owen was ever going to call again.

He answered on the first ring.

"Marc? Hi, it's Kate Markham."

"Kate." He sounded happy. Happy was a sound I hadn't inspired in a while. It felt nice. "How are you?"

"Okay," I said. A lie. "You?"

"Better now. I've been sidelined with a knee injury, so it hasn't exactly been a banner couple of days."

"Oh." I should have known. I'd read in a singles guide once that women on the dating scene should watch ESPN highlights. Not that recommendations from singles guides ever mattered to me before. "I'm sorry to hear that."

"No problem. I was hoping you could join me for dinner at Bomboa. That's in your neighborhood, right?"

"A few streets away, not far," I said. A thoughtful choice, Bomboa was close enough that I could make a quick escape if things went awry.

"Great. I have reservations for eight o'clock. Shall I pick you up?"

"No," I said, hesitant. Picking me up meant dropping me off, creating the awkward moment of truth where I had to decide if I would invite him in or not. The moment of truth hadn't been going so well for me lately. "No, that's okay. I'll meet you."

"Great. See you at eight, then. And Kate?"

"Yes?"

"I'm really looking forward to it."

"Me too," I said, surprised that I actually meant it.

Kate Markham, back in fighting form. I wasn't cut out for wallowing in self-pity after all.

Bomboa, one of the trendy new South End restaurants, specialized in French-Brazilian fare. In honor of the eclectic cuisine combination, I'd thought about pairing my salsa-inspired ruffled red dress with a jaunty beret.

After getting dressed, I looked in the mirror. The world wasn't ready for Parisian Flamenco. Quickly, I changed to a basic black wool skirt, a plum cashmere wrap sweater, and my trusty Prada boots. Simple, elegant, perfect.

I got there early and had a mojito at the bar before I remembered that I wasn't supposed to drink. A shame. I loved the mojitos at Bomboa. Marc came in as I was signaling the bartender for water.

"You look great," he said, leaning in to give me a chaste greeting hug. "I mean, wow."

"Wow?" I could deal with wow. "Thanks. I like a man who recognizes the power of wow to make a good impression."

"Rafael, how's it going, man?" Marc greeted the bartender. "Get the lady a new drink, but bring it to my table."

"Sure thing," Rafael said, and was gone before I could request water instead of another mojito. I made a vow to my stomach region to only have a sip or two to make it look good and then switch to water.

Marc kept his hand around my waist and led me to a coveted table right near the restaurant's gigantic aquarium, a table I later learned was "his" table. As easy as Marc's relaxed manner made it easy to forget I was dining with one of Boston's most celebrated sports treasures, the restaurant's staff reminded me with impeccable service and constant deference to Marc.

We didn't even have to order. Food just magically appeared at well-timed intervals, a perk I appreciated on a night when I had no desire to make decisions, or even to use my brain.

"What is this?" I asked Marc as I dipped my spoon into something delicious served in a miniature copper cauldron. It had chicken, sausage, beans, and just the right amount of spice.

"Feijoada," Marc said. "My favorite. But if you don't like it, we can get you something else. Anything. Whatever you want." He signaled the waiter.

"No, I'm fine. I like it," I said in time to stop him. "It's like Brazilian comfort food, really good."

"Hm, especially on a cold night like tonight," he said. "Thank God we play in Miami this week. I could use a little heat."

"Lucky you," I said.

Conversation flowed easily for most of our evening. It came as a surprise that I honestly enjoyed Marc's company. I could talk to him without the usual date jitters stalling my wit. By dessert, we'd covered a number of topics, from childhood insecurities to adulthood hassles—including dating, a normally taboo topic for a first date. It was nice to know he *had* a childhood.

It was a point in Marc's favor and was supposed to

make me feel better. Instead, it made me ache for Owen. No childhood? What he'd missed . . . No wonder he yearned for light.

As we chatted and I sipped my herbal tea, I noticed the place was emptying out. I had no idea how long Marc and I had lingered but I realized it must have been getting late. I didn't care.

"I really had fun tonight, Marc."

"I did, too." He seemed sincere.

"I enjoyed your company. You enjoyed mine. Let's leave it at that. Friends?" I liked Marc, but I couldn't stop thinking of Owen. What had he been doing these past few weeks? Had he given in to the darkness? Did he even know how much I thought of him?

"Friends." As if considering the word, he nodded his head. "You think we can stay just friends and still go out sometimes? I would love to take you to the new bistro on Tremont. My football friends are more the beer and pizza types."

"That sounds great. I'd love to spend more time with you, but I'm not ready to be more than friends. I hope you understand. It isn't a brush-off."

"I understand. But it isn't too *When Harry Met Sally,* is it?" He raised his eyebrows and I realized he had waxed them, just enough to give them some shape and highlight his stunning blue eyes. "I mean, if there's any chance we can be friends and fall into bed now and then, I'm all for it."

"Uh-huh." I laughed. "I'm sure you are. But no. Friends. Not *special* friends. Just friends. For now. But if you're really into the whole Meg Ryan thing, I can treat you to a fake orgasm. Just for kicks."

"Really?" He seemed interested. "Right here?"

"Next date," I said. "I never fake an orgasm on the first date."

"Technically, this could be our second date," he said.

"Ha, don't push your luck."

We laughed together. For a day that had started out pretty bad, I had to say that it had ended up all right. So why didn't I feel any better?

Coming home, my empty apartment made me feel all the emptier on the inside. Did I seriously think I could just forget Owen? Move on? I yearned to know where he was, how he was. I had given up too easily. Why hadn't I fought harder to find him if he wasn't going to come to me?

I sighed, the weariness taking over. It had been a big day. I needed my rest. Tomorrow I would fit in a trip to the main offices of Glendower Enterprises. I had just started to undress and prepare for bed when suddenly, I felt energized again. *The tingle.* My blood perked as if I'd had ten cups of full strength coffee.

On instinct, I threw on my nightgown, ran to the door, and looked out. Owen stood on the other side.

Chapter 18

"Owen." I opened the door and greeted him. "What are you doing here? It's late." My knees practically knocked from the force of the full strength tingle when I met his heavy-lidded gaze.

His hair was slightly longer than I remembered, a disheveled mess, as if he'd been running his hands through it to the point of distraction. He was unshaven, unbuttoned, and all around unforgettable. He wore only a thin white shirt, untucked from plain black trousers. He may have been pacing outside my door for who knew how long, or he may have just arrived. Devil or no, I *wanted* him.

"I couldn't stay away." He stepped inside, his body brushing against me with feral grace. I moved with him, unable to distance myself, as he swept in and shut the door behind us. His dark gaze pierced straight through me as he took me in his arms. "I've missed you."

"I'm sorry," I said. "I don't know why I ran away, why it was so hard to accept." I ran my palm along the sharp edge of his jaw and felt some of the chill fade from my veins. "I know what you mean now, about being frozen. I'm so cold without you."

My thumb paused to stroke at his full lower lip, the urge to taste him coming on strong.

"No." He held me away from him and looked directly into my eyes. "I don't want to pressure you. Perhaps I shouldn't have come."

He stepped back to the door, his hand closing on the knob. I reached for him, tugged until his feet were back on the rug in the entryway, too far from the door to walk out. "I've been so afraid you wouldn't come. I was afraid I'd lost you. Please. Please stay."

As if against his will, he stopped and stared with an unmistakable hunger, letting his gaze drop down my body. The crooked smile let me know he approved of my sheer white cotton nightgown. A lazy tendril of heat, smoke in my belly, curled up inside me.

"Then you're ready for me?" He slipped a finger under my chin and directed my face to meet his. "You're willing to give us a chance?"

Desire held my heart in a viselike grip. It hurt to as much as breathe another second if I couldn't inhale him straight into me. "I'm willing." But somewhere inside of me, fear flickered.

I gripped his hand and his hollow, empty ache ripped right through me. It was the same ache I'd felt for him in the cave, the same cold, painful burden I'd been carrying for weeks. We *had* to be together. Together, we stood a chance to ease our torment. Apart? There was nothing.

"I know it has been hard on you, Kate. I want nothing more than to make love to you right now. But I won't until I'm certain you're ready."

All I knew was that I wanted him now. I couldn't bear the thought of spending the night without him. Only *he* could make the desperate emptiness inside me go away. There was no alternative, no avoidance.

"I need you," I croaked, my throat dry as ash. I trembled as he stepped closer.

"Are you sure?" His voice held an edge, as if he asked for so much more than a mere night of intimate surrender.

I thought of my work, of my family, of the baby I might even now be carrying. I couldn't make any promises. I looked to him for reassurance, for some guidance. But deep down, I wanted to be pushed over the edge, to the point of no return. I didn't want to think of later. I only wanted now. I wanted to lose all control. Unable to resist any longer, I reached up to tangle my hands in his hair, to guide his face down to mine. I never imagined I'd be forced to make such a decision. To walk away from everything I'd ever known for love. "I know I need you now. Beyond tonight, I don't know what to expect, what I can give."

He paused, his lips not an inch from my own. "I want you, all of you, and nothing more."

"That I can give," I answered, barely a whisper. I stood up on my toes, brushed my lips to his, and darted my tongue out to taste him at last.

He broke from the kiss. "Where does it hurt?" He stroked a hand down the length of me. "I can soothe your pain."

His eyes, darker than the night, held a promise to love, to cherish, to care for me as he had no other. I could hear it all in his head without his saying a word. It was odd, mysterious, and incredibly sexy.

"The cold is the worst." Most of the cold had gone,

ice melting to pools, but I needed to feel him inside me
to be sure. "I've been so cold."

His lips curved in a slow, lazy smile. "Let's get you
warmed up."

I almost protested when he stepped back instead of
moving closer. Then he held my gaze and flooded me
with warmth as he urged me, using some otherworldly
power, flat against the wall behind me. I gasped at the
sudden shift. My feet lifted right off the ground. He
hadn't moved an inch.

The heat inside me was so delicious, so overwhelming, that I didn't want to ask for an explanation. I let go
of the tension, rolled my head back, and gave in to the
feeling of being weightless, light as a feather. His gaze,
warm as a human touch, stroked my nipples until they
smoldered like embers against the thin fabric of my
gown.

He closed the distance, reached down, and caught
my hem in his fist, tugging the white cotton flounce
aside to ease his hands up my legs, from ankles to
calves. My breath caught. I remained suspended before
him, hung like a new work of art on the wall between
my beveled mirror and the antique pewter candle
sconces. The candles lit into flame one at a time down
the row, nearly in synch with my own fast-rising temperature as his fingers traced the dimples on my knees.

His hands continued a slow journey until he paused
to stroke the delicate white skin of my inner thighs
before forcing them open for him. I inhaled sharply,
but did not gasp. I wrapped my legs around his waist
and pulled him closer. It was my turn to flash the
wicked smile, which he answered with one of his own
as his finger traced the damp lace edge of my panties.

No longer held by unseen forces, my weight fell on

his hips, his growing erection brushing at my core, burning through his trousers and my underwear.

"Your skin," he said, leaning into me, his breath hot in my ear as his hands slid over my back and down to cup my backside. "It's softer than angels' wings."

I didn't want to ask about angels' wings, or if I should be jealous of any particular angels. Instead, I took it as a compliment and tightened my legs, unable to keep still against him.

His tongue, liquid glass, slicked expertly between my lips. I drew him to the far reaches of my mouth. I wanted him as deep inside as he could possibly go. For the first time in my life, making love represented a solid bond, a solemn vow.

He held my waist and let my feet slip back to the smooth wood floor. Suddenly, we stood in my bedroom, next to my four-poster bed, but I had no idea how or when we'd moved. My deep purple taffeta comforter was already, magically, turned down to the smooth, imported cotton lavender sheets. The candles of various sizes that I kept on my dresser and side tables were all lit and glowing.

Fleetingly, I wondered if there were beds in hell. Maybe we would sleep on clouds or steam licks. I laughed out loud. It was all so unreal, I couldn't even comprehend it.

"I love your laugh," he said. "When I was away from you, the sound of your laughter is what I missed the most."

Then the need for conversation died as he slid my nightgown down over my shoulders and sucked in a breath at the appearance of bare skin. His gaze moved with aching deliberation from my breasts to my belly, and lower. He moaned from low in his throat, then stepped closer again to drop a trail of light kisses down my neck. With his tongue, he licked a path down the valley between my breasts. His fingers rolled around a pebbled nipple, and then his lips closed on me and he sucked my entire areola straight to the core of his scorching mouth.

I could hardly stand still for it. In desperation, I reached for him, grasping for a hold to steady myself, and then tugging at his shirt and running my hand down his taut body to his zipper. *Slowly,* I cautioned myself, but instinct took over. Frantic, I tore at his clothes until he stepped away and shed them on his own.

My first sight of him, naked and glorious, took my breath away. Michelangelo himself might have used him as a model for *David.* Every inch of him was perfect. Lean, muscled, taut. Long. Very, very long.

I wanted to touch him, but my eyes could hardly get enough of him first. Until he gathered me in his arms and kissed me again, insistent and deep, and I couldn't think of anything else at all, just him and the comfort of his body, the way we fit together, the delight of being with the man I loved.

"So beautiful," I said, and he was. My hand splayed down the rigid muscles of his stomach. He was absolutely perfect, no flaws, no scars. Not even a freckle. I closed my fingers around his shaft, as hard as the marble that might have been sculpted to such perfection.

But I didn't want to take our time, to map each other's bodies as lovers did in luxurious hours. That would come later. For now, I wanted him hard, fast, and in me. I wanted him deep inside my soul. I wanted to take him so far inside me that I'd never let him go.

Owen was more patient. He pushed my hand away

and nestled into me as we embraced. With lingering, glorious strokes, he caressed my back, then around to my breasts and belly before easing me to the bed and falling atop me, parting my legs with his thigh. Propped on an elbow, he lowered his head to my navel, laving a slow circle then working his way down. With one smooth motion, he eased my panties down my hips and off, then he blew a steady stream of air over my damp curls until I bucked against the heat, wild for his exploration.

He replaced the air with his hand, parting my folds and slipping a long finger inside. I rocked into it, urging him deeper, but instead of finding a rhythm, he centered his attention on my clitoris. With expert strokes, he circled then slicked his thumb over my swollen pearl while his finger delved. He stroked until I was bleary-eyed and crying out, but he didn't stop there. He leaned down and repeated the exquisite torture with his tongue, lapping at my nectar as if he couldn't get enough.

My toes curled, catching in the tangled sheets.

Every ounce of my control slipped away. I cried out, ragged, and cried again.

"Now," I begged. Screamed? "Finish or I might die."

He laughed, a wicked rumble that echoed off the walls.

"You won't die, sweetling. I've got what you need."

I reached for him. He gripped my wrists and smoothed his hands down the length of me, his fingers catching at my nipples for the barest second before he leaned in for one more kiss. It was then that he thrust into me, sinking deep. So blessedly deep. It was as if a silent hush fell over the entire world as he entered me. Even the air became still. He pulled back just as quickly to tease at my entrance with his glistening tip. I watched, not taking my gaze from him, as he slid in again with agonizing slowness. I'd already climaxed a number of times, but I came again and again until he finally joined me and bellowed my name. I completely unraveled at the sound. The sheets, bunched in my hands, hung down and I realized we'd lifted somewhat off the bed and there was a golden glow all around us, radiating from us. Amazing.

In that second, I finally felt completely whole, completely loved, and completely at home.

Home at last.

After we had exhausted ourselves, I settled in his arms. Bathed in sweet ecstasy, I had no fears, no worries. I didn't think about the past, the future. There was only now. Only us. Only love. I drifted to a blissful sleep.

Not long after, I jolted awake at the sound of the phone, but I didn't move to answer it. It was late, but a dim glow filtered through the window, fending off complete darkness. With Owen, Hades, curled at my side in all his golden perfection atop the sheets, there was nothing important enough to pull me out of this perfect warmth. I let the machine pick it up.

"Kate, there's been a terrible accident." I startled at the sound of my mother's tearful voice. "Come quickly. It's Patrick."

God, no. My stomach bottomed out. *Patrick.*

I pulled myself together somehow, alarm calling me to my senses, and darted for the phone.

"Mom, what happened?"

"Bennie tried to reach you earlier. We're at the hospital."

"Hospital, good Lord." Or bad. I shot a look at Owen,

dread erupting like slow-rolling thunder through my soul. Had he known? He lay, awake now and propped on one elbow. He looked as if he knew. I shivered. "How bad is it?" I stood by the bed, holding the phone out, unsure of who to ask, Mother or Owen. The question hung in the air between them, but it was Mother's voice answering from over the phone.

"He ran off the road. It's critical. Your sister needs you. Just get here. Hurry. Please hurry." With a sob, she hung up the phone.

A cold knot of fear tangled deep in my stomach, freezing me from the inside out.

Patrick.

I put the phone back on the table and turned on Owen. He was already back down in bed, pulling the sheets around him as if to settle back to sleep. "You knew," I said. My voice held a venom I barely recognized. "You knew and you didn't say anything."

Naked and devastatingly handsome in his dishevelment, he sat up again, slowly. I cursed myself for even noticing the way he looked.

"We needed this time." He ran a hand through his hair. "You couldn't do anything to help."

"I can be there for my sister." I went to my closet and started pulling out clothes. "This is my *life*. My family."

"What about us? I need you."

"Not like this. Not now."

He got up. "Exactly like this. Exactly now. I needed to know where your heart was. With me, or with them."

I felt the tears coming. "Why does it have to be a choice?"

"You know why. You're leaving them. You'll never come back."

I shook my head. "I don't have time to think about that now. I have to get there."

"You're choosing them after all?" He looked hurt.

My head was spinning "No. I don't know. All I know is that my sister needs me. I have to be with her."

"What if I said that we have to leave now? Now or never, Kate?"

I stared in disbelief. The lovemaking, the intense attraction between us, the way he felt like home, it was an illusion. It had to be if he didn't understand why I needed to go. Reality called. My sister needed me. I'd wanted fate to choose for me, but not this way. Not now. And certainly not on an ultimatum from him. I wasn't about to be forced into a decision.

"Life means so little to you," I realized it all as I spoke. "It's nothing to you. What you're asking me to do, you have no idea. Life, death, it's just a state of being. All the same to you, is it?"

He shrugged. "It is a state of being. You're one way, then the next. It's really not that different. Come back to bed." He patted the space beside him as if it was so easy to tempt me.

"Not that different? The fragility, the wonder, the sheer delight of being alive. Is all of that lost on you? Do you really not understand?"

He didn't say a word, but he did toss off the sheets and get to his feet.

"I'm sorry, Owen. If you're going to make me choose right now, I'm choosing them." Choosing life. "I have to. Come with me."

"It wouldn't look right. They won't understand. I'll be an intrusion." He reached for his clothes and started dressing.

"No. You're wrong. You'll be family." I held out my hand but he didn't make a move toward me.

"Not this time. Trust me on this. I know."

"*Trust* you?" It hurt how much I wanted to trust him. But I didn't know how. "Did you have something to do with this?"

"I promised never to hurt you. Of course I didn't."

"But you know what's going to happen. Don't you?" I narrowed my eyes. "You knew when you came. You knew when you made love to me. You knew when you were asking me to make a choice."

"Yes, I knew. I know. That's why I can't be there." He closed the distance and hugged me to him. How could he be so warm, so comforting, and so cold all at once? "I'm sorry, Kate. I'm not allowed to intervene. I'll check with you in a little while." How could I love him when he had so little regard for all I held dear? And yet, I did love him. I knew how much when the darkness started to cross his features again and the fingers of ice-cold started to creep up my spine in reaction. I had to go to Bennie, but I wanted to save him from the darkness, too. "Don't go. We can work it out. Together."

"Now?" He raised a brow.

"Not now. I have to go." Tears clouded my eyes. I wanted to make him understand. But how?

"And so do I."

Without waiting for my response, he was gone. Poof. I wiped my eyes and looked around, but not a trace of Owen remained. He'd just disappeared. He must have headed for the door and my eyes were so filled with tears I just couldn't see. I squinted through my crying and pulled on my jeans and a blouse. I didn't have time to run after him. Bennie needed me and, as usual, I was running late.

On the way to the hospital, I checked my messages. Sure enough, I'd missed a few calls, two from an eerily calm Bennie and the rest from my mother. I'd shut the phone off at the restaurant and hadn't thought to check it. It must have taken them a little while to give up and try my apartment line. Or they *had* tried and something had happened to keep me from hearing the phone.

A chill shot through me. Had Hades done this to Patrick? He swore he'd never hurt me, but to what lengths was he prepared to go to convince me to follow him to hell? I loved Patrick like a brother. I struggled to get my mind around the fact that something bad had happened to him. How could it be? God help me if I was somehow responsible, no matter how inadvertently.

Mother said Patrick had run off the road, but perhaps his injuries would turn out to be superficial. People walked away from some terrible things. Patrick was young, strong. He would do anything for my sister. The human will was amazing. I couldn't count out the possibility of a miraculous recovery.

I drove to the hospital and parked the car, then ran for the emergency room entry. Inside, a kind-faced older woman greeted me as if she knew me.

"Kate?" she said. "Your family's over here. Follow me."

For a second, I wondered how she knew who I was. Then I realized it was my striking resemblance to Bennie. Who didn't know we were sisters?

"I'm the hospital's family advocate," she said, tenderness in her eyes. "Ellen."

Dread snaked through my bowels. Family advocate? This was no broken leg.

"Thank you, Ellen." I followed her brisk steps. She led me to a room off the main hallway, a private waiting room. Through the glass door, I could see Bennie inside on a couch, with Mom right next to her. Gran and Pops perched on the couch across the way. Upon seeing them, my fear became a steel claw, gripping at my insides, threatening to tear me in two. It had to be the very worst-case scenario for anyone to get Gran and Pops out of bed.

"What happened?" I asked, taking Ellen's arm and pulling her aside before she could swing the door open. "Is he—" the words froze. I couldn't even say them.

"He's alive," Ellen said, before ushering me in to my family.

"Kate." Bennie shot across the room and into my arms. "You're here."

Bennie was wearing her battered gardening jeans and a faded tee, no makeup, her hair a disheveled mess. It was an outfit that, on a normal day, Bennie wouldn't be caught dead in outside the house. But this day was shaping up to be anything but ordinary.

"He's going to make it," I said, without even knowing if it was true. The need to reassure my sister, to make things better, took hold.

"Now that you're all here," Ellen said. "Let's talk."

As if we were a single unit, I moved with Bennie to the couch and sat us down. Ellen took the chair across from us, directly in front of Bennie. Personal service and private waiting rooms weren't part of the normal hospital experience. I braced myself for the news.

"At eleven forty-five, Patrick St. James was driving

east on the Mass Pike. He took exit eleven and lost control of his car. He hit a utility pole head-on."

Gran gasped. I shot her a look and squeezed Bennie's hand.

Ellen went on. "A friend of his following close behind witnessed the accident and called 911 from his cell phone. Thankfully, the friend knew CPR. He was able to pull Patrick out from behind the wheel and begin taking lifesaving measures, which he continued until the ambulance arrived. Patrick hasn't regained consciousness, but he does have a good solid heartbeat. We'll know more as we have time to evaluate."

Bennie stared straight ahead as if in some horrific trance. I rubbed her back and exhaled deeply. Okay, it was bad but there was hope. A good solid heartbeat said something about Patrick's ability to survive the worst. Maybe this was meant as some kind of wake-up call, a shock to the system to make me truly know my heart before running off to hell. But why should Bennie suffer? Patrick? Maybe it had nothing to do with me at all.

Still, I couldn't imagine that Owen had no idea what was about to happen. For all Owen's previous shows of concern, he'd picked a crucial moment in my family's history to make love to me at last. Hardly an hour ago, I'd been so happy, overwhelmed with love and contentment, released from all cares and concerns. And now? But this wasn't about me. It was about my family. I launched into "take-charge" mode.

"Can we see him?" I asked.

"I'm going to take you all up to the waiting room of the Critical Care Unit. That's where Patrick will stay for tonight." Ellen's voice was low and modulated, a calming influence. "Only two visitors at a time."

"Will we be able to speak with a doctor?" I asked.

"They're still running tests," Ellen said, matter-of-fact. "As soon as they have information, they'll find you."

I sensed Bennie didn't need to hear grim realities. She needed hope. I planned to be optimistic, for the sake of my sister.

Chapter 19

Once upstairs in the CCU family waiting area with late night television as a distraction, Ellen placed her hand on Bennie's shoulder.

"I'm going to let you in to see him now. You need to know that he isn't conscious and he can't speak. His appearance may be alarming at first, but try not to let it frighten you."

"All right," Bennie said, barely a sniffle interrupting her steady voice. I wasn't sure if it was shock or forced calm, but I was impressed by her sudden composure.

"You may bring one person in with you, if you wish."

"Kate," she said. "Come with me, Kate."

Mother's face crumbled, betraying her pain at not being chosen as her daughter's comforter. For a fleeting second, I was sorry for Mother. Even in the worst of circumstances, she was only thinking about herself. But this wasn't about her. It was about Bennie.

"All right, sweetheart," I said. "I'm here."

We followed Ellen in through the large double security doors of the Critical Care Unit.

The rooms were merely glassed-in cubicles, no bigger than the space needed for a bed and equipment. We passed trauma patients lingering in beds, attached to tubes, machines, and various lifesaving measures. It only took a second to realize the gravity of the situation. Every patient here fought hard to hold on to the remaining shreds of life. Patrick would be no different.

Life. Not exactly a specialty for the lord of the underworld. I tried not to think about the role of Hades in the great scheme of things.

We stopped outside of Patrick's room and Ellen motioned to the door. I reached for Bennie's hand. Inside, the man stretched out in bed and barely covered by a sheet bore no resemblance to my red-haired, robust brother-in-law. He was pale, slightly yellow, and every piece of skin that was not covered by sutures or bandages or lifesaving machines was covered in bruises. Even his hair had lost some luster.

He reminded me of a candle snuffed out and melted down to an oozy pile of wax. The shock of seeing him, of wondering what he was going through, nearly made me lose control. For Bennie's sake, I swallowed hard and maintained my outward calm.

Surprisingly, Bennie had found an iron will of her own. Without hesitation, she went straight to the edge of the bed, took one of Patrick's hands, and spoke to him in a loud, clear voice. I was proud of how well she held it together.

"Patrick," she said. "I'm here."

She'd put her emotions aside and snapped straight into Bennie Show mode. Bennie, life of the party, had always been a source of amusement to Patrick. He loved her acting out, her acting up. Now, she used it to anchor him, as if to say everything was business as usual. Just another day. Everything would be just fine.

"You know, you didn't have to go to such lengths to convince me to get a new car." She joked with him. He'd always hated their minivan. "I've planned on surprising you with the new Lexus hybrid you like on your birthday. Oops, I ruined the surprise."

"It's okay, Ben." I fell into place beside her at the bed rail and stroked her arm. "Now he can pick the color. You'll probably choose something girly, like champagne gold."

She shot me a look. "That's not girly. You'd like gold, Patrick?"

Despite our banter, Patrick didn't stir. I had no idea if he heard. I didn't even feel his spirit in the room with us, a fact that frightened me beyond belief. His eyes were opened to slits but it was clear he wasn't seeing. A mask covered his mouth, apparently hooked to the machine that did his breathing for him.

"He's being diplomatic, as usual," I joked.

"No seatbelt. His lungs collapsed," Ellen explained in a whisper as she stepped into the room and stood near the machinery across from us, at the head of Patrick's bed. "He broke his palate, his nose, many of the bones in his face, including eye sockets."

I winced involuntarily. That explained his mushy appearance. Bennie, in the midst of her private conversation with her husband, didn't hear, or pretended not to as she leaned closer to Patrick to smooth his hair.

"Can they fix that?" I asked, naïve.

"Cosmetics are not a concern now," Ellen said. "They'll do whatever it takes to keep him alive."

I felt like an idiot for asking, for worrying over

something as foolish as the way Patrick might look. "Of course," I said. "Absolutely."

"I'll leave you," Ellen said with a wan smile. "The doctors should be in soon."

Sure enough, a doctor appeared within minutes of Ellen's departure. He was a forty-something, dark-haired man with a pleasant, no-nonsense appearance. Green scrubs, white lab coat.

"I'm Doctor Chen," he said. "Let's step outside and talk."

We followed him to the narrow stretch of hall outside Patrick's room.

"I'm Kate, Patrick's sister-in-law," I said, once he stopped, "and this is his wife, Bennie."

"Bernadette St. James," she corrected, suddenly formal. She hated Bernadette, but it must have been nerves taking over.

The doctor nodded. "Your husband's condition is delicate. It's still too early to tell much of what's going on with him."

"But he's going to be okay," Bennie said, not a question, but an imperative statement, as if believing it made it true. "He'll have to stay for a few nights, maybe?"

The doctor met my gaze, his concern apparent. "It's not that easy. The accident did some damage, but we can't tell to what extent until he regains consciousness. There's swelling. It can take time."

"Brain damage?" I asked, hesitant to bring it up but understanding the possibility.

Bennie's eyes grew wide.

"Let me show you the film." From some files tucked under his arm, he grabbed and held up what looked like an X-ray of Patrick's skull. "The dark parts indicate where there is bleeding."

The entire inside of his skull looked dark. It wasn't good.

"Now, it's possible that it's all temporary. It always looks worse at first," he said.

"So the bleeding will stop?" I asked.

He nodded, probably more hopeful than certain. "If so, we'll get a better sense of what kind of damage we're dealing with. In some cases, the patient regains consciousness and seems perfectly fine. In others— well, we have to wait and see. If he comes out of the coma in the next twenty-four hours, we'll have a better sense of where to go from there."

"And if not?"

"Sometimes it takes longer. There's no set diagnosis right now. We're better off to wait and see." He gave me his card, as if sensing Bennie wouldn't be the one in any shape to call him later.

"Wait and see," Bennie said, still keeping it together. "Yes. I'm sure he'll be up and talking in no time. We'll wait."

I thanked the doctor and watched him go. Bennie headed right back to Patrick's side.

"Okay, babe." She stroked his head. "You get a little rest and then wake up and tell us how you're feeling. It's all up to you."

I joined her again, this time choosing a spot across the bed from her.

"I should have stopped him," she said. "I should have known."

"You weren't even with him," I said. "Accidents happen. You can't blame anyone."

But I could. It wasn't that I blamed Owen for what

happened. I still held some resentment for him not telling me. But maybe he was right. If I couldn't prevent it, then what good could it have done to know? Fate. I'd wanted to play the odds, see if fate pushed me closer to Owen or away from him. If only I had guessed the power of Fate. I couldn't fight it. I'd been a fool to tempt it. And now, I could only sit quietly by my sister's side and see what it had in store.

But in the back of my mind, I still had some fight left in me. I didn't feel entirely powerless.

I would do anything in my power to make it right for Bennie, even if it meant sacrificing something of my own.

"You need to get some rest," I said, cradling Bennie to support her on the way to the waiting room after over an hour by Patrick's side. "It doesn't look like anything's going to change tonight. Why not let me stick around here while you go home and get some rest?"

"I'm not leaving." But she could barely even walk on her own. I held most of her weight, or so it felt.

"What about the kids?" I asked, trying to refocus her attention. Maybe she would go home if she thought about the children. "What do they know?"

"They're with the nanny," Bennie answered, as if in a fog. "She was still around getting the kids ready for bed when the call came in. She offered to stay overnight. They don't know anything yet."

I had always thought it was a little silly that Bennie, a stay-at-home mom, needed extra help with the kids, but she argued that it kept her schedule free for things like Pilates class and her scrapbooking activities. Now I was glad Bennie had the extra hand to rely on.

"All right." I checked my watch. It was two A.M., hours before they needed to get up for school. "For now, we need to get you something to eat."

"I can't eat," Bennie said. "I can't do anything. I'm just going to wait here until they let me in to see him again or come out with news."

"Okay, Ben," I said, indulgent. "You sit here. I'm going to go get a coffee and be right back."

Gran, Pops, and Mother stayed with Bennie while I left to get sustenance for the troops. We would all need coffee and strength-sustaining snacks. But I had an ulterior motive as well. I needed to get hold of Owen.

I walked out of the emergency room doors and dialed his number, relishing the cold night air on my hot skin. No answer on his work phone. It went straight to voicemail. I didn't leave a message. I had a macabre vision of calling the hotline straight out of *The Year Without a Santa Claus,* the Heat Miser on the other end to answer the phone.

"Where are you?" Outside, I spoke aloud into the night. "I need you. Please come." I breathed deep, waiting for a sign. No answer. No ghostly arrival on a chill wind or sudden appearance from behind. No Owen. The tingle didn't come to warm me or thrill me or even let me know he was alive. Maybe it had all been a dream and I was slowly losing my mind. I couldn't afford to go nuts with Bennie hanging in the balance. She wouldn't make it without me. Even if I wanted to leave now, my obligation to my sister was too great.

If Owen loved me, why couldn't he wait for me? Why the sudden urgency from one who'd previously professed a desire to "court me properly?" Being properly courted would take some time. He couldn't tell me he hadn't expected it to take a while for me to come around. I had a whole life to lead. Things to do. Perhaps a child on the way, and now a sister to take care of. Leaving Bennie now was out of the question. If Owen couldn't accept that, then maybe he couldn't really accept me. I'd grown up believing, through media messages and living examples, that women could have it all. It fed my determination to find a way.

But all I could see was his face the last time I saw him, the darkness shrouding his features as he took on an increasingly sinister air. I wasn't dealing with an ordinary man. There were forces at work I'd only begun to understand—forces possibly stronger than all the determination I could muster. Perhaps there were two sides of him, and I'd been dealing with the best of him up until now. I only hoped I had it in me to stand my ground against the darkest possibilities, to let my light shine out and defeat anything that stood in my way.

Even if it was the devil himself?

I steeled myself for a long night and went to get the coffee.

As I struggled to get out of the elevator and down the hall with a tray of coffees and bags of convenience store snacks, I felt a rush run straight through my veins. *He's come.*

I rounded the corner and there he stood, talking to a man I recognized as one of Patrick's friends—someone I'd met at a dinner party once or twice—just outside the waiting room. Owen. *Hades.* My lover, my enemy, I didn't know which. Sturdy build, strong posture, he looked all man. *My* man. My body felt a surge of possession over him.

His appearance was polished. He wore one of his signature dark suits, his hair neatly combed as if he'd come straight from work and not fresh out of my bed. I wished I could run into his arms, but I struggled to kill the image. He was *not* a man. For all I knew, he'd come in an official capacity. The grim reaper.

I braced myself as I approached him. No sign of the darkness. He looked almost pleasant, except for the serious concern that marked his features. I couldn't let my guard down. I had to be cold and hard. I had to deny that I felt so much warmth inside the closer I got to him. My heart and soul were at war. I could hardly tell which part of me was fighting for me to be with him and which was telling me to run.

"Kate," Owen said, strictly formal. "This is Larry West. He saved Patrick's life."

As I reached for Larry's hand, juggling various coffee cups and bags, Owen's voice hummed in my head. "There will be time for us, Kate, but now is not the time." I glanced at Owen, but his lips were not moving.

Fear leapt into my heart. How could I hear his thoughts? Had making love with him given me special powers? Or had I always been privy to his thoughts and just never bothered to listen?

I kept my composure and turned my attention back to Larry, where it belonged. "Thank you, Larry. Thank you so much."

Owen took my bags, our fingers brushing for the briefest of moments, and I relished the heat. "I'll bring these in to the troops. Why don't you tell her what happened, Larry?"

Larry, clearly uncomfortable, stared at the floor. "I didn't do anything special."

"I'm not so sure. Not everyone thinks fast in a crisis. From what I understand, you got Patrick out of the car and did CPR."

He met my gaze at last. I noticed his shirt was on inside out and covered in patches of brown. It took me a moment to realize that he was covered in Patrick's dried blood, and thoughtful enough to try and hide that fact. Larry was a good guy. A typical brown-haired, brown-eyed, beer-bellied, everyday average Joe who had done the best he could in a bad situation.

"I would have been here sooner but I had to make statements. How's he doing?" His eyes clouded over, a mix of fear and regret.

"He's hanging in there," I said, cautious. "How are you?"

His eyes lit with surprise. Apparently, no one else had bothered to ask. "I'm fine. Not a scratch. I saw Patrick go over the edge and pulled over to see what I could do."

"So, it was an accident? Just a random thing? No other cars or trouble on the road?"

Again his gaze met floor. "We were drinking. He shouldn't have been behind the wheel."

A hollow shiver went through me.

"We were at the Olde Hadley tavern," Larry said. "Blowing off steam. Same old stuff. I stick to beer but Patrick usually has a few shots, some whisky. I don't know."

"You don't know?"

"Who keeps count? He's a good guy. Solid. Knows what he's doing."

"Apparently not," I said. I didn't need to hear any more. I knew. Images of Patrick through the years flooded my brain. Patrick, the life of the party. Patrick, always a drink in hand. Patrick, the perfect host, refilling everyone's glass. But never all that worried about his guests getting behind the wheel. Outside the house, why would he worry about himself? What hadn't I ever considered the possibility?

"She never wanted you to know." Owen's voice filled

my head once again and I tried not to flinch. I glanced up to see him standing just outside of the waiting room. I met his gaze then turned my attention back to Larry as if everything was normal, as if it came as no surprise that Owen and I could carry on a conversation in our minds.

"Thanks Larry," I said, heartsick. Suddenly, I barely had the strength to stay on my feet. "Why don't you go home and get some rest. They're only letting family see him. We'll keep you posted."

"That'd be great. Thanks. I'll come back in tomorrow."

Vaguely, I was aware of Larry walking away, of the floor moving under my feet as I found my way to the wall for extra support, but I didn't need the wall. Owen slid his energy around me, supporting me even as he stood some five feet away. Seconds later, he stood next to me, replacing his psychic energy with his own solid strength as he slipped his arm around my waist.

My mind flooded with images, courtesy of Owen. A glimpse into Bennie's private world. Patrick, passed out on the sofa night after night, and Bennie's secret shame about her husband's addiction. Something she struggled to deny, to fight, to hide all on her own. She'd made a life to be proud of in public, and to cry about behind closed doors. I'd never had a clue. Next, I saw Thanksgiving, the aftermath. Patrick, arguing with Bennie once the rest of us had gone home. Patrick, passed out, this time on across their bed. Bennie putting the kids to bed on her own. She'd made herself a world, built a solid wall of good times to cover up the bad. She loved Patrick with all her heart. She was simply powerless to help him, as I felt powerless now. If I'd

been a more attentive sister, might I have caught
it sooner?

I ached for all she must have been through. The perfect couple, the perfect marriage, all a sham.

"It wasn't *all* an act," he said, out loud now, his arms
still around me.

I backed away. "Stop reading my thoughts. I told you
to stop."

"It seems you've picked up some gifts of your own. I
told you we were meant to be together. I'm a part of
you and you of me. You can't shut me out. No matter
how you try." He smiled, but the crooked grin that
once seemed slightly wicked looked more on the edge
of sinister. A trace of the darkness lurked in the back of
his eyes.

A slow spiral of fear began to climb within me, but I
tamped it down and stepped back into the circle of his
embrace. Owen didn't scare me, and this darker side of
him wouldn't win out, either.

I held his gaze. The darkness prowled within him, a
caged animal desperate for release. I wondered how he
found the strength to control it, or if it took all that
much effort to force his humanity after all. I wouldn't
look away. In a glimmer, the darkness disappeared and
his eyes turned from black to a softer brown. Perhaps
I had imagined it after all. Or perhaps my light had
more power than I imagined.

He laced his fingers with mine.

"Together," he said. "Dark and light. I need you."

"You can't be all dark on your own." I struggled to
raise a brow.

He shrugged, as if it was true but he wouldn't own
up. "We're better together. Both of us."

"I can't be better if I turn my back on my sister now

Don't you see? You've survived centuries without me. You can make it a bit longer. My sister needs me, too."

"She's stronger than you think." He squeezed my hand and led me down the hall, away from the waiting room. "You heard Larry. It was an accident. Patrick had been drinking. His free will put him in that car."

"But you knew it was about to happen. Why didn't you tell me?"

"There was nothing you could do. We needed a chance. If letting you go would have changed anything, I would have done it. I would do anything *for you*."

He didn't understand. My heart broke on the spot. How could I be put in the position to choose between Owen and my family?

"Then do it," I said, calling him on it. I let go of him, stopped walking, crossed my arms over my chest, and stared him down. No trace of darkness. Good. "Walk away from your duties. Elect a stand-in. Can't you do that? Just for about forty years or so? Compromise."

He jammed his hands in his pockets, a man exasperated, and shook his head. "I can't. I have no say in the matter. There's not the slightest possibility."

"Then we're at a standstill. There's nothing I can do, either. My family needs me. I'm staying here."

"Oh, Kate." He crossed the floor and pulled me back into his arms. "I never knew it was going to be like this. I had no idea what it would feel like to love so much. I can't do anything, say anything. I stand before you absolutely powerless, so insignificantly human that I wonder how you stand it. How do you live so? Without any ability to change things or help? All you can do is wait. So it is with me, now. I wait."

Nothing was fair. There had to be more. More than

free will. More than horrible accidents. More than life and death, startling and sudden.

"What do you mean, wait?" I looked up at him, realization dawning. "You're waiting for him. When do you take him?"

"I can't say."

"What can I do?" I grabbed his arm. "There's something. Tell me. Take what you want, but leave him. Leave Bennie be. She can't handle losing him."

Tears clouded my vision. I fell to my knees. My soul may as well have been ripped out through my chest, or so it felt by the burning, heavy pain I felt there.

"There's nothing I can do, love," he said, reaching out to brush my hair back off my face. "It's all settled. I have to go now."

He turned to walk away, the darkness a shadow trailing his feet. How could it be?

"Don't go," I said, desperate to stop the darkness from following him, as if filled with the sudden awareness that I could still help Owen, even if I couldn't be with him. The darkness had to stop. I got to my feet, but he kept walking. I ran in time to catch up with the shadow. In an instant, I could feel the aching, hollow coldness of it coursing through my veins. I reached out and caught his shoulder.

He paused before stepping onto the elevator, though he wouldn't turn to face me. I looked down in time to see the darkness shoot out around us in a rim and disappear as if repelled by some unseen force. By me? Or by Owen and me, together? Whatever it was, the darkness was gone. I struggled to catch my breath.

"Walt Disney World," I said, on a whim, trying to get him to look at me. I needed to be sure that the shadow had gone out of his eyes. "This is why you sent them on the trip. You knew he wouldn't be around much longer."

"I gave them memories." He faced me, his eyes beaming as if lit from within by a soft golden glow. I gasped, amazed. Our love was that perfect mix of dark and light. Together, we had some cosmic sort of balance we would never have alone. Without him, I would never find it again. He smiled, a pure beatific smile, his eyes tender with emotion. I loved him more than ever.

"It was all I had in my power to do. Let the memories sustain you, Kate." With that, he stepped into the elevator and the doors closed, swallowing him up.

"No, wait!" I pressed madly at the button, as if I could open the elevator and bring him back. *He was gone.* Patrick would soon be gone.

Memories. They were all we had now. Bennie needed me and I would be there for her, but I felt as though I, too, had been left a widow.

I fell against the wall and sobbed. I let myself feel it, allowed myself to mourn. It was only for a minute, but it was enough to release some of the wild emotions raging inside me. After a minute, I pulled myself to my feet and took a deep, steadying breath. Bennie needed me now. I didn't have time for my own pain.

Where I'd failed myself, I could still be strong for her. I straightened up, turned away from the elevator doors, and went back to where I was needed, at my sister's side.

Chapter 20

Bennie sat in the same place I'd left her. She stared off, catatonic, while Mother stroked her hair.

Gran, as I discovered, had gone on a hospital scavenger hunt and rustled up some spare pillows and blankets.

"Where'd you get these?" I asked.

"Closet in the maternity ward," Gran said with a sly smile. "I remembered they left it unlocked from back when Bernadette was here to have Sarah."

Another family had moved in to the waiting room. Motorcycle crash. They kept to themselves on the other side, but it wasn't long before Pops started talking to one of the men about the infomercial on television. I offered snacks. Gran took one of the women to find more pillows. It became one big sleepover with plenty of dour faces and no laughter or games.

"You should take Gran and Pops home," I said to Mother after she attempted to stifle her fifth yawn in an hour. "They need their rest. And so do you."

"But what if—" She caught herself before saying more.

"Go. The doctor didn't seem to think anything would change tonight," I reassured. "I can handle things here for now. By tomorrow, I may need to call in reinforcements. We should probably take shifts."

Plus, I could sense Bennie's annoyance at Mother's hovering. Giving my sister peace from the rest of the family was probably the best thing I could do for her right now.

Tomorrow, she would need all the support she could get. Tonight, she needed to let it all sink in. Unfortunately, I knew the feeling all too well.

We went in to see Patrick as often as they'd let us, about once an hour and never for long. He looked unchanged. The monitors beat out a steady beep, indicating a steady pulse.

Bennie gripped his hand, stroked his forehead, and whispered soothing words. She would stay by his side, for better, for worse. I remembered watching her make those vows in St. Mary's church in front of all our friends and relatives. She'd worn a white dress, off the shoulder with beaded cap sleeves, a tight bodice, and a full skirt. That day, I saw my sister as a fairy princess come to life. She was beautiful, the kind of beauty that started from within and shone out like a bright light on everyone in proximity.

Marrying Patrick was her dream, even though she was barely twenty-one. I didn't understand it at the time, didn't see how it was a fitting ambition. Still, she had my full support. I would do anything for Bennie, as I proved by walking down the aisle in the bridesmaid's dress, a frothy concoction in a shade named Cotton Candy Pink.

Bennie was supposed to have the happily ever after.

None of us had ever imagined she would end up with a nightmare.

I ached for her in a way I'd never ached for myself, not even after watching Owen walk away. Perhaps it was too fresh, my love too new. But Patrick was a brother to me, and so much a part of Bennie for so long. The pain was visceral, a burning tightness deep in my chest. I would have given anything to spare Patrick, to save Bennie from the agony of losing the man she loved.

"Why did this have to happen?" Standing at Patrick's bedside, Bennie shielded her eyes with a well-manicured hand as she started to cry again. They'd brought her a chair, but she refused to use it in favor of hovering over her husband like a guardian angel. I knew better, but I couldn't help hoping her love was enough to protect him. I walked to the other side of the bed and put my arm around her.

As I held her, I searched the floor for shadows. With relief, I found none, no trace of chilling darkness in the room. I held my sister and let her cry for a few minutes until she dissolved into big, silent, heaving sobs. Silent, I guessed, because she wouldn't want Patrick to know she was crying. Silent wasn't one of Bennie's normal operating modes.

"Why didn't you tell me he had a problem?" I asked when the sobs quieted to huffs as she struggled to catch her breath.

She shook her head, no denials, no surprise in my question. She took my hand and led me across the room, away from the bed. "I thought I could handle it on my own."

"But I could have helped." I doubted Patrick had any sense of our conversation but I whispered out of respect for Bennie. "I could have done something."

She looked at me. "You can't fix everything, Kate."

"You could have at least talked to me. I would have understood."

Bennie sighed. "Let's not discuss it here."

"How about over breakfast?" I shot a glance at the clock over the bed. "The cafeteria should be open by now."

"I can't eat." She walked back to Patrick's side.

I followed. "Coffee, then?"

A nurse came in to check Patrick's vitals and gave Bennie a long look. "Coffee's a good idea," she said warmly. "Take a break. You'll need your strength."

"*Patrick* needs *me*." Bennie said, squeezing Patrick's hand.

The nurse put a comforting hand on Bennie's shoulder. "He'll need you more tomorrow. I'll be honest. People want to be here. They think it makes a difference. Later on, maybe it does. Right now, he's so doped up he has no idea you're even here. We'll be reducing the Ativan later today and maybe then."

Bennie looked on the verge of crumbling. I thanked the nurse, came around the bed, grabbed Bennie's arm, and whisked her from the room.

Over coffee and a muffin in the cafeteria, Bennie opened up.

"He's always been a drinker."

"I know." I remembered Patrick in high school. He graduated one year ahead of me. Star athlete, honor student, big partier. He'd been the "it" boy of his class.

"It never bothered me. He was a happy drinker. Social. It made him lively."

As I recalled, Bennie enjoyed a good party as well.

She'd always been Queen of the May in her own mind. I think it had actually been her ambition to achieve universal adoration at some point. In fact, it was what she'd written in her high school yearbook. Bernadette Markham's Future Plan: To achieve universal adoration.

"Some people don't make good drunks. Patrick didn't make a good sober," Bennie said. "He had such low self-esteem. His mother did a number on him growing up. Drinking made him warmer, more accepting."

I remembered his mother. Roberta St. James had passed out on the dance floor at Bennie's wedding, only after loudly berating Patrick's father and trying to pick up half the groomsmen. They'd never been close.

"I could call her," I offered, thinking of it now.

"No. I'll let her know when the time comes. He wouldn't want her here. She'll poison his environment."

"Okay." She was still his mother, but I trusted Bennie to know best and I wasn't about to push.

Still, Bennie traced the rim of her Styrofoam cup as if there was something more on her mind, something she had to get out but was somehow hesitant to say. She gnawed on her lip, then met my gaze.

"We haven't had sex in two years," she blurted out.

"Two years?" I repeated, trying not to sound too shocked. Until recently, two years was not too unusual for selective, single me. But for a married couple?

"At first, it seemed normal, with our busy schedules and the kids at home. I was fine with it, thinking we were settling in to that older, more comfortable stage. But then it just continued on. He was tired, or I was tired, and then he just stopped being interested at all."

I put my hand over hers on the table. "I'm sure he

was still interested. His schedule got crazy there when the market took off."

Bennie blushed. "He showed signs of interest, but . . . there was just no follow-through. I should have asked him to see a doctor, but deep down I think I knew it wasn't a matter of needing a little blue pill."

"The drinking?" I asked, hesitant. Bennie and I were close but bedroom topics were not in our usual range of conversation.

She nodded. "That's the one thing that really upset me. Everything else I could handle. The late nights, the bleary mornings, the forgetting conversations, the falling asleep in the middle of the day, the occasional bottle tucked away and forgotten. No problem. But what about me?

"Plus," she went on, "even at the best of times, Patrick was kind of a wham, bam, thank you ma'am kind of guy. He wasn't into physical affection. No matter what he does, he never feels good enough. Classic behavior of a middle child of an alcoholic. We've read up."

"That's a start," I said, gently.

"So, we didn't have sex. For a while, I thought it was enough. Patrick forgets to be so worried about every little thing when he drinks. He doesn't drink at work. He manages to function on a regular basis. I hate to fight with him. I figured if I let him find his own way and stood back, it would all work out."

"But you weren't happy?"

"I wanted *him* to be happy. What I wanted never mattered so much. As long as nothing ever affected the kids, I was willing to be the enabler." She made air quotations when she said "enabler," as if to demonstrate just how much she really had read up on alcohol abuse issues.

"You deserve to be happy, too." All this time, I'd really thought she had it all in the domestic department. Great house, loving kids, attentive husband. It never even crossed my mind she may have wanted more.

She shrugged. "I have the kids. Besides, I'm not saying I'm unhappy. I love Patrick, Kate. He's funny, sweet, charming. We think alike. We have a lot of fun together. He's my best friend. It's just, at some point, he stopped being my husband. My lover."

"I'm sorry, sweetie." Watching her eyes well up, I got up and came around the table to slide into the seat next to her, to hold her.

"Me too." She wiped at her eyes. "Oh, Kate. I'm going to lose it right here. What will people think?"

"We're in a hospital. It happens all the time."

"I'm okay. I can get ahold of myself," she said, fanning at her eyes as if the air would magically evaporate her tears.

"When he's out of here, maybe you can work on your relationship. I didn't know how things were for you, but I do know that Patrick would do anything for you, Bennie. *Anything*. If you asked. He loves you."

I covered her hand with mine. Love like that was priceless, hard to find, and even harder to hold. It was a feeling I'd known for all of an hour before life interfered. Owen had said he loved me, but he wanted me to make all the sacrifices. What about him? Would he have been prepared to do anything for me, as he'd said? I shelved the thought as something to get back to later.

"I should have been more worried about the driving. I never thought anything bad could happen. He's careful."

"I'm glad you and the kids weren't with him," I said, for lack of more encouraging words.

"Speaking of being with someone," she said, suddenly sly. I recognized the tone as her interrogator voice and knew I was in for some temporary discomfort. "What was Owen Glendower doing here?"

I tried to keep a straight face, but the heat of my blush gave me away. "We were together when Mom called."

"I *knew* you wouldn't take my advice. I haven't seen you look at a guy like that since Bart Haywood. Actually, you never looked at Bart quite like that, either, Kate. What's up?"

"Nothing now. Don't worry about it. It's like you said. He's the devil." I gave a brittle laugh.

"Maybe he's not so bad. If you like him, I'll give him a shot."

"We'll see." I finished my coffee to avoid further discussion. Now was not the time to fill her in about Owen. And what could I possibly say? That Bennie was right, and he really *was* the devil, after all?

"We'll see." She echoed. "Sometimes, you make me feel like I'm the older one. I've done the marriage thing, the kid thing. You have so much ahead of you. You have no idea."

"Maybe I'm better off having no idea." But I knew as soon as I said it that it wasn't true. He wasn't in the business of possessing souls, but he held a piece of me anyhow. A very large piece. I felt practically rent in two.

"Don't be so quick to deny it." She reached for my hand. "You have so much to look forward to. Good times and bad. Don't lose faith before you even try. No matter what happens with Patrick, I wouldn't give up on what we have. I'll never give up."

That was the biggest difference between us. I wouldn't fight a battle I didn't think I could win.

Bennie fought, no matter what. "Maybe I need to be a little more like you."

She smiled. "That's probably the nicest thing you ever said to me. We're in this together. You're always here when I need you. We're *sisters*. No matter what happens, I'm here for you, too. I love you."

And that's when it occurred to me. I did need to be more like my sister. Hadn't Owen always encouraged me to have faith? I needed to believe that I would see him again. I had unfinished business. Even if it didn't seem possible, I had to have faith that I would find him.

I had to do something. I couldn't sit back and let my sister lose the chance to make things right with the love of her life, not if I still had the power to fight it. I had to find a way.

The hours passed, and Patrick's heart remained strong, but it wasn't much encouragement. I began to wonder what would happen if his body got better but his brain didn't. It seemed a fate worse than death.

"What about the kids?" I asked again after time had passed. I'd finally gotten Bennie to take the chair at Patrick's side while I, desperate to think of a way to convince her to go and get some rest, paced the floor.

"I don't know," Bennie answered. "I'll have Kristin take them to school and worry about it later."

"No. You have to bring them in." I thought it was time for Bennie to get more realistic about Patrick's situation. It wasn't going to be easy, but they needed to go forward as a family.

"I don't want them seeing Patrick like that." Bennie buried her face in her hands.

I kneeled next to her chair, pulled her hands away,

and forced her to make eye contact. "No one does. But what if they *need* to see him? What if they don't get another chance?"

For a second, she looked as if she would wilt and I almost backed off. Then I remembered her strength when we'd first come in. Despite what I'd thought of her before, Bennie had proven she was no delicate flower. The worst could happen to Patrick and she wasn't going to wither and die at his side. She would go on. She had no other option. When her strength began to falter, I would be at her side to build her right back up again. Just like she knew I would.

"I'm not sure about Sarah, but Spence is like me," I said. "He needs solid proof to believe in things. He needs to see his father, to know how bad it is. If not, he'll always wonder if there was something else that could have been done to save him."

Bennie looked at me, eyes wide and bloodshot. "You think so?"

"Think about Dad," I said. He had been on my mind a lot since Owen showed me that he was out there. "If Mom and Dad hadn't tried so hard to hide their problems from us, we may have been more understanding when Dad walked away. How much easier it would have been with a chance to know our world was about to change."

"This is different," Bennie said.

"Yes. There's a lot more at stake," I said. "Spencer will never forgive you if you deny him a chance to see his father now." *To say good-bye,* I thought, but couldn't say aloud.

Bennie got up and stood gripping the bed rail at Patrick's side as she looked him over, as if looking for answers, but he did not stir. After a moment she asked to borrow my phone to call the kids.

A strange urge came over me while Bennie stepped out to make her call. I wanted to pray. No, I needed to pray.

Not to Zeus. Not to Hades. To God. I prayed silently to the image of God I'd known as a child, the only God my heart would recognize in the midst of a crisis, the wise old man with the flowing robes and white beard. The one who loved everyone and made miracles happen.

"Please God," I said to myself. "Don't let Patrick die. Let Bennie have her happily ever after."

His heart monitor beat out a steady answer.

As soon as Kristin came in with the kids, I would have my chance to slip away. I knew what I had to do.

Chapter 21

Before I went in search of Owen, I went home to shower and change. Eau de hospital wasn't exactly a flattering scent and I needed all the help I could get.

I changed into my favorite black dress, a figure-enhancing wrap number that was pretty but professional at the same time. It always made me feel confident.

I slipped on my ankle-strapped Weitzman heels to add a little sex appeal. It wouldn't hurt to remind him of all I had to offer. I needed to convince him that helping me held advantages for us both.

Now where to start? In my mind, Owen was still Owen and I had a chance as long as I could locate him. If the darkness had overtaken him, I had no idea what I would find, or if I could even convince him to listen to my proposal. And if he did listen—my heart skipped a beat—what would become of me, or of my baby, if my attempt to get pregnant had worked? Fate hadn't been working too well for me. Baby or no, I had to take matters into my own hands, to do what I could for my sister while there was still time to act.

The idea of the underworld still scared me. Would my light have any effect, as it had outside the elevator before the doors closed to take him away from me? Or would it be powerless in the depths of hell? Perhaps he'd overestimated me and we were both doomed the second I stepped foot in his territory? No light for him, no holding off the darkness for me.

And in truth, the thought of seeing Owen again, on any level, in any form, seemed more like a pleasure than a punishment. Now that I knew what it was to lose him, I was ready to face my darkest fears just to have him back, to try to recapture that feeling of being loved and complete at his side.

My luck with silent chants and phone calls seemed to have run out. No answer, straight to voicemail on the phone. No one magically materializing in front of me. I headed to the car and just hoped I would find him at the house or office. If I had to, I would go all the way to hell.

I started at the Prudential Center. I parked and made it to the elevator before I realized I had no idea what button to push. What floor? I didn't have to worry because the doors closed and the elevator proceeded without my intervention. A fluke, or did he know I was here?

The elevator doors opened again on what appeared to be the floor I last visited with him—same blue carpeting, same potted plants. But when I opened the door to the office, a different scene met my eyes. No empty office or incredible view, but a sterile corporate reception area with waiting-room furnishings around a large, central desk.

I stepped forward. "Kate Markham. I'm here to see Owen Glendower, please."

The secretary, a dark-haired man, looked up. Apparently, hell was an equal opportunity employer. I eyed him carefully, my blood chilling to ice. Was this a minion? I shouldn't have been surprised that he looked like any ordinary man. Well, not entirely ordinary. Like Owen, he was handsome and fit. Unlike Owen, it wasn't in a way that might draw undue notice on the street. The minion could blend in to a crowd.

"Miss Markham. Of course." Instant name recognition. His eyes narrowed as if he'd been about to bar my entry. "He's been expecting you."

I should have known. He knew everything, after all. "Indeed."

"Through the door and down the hall. Let me show you the way."

"No. I'll find it myself." I was driven in part out of confidence that Owen's presence drew me even now, and in part because the idea of the minion still creeped me out a little. Minions, something I would possibly have to get used to around hell.

Through the door, a long hall led to another door. My heels echoed as I walked the slick bare tile to his door. I felt like Dorothy on her way to the wizard. I wanted to click my heels together. *There's no place like home.* The most at home I'd ever felt was in Owen's arms right after we'd made love. The door opened on my approach, spilling bright light across the floor. I stepped into the light, trying to stifle the mental soundtrack that echoed "step into the light" in the voice of the little psychic lady from the *Poltergeist* movies. Actually, I was relieved to see light instead of being greeted by a wave of darkness. So he did have some light of his own. I'd always suspected it had to be true. But it was an eerie, artificial light and nothing like the sunlight he cherished.

After a second, the light dimmed to a more pleasant, but still fluorescent, glow and my eyes refocused. I was in the middle of a blank white room, empty except for a transparent acrylic desk, chair, and Owen dead center. Owen, the spot of dark amidst all the light. *The devil.* But instead of his usual Armani, he was clad in voluminous dark robes, like a character right out of *The Matrix.* He radiated power. I struggled to keep my body from trembling.

"Very Angel at Wolfram and Hart," I said, a reference to the *Buffy the Vampire Slayer* spin-off. I didn't think he'd get it. "Straight from the weird room at the top of the building."

"Is that what you're here for, Kate? A little demon-hunting?" His eyebrow shot up, but he barely seemed interested, as if my presence barely registered a blip on his radar.

Determined to appear nonplussed, I met his gaze to find his eyes an eerie black instead of the soft brown I preferred. The darkness. He'd become so cold. I marveled at the change. Was this the Hades I would find in hell?

"Nothing of the sort." I approached and paused at the edge of the desk, trying not to flinch at the sound of the door slamming shut behind me. I had to believe I still held a place in his heart, that I had some influence. Some light of my own. I struggled to force out the coldness that crept in my veins. "Can't say that I like what you've done to the place."

"It's *your* imagination at work." He tented his fingers and avoided my gaze. "Hell is what you make it. You've yet to fill in the blanks."

"I rarely do minimalist to this extreme." The white and cold extreme. It most definitely did not appeal. "Are you sure it's my work?"

He nodded. "You don't know what to expect yet. You haven't quite realized a vision. It will come. Think of it as a blank canvas. You have to furnish the room."

"Let's start with some heat. Who cranked up the AC? It's freezing." I shivered involuntarily. "Besides, we're not *really* in hell. We're in your building."

"My employees would beg to differ." He threw back his head and laughed, a deep rich chortle. His teeth reflected light from an unknown source. Eerie light, odd beyond industrial fluorescence but far from natural.

"I never do white walls." I strolled casually to the edge of the room and ran my hand over the smooth, white surface. "I don't think I want to take any credit, or blame, for this design."

As if on cue, the color dimmed from stark white to a warmer shade of eggshell. I bit my lip to stifle a gasp and turned back to face the devil.

He waved me into a chair. "Have a seat. You've got something on your mind."

"Yes." I said, unsure of where to begin. I met his gaze. Dark, but no longer pure black. A hint of rich brown glowed through the coldness. His eyes lent a fire to the room. Instantly, I warmed, and I was done with keeping up appearances. I sat on the edge of the chair and stretched a hand across the desk toward him, though he remained out of reach. "Please save Patrick. I'll give you whatever you want."

"You're offering yourself in exchange for your brother-in-law?" The devil said, as if considering. "Very noble."

It sounded colder than I'd expected, a bit too no-nonsense, all business. I struggled to lighten my tone.

"It's a decent trade. My life for his. Bennie gets her happily ever after. You get an eternity with me."

I smiled.

"Giving yourself to the big bad devil?" He stood, darkness radiating out in a ring around him, and leaned across the desk, teeth bared as if about to bite. "Are you sure it's what you want?"

"You're not bad." His hand was close enough to touch now and I reached out, covered it with mine, watching to see if the darkness receded around him. It didn't.

"Just not good enough?" His wicked smile held a hint of triumph. "Not enough to tempt you, the steadfast Kate. Reliable Kate. Always there in a crisis Kate. There for her family, at the cost of all else. Of me. You walked away. I wasn't worth the risk of giving it all up to go to the underworld, but your family is. You'll take the chance for them. Your choice was clear. Now if you'll excuse me, I have business to attend."

He sat back down but his hand remained in place under mine at the edge of the desk, as if he couldn't bear to break off contact.

The darkness surged, widening the circle around him, spreading over my hand. My fingers went prickly as if nearly frostbitten, but I refused to pull away. I gripped him tighter, as tightly as I could with frozen fingers. "Owen, don't. It doesn't have to be this way. Why should it have had to come to a choice?"

"Call me Hades." His voice held a dare.

"Hades." I accepted the challenge, struggling to hold on and ignore the needle-sharp pains in my hand. He

pulled away before the pain dulled to deathly numb-
ness. I rubbed my fingers to try and restore circulation.

"It hurt when you thought I could be responsible for
Patrick. I *don't* kill." He got up and paced the room,
except it was one smooth motion, as if under the robes
he had no human feet. Surreal. I sat transfixed until he
turned and gazed sharply at me. "I don't take lives,
Kate. I simply decide what happens afterward."

I could hardly think with the infernal chill seeping
straight into my bones. The temperature dropped
maybe fifty degrees with the ice that came over his
tone.

"Please forgive me. I know that now. I knew it at the
hospital, when you came to see me. I didn't want to let
you go. The doors closed around you and all I wanted
was for you to come back. I called for you." Shouldn't
he know as much? Didn't he know everything? Could
he not feel how I'd cried for him? But he hardly
seemed to believe me and I didn't know what more to
say to convince him. My teeth started to chatter,
making it hard to speak. "It's cold in here again."

"It's all in your perception," he said. "That's why the
underworld is such a powerful place. It acclimates to
the occupant."

"Meaning?" I looked at him, trying to understand.

"For some, the underworld's unbearably hot. For
you, it's frigid. Unfortunately, people save their darkest
fears for death. Your fate in the afterlife becomes what
you've always believed it would be, what you truly think
you deserve. You're apparently afraid of being frozen.
Interesting concept. Frozen in place, immoveable, or
frozen out? What's your idea of hell, Kate?"

Being alone. Being left all alone. I knew it as soon
as he asked, but he didn't wait for an answer. Up until

now, I'd thought dependency was my greatest fear. Having to rely on others scared me. But really, what I feared was having no one to rely upon, no one in the end but myself.

"You won't have to worry. You won't be dead. You'll be my guest."

"How does that make it any nicer?"

"You'll get my vision instead of yours. With you around, it will be constant Elysium. Sunshine every day. At least, that's how I'd imagined it would be with us together."

A hearth appeared on the back wall, complete with a blazing fire. I blinked, then turned my gaze back to Owen.

"Elysium being heaven," I said. "The place for pure souls."

"Not technically. Elysium is my brother's domain. I send the good ones on to him. For the rest, I mete out justice. Purgatory, Tartarus. Whatever the situation warrants."

Behind the coldness of Hades, there was Owen. My Owen. Thinking of Owen having to choose who suffered and thrived, having to assign tortures, made me ache for him. Could I really make it easier for him by just being there?

"Tartarus, that's the true hell?" I asked. He nodded. "What about Purgatory?"

"Purgatory's not so bad. The soul has to carry out some assignments and then face me again. Usually, they get to go on to Elysium after some soul-searching, if you'll pardon the pun."

"So it's like a job? You're the ultimate judge?"

"Not just a job, an adventure." He was being flippant, but the coldness of the room told me there was something going cold inside him. Inside me? I couldn't tell anymore. Everything felt upside down. I only knew that the usual Owen tingle had become a constricting hellish ache. The darkness remained around him as if threatening to wash over the rest of the room in a wave.

A little afraid of the dark and the cold, I willed away the urge to go to him, to hold him. To make us both feel better. He looked like my Owen, but I knew he was the devil. Inside the hearth on the wall, a fire lit as if by magic. He jumped at the sound of the flames. Did they surprise him, too?

"You can't imagine what it's like, trying to comfort the soul of a frightened child," he said, turning away from the fire. "They all feel so lost when they get to me."

"Actual children? Or do you mean souls?" Despite my fear, I stepped forward. His voice was so pained that I couldn't help reaching out for him, softening toward him again. This time, the darkness didn't spread as if contagious. My hand met with the warmth of his skin, no trace of cold.

No murky shadows clouded his dark brown eyes when he looked at me.

"Actual children. Children die. It's a sad fact of life." And here I was arguing for the soul of a grown man. A grown man who'd done something foolish. Hardly an innocent.

"Children. You comfort them?" I formed a mental picture of Owen with a child in his arms. A vase appeared on the wood mantle of the hearth. Flowers bloomed. Peonies.

"As best I can. It's much easier on them once they pass to Elysium. Everything's light and warmth there." His voice held some resentment. "Hell is no place for a child."

My hand automatically dropped to my stomach, and

I quickly moved it away, hoping Owen didn't notice. I was suddenly more afraid than ever. What if I was pregnant? What would happen to my baby?

He walked back to the hearth, darkness fading as it trailed him. "Creation is entirely out of my control." He picked up a flower and looked at me. The flower wilted and died in his hands, turning to a fine dust that he casually brushed away. "Do you understand, Kate?"

"I do," I said, after my heart skipped a few amazed beats.

I understood too well. It all made sense. Hades was not in a position to give life, but to sort it all out afterward. But what if I carried a child?

"If you come with me, you'll never have a child of your own. It's impossible." He studied me for a reaction. I tried not to give him one. "No changing your mind on that one. Something else to consider, hm?"

He looked at me knowingly. A pregnancy weighed on my mind, yet another reason to change my mind and back away. But I had come too far to back down now. Patrick's life hung in the balance, and my sister's happiness. I couldn't give them up for the mere possibility that I carried a child. Not now. I bit my lip, the sacrifice greater than I ever imagined possible.

"So you mean to take me up on my offer?" I asked. "You can spare Patrick?"

"I have the best intentions," he said, an evasive answer.

"The path to hell is paved with good intentions," I said.

"Vastly untrue," he countered. "Actions count for more than intentions in the end. Your actions speak for themselves."

He pursed his lips, and I suddenly felt very cold again.

"Your actions. You gave me your word that you wanted more than anything to be with me, and yet, the second you had a crisis, you gave me up for them."

"I'm here now."

"Not for me. It's a sacrifice for your sister. I don't want you that way."

I looked around, expecting the darkness to have spread, but finding no trace of it. It was truly the way he felt, no sinister force overwhelming him. Just him. It was an unmistakable rejection. He no longer wanted me.

Anger flared deep in my core. The fire flared up along with it, then just as quickly faded away. He was being the selfish one. Not me.

"It's not exactly fair to force me to make a choice. What am I supposed to do? Turn my back on my family? For you?"

"Why not?" He shrugged. "You won't cease to exist for them. You'll be in their hearts, in their memories. And you can watch them from afar. It's really not so great a change."

Not so great a change? I remembered now why I'd been frustrated right after the news came about Patrick. Owen really had no idea what he was asking me to give up. Just life, that's all. Not so great a change.

I'd put myself on the line for him. I'd come prepared to plead. To beg. To give up any life I knew. To recognize our love for what it was, honest and true. But that he failed to understand the importance of my life—of my family—to me? It was a slap in the face and I felt every bit of the sting. The fireplace disappeared, leaving a blank wall. The vase and flowers crashed to the floor and vanished as well, as if sucked into a white vortex.

"Let's see you do the same for me," I said, cold again and struggling to make sense of everything. "Walk away from your job, from your family. Give up everything you have for me."

"It's not an option." He slammed a fist down on his desk and the impact sent sparks, like little bolts of lightning, flying from his hand.

I refused to be intimidated.

"That makes it so easy for you, doesn't it? You've no idea what I'm going through. You can't even imagine." I looked at him. Hard. I saw a man full of himself. Expecting everything. Offering nothing. A god unaware of human reality. *The devil,* I reminded myself again, as if I needed reminders.

"To love me is to understand what I'm going through, *Hades.*" I could not bear to use his human name. "I'm not sure you can truly fathom what this whole experience has done to me inside. And if you really mean to make me choose, then maybe you don't know what it is to love, after all. I'm sorry for you. Truly sorry. I did come here to make a trade, it's true. I would do anything in my power to save my family. But that doesn't mean I loved you any less. It's clear you don't understand."

"Perhaps I don't understand." His voice held an icy edge to match the chill seeping back into the room, but his body radiated heat as he came around the desk and tipped my face up to meet his smoldering gaze. "I thought you were strong enough to come with me, but I see now that you're still so afraid. Hell's no place for you, my love. Consider yourself spared. I'm very sorry for your loss. Byron will show you out."

He dropped a light kiss on my forehead and walked away to take a seat at his desk.

"My loss? But you'll help Patrick? Please."

His secretary appeared as if from out of thin air.

When I looked up, Owen was gone. The room was completely furnished, one of my better jobs. Rich wood accents, deep red walls, a pair of matched overstuffed chairs in front of the fireplace.

"Come back," I called out. "Owen, please."

Afraid? I'd stood up to him, hadn't I? But somehow, I felt like such a failure. I was afraid of leaving the people I loved, of going to who knew where, of not being able to constantly chase the darkness that hung on him like a shroud. He was right. I was afraid. I needed reassurance that he had been hard-pressed to give, and he needed a partner ready to give it all up without a glance back, no need for reassurance. I couldn't be that partner.

I stood, frozen in place, as tears formed in my eyes.

I'd come to save Patrick, but I'd ended up losing so much more.

"You have to get back." The secretary took me by the elbow to guide me from the room. "Your sister needs you."

I shrugged out of his hold. "I'm not leaving until he comes back."

"Then you'll be here a very long time. He's away on business. I don't expect him back."

"At all?"

Byron, a well-trained minion, would neither confirm nor deny. He merely shrugged. "He's not coming. You want to help your sister, I suggest you get back to her now. As soon as you can."

I stared at the room, no trace of the desk, chair, or Owen ever having been there. I knew Byron was right. He wasn't coming. I had to get back to Bennie.

Chapter 22

There was no time to lose, but how could I explain showing up at the hospital in a dress and heels? No one would believe that I was working at a time like this. Before heading to the hospital, I rushed home to change back into jeans and a sweater, with the addition of my warmest jacket. The weather report predicted light snow but it was nothing compared to the deep freeze that had returned to my soul.

In the hospital parking garage, I blinked back the tears that burned at the back of my eyes, took a deep breath, and buried my emotions as deep as I could. There was no point dwelling on my failure, on my loss. I had to focus on my family.

It became easier to forget my own misery with every step toward the Critical Care Unit. Patrick was fighting for his life. Anything I had to cope with in the meantime paled in comparison. When I got to Patrick's floor, I was surprised to find no one in the waiting room. Perhaps they were in with Patrick or down in the cafeteria. Normally, I had to use the waiting room phone to call ahead for admission to the closely-monitored CCU, but a doctor was going in and I followed after him.

When I got to Patrick's corner room, a nurse hovered, resetting machines.

"She went home with the children." The nurse looked up from her ministrations of Patrick to greet me. "She looked real worn out, poor dear. I told her things were fine here, to go on home and get some rest. Wouldn't you know it, as soon as she left . . ."

I noticed that Patrick's monitors were still, no lights or sounds. "Oh. Oh, God. No."

The nurse followed my gaze to the equipment. "Heavens no. He's still with us." I breathed a sigh of relief. "I have him unhooked to clean him off a little. What I meant was that he started waking up a little as soon as she took off. He's sleeping again for now. We called her. She's on her way back in."

"Did he say anything?"

"He couldn't speak with the tubes. When he comes out of it again, he might be able to respond with blinks or nods. It's wait-and-see time."

The whole hospital stay felt like "wait-and-see" time, but I nodded eagerly. "Thanks so much."

Now that I knew Patrick held on, I let out a sigh of relief that the nurse had convinced Bennie to go home at last. She needed a break from the hospital and some time with Spencer and Sarah.

"I'm just going to hook him back up to the monitors and I'll be out of your way." But after she hooked him up, she made a face that indicated things weren't as rosy as they seemed.

"What is it?"

She studied a printout from the machine. "Well, his

heart rate's down. I don't like his oxygenation. We'll give it a little while to stabilize."

"And if it doesn't?"

"We'll see." She smiled reassuringly. "I'll be back in a bit."

At last, she left us alone. Patrick and I, co-conspirators against the rest of my crazy family. Against the devil. Against death. I stroked his hand. "Come on, Patrick. Who's going to help me fend off Gran's little zingers? I need you."

Silence, save for the erratic pulse of the monitor.

"Remember when she said I would never get a date if I kept wearing jeans in public? That women over forty shouldn't wear jeans? And I had to remind her that I had just turned thirty-four?" Not to mention that I planned on wearing jeans well into my sixties, at least, and why not?

I laughed, to no response. Patrick looked more peaceful somehow. His face was a mess of bruises from the steering wheel, but he looked more like the Patrick I knew. As I studied him, his eyes fluttered open.

"Hey, handsome," I said, reaching out to smooth his hair back off his clammy forehead. "How's it going?"

He made a funny noise from the back of his throat and looked like he was trying to sit up. "Up? You want me to fix your bed?"

He nodded. I adjusted him to a slight incline.

"Flirt," he said. I heard it loud and clear though he couldn't have spoken.

"What, me?" I tried to keep it light.

"Ben hates it when you flirt with me." His expression clearly indicated that we were having a conversation, but I couldn't imagine how, unless I'd picked up some of Hades's powers, or somehow Patrick had a few of his own. What did it mean? I tried to hide any concern in case he could feel that as well.

"She's not here. We're free to carry on." I waggled my brows. He recognized me. He knew his wife's name. All good signs. But the mental dialogue? I couldn't imagine what made it possible and it still worried me.

"I don't think Hades would be too pleased," he said suddenly, quite clearly.

I stifled a gasp. "What do you know?"

"Don't look so alarmed. You're the one who asked for me to be spared."

My heart soared. Owen had committed an act of pure love. For me.

"Patrick." I squeezed his fingers. "So he did? He saved you?"

"Not so fast." Patrick glanced at the door and back at me. "I can't stay."

My pulse picked up speed. "What? Of course you can. I asked for it. *For you.*"

"I'm not going to make it, Kate." His blue eyes watered.

My heart did the broken elevator drop, straight to the floor. "What?"

"That I'm even able to talk to you now, it's a gift. From him."

"From Hades?"

Patrick nodded. He reached for my hand. His limited ability to move allowed him to only graze my fingertips. "You have to listen, Kate. I don't have long."

My breathing slowed. I didn't want to blink for fear I would open my eyes and find Patrick gone.

"He didn't want me to say anything. He threatened me with a longer stay in purgatory if I told you but—"

"Told me what?"

Patrick shrugged. "You deserve to know. I want you to know. It's worth the extra time in purgatory. What the hell, right?"

He laughed at his own little joke. *What the hell.*

"Hades doesn't have the power to restore life, as you know, and yet he offered to grant mine back to me. How do you think that is?" he asked.

"I don't know. The main thing is you're back. Bennie will be so thrilled!"

"She isn't to know all this. Not for anything. Right now, this is about you. I'm glad you're there for Bennie, Kate. So glad. She'll need you. But you also have needs."

I rolled my eyes. He sounded like Owen.

"You love him, Kate. Stop denying it. I can see it. I saw it over brunch three weeks ago."

"I do," I admitted, and it felt great. There was no need to hold back confidences or play games now. "I love him. And Bennie loves *you*."

"I just don't have it in me anymore. She's going to be fine, Kate. Trust me on this. I've seen it."

"You've seen it? How?"

"The underworld is a different dimension. Hades loves you, too. He had to call in major favors to grant my life back."

"Zeus." I knew instinctively. "He had to get help from his brother. Zeus is the only one who can grant life."

Patrick nodded. "He had to give up something in return. I'm not at liberty to say, but it was precious to him."

"How precious?"

"*The air we breathe* kind of precious. He had to give up something that means as much to him as air does to us. Something vital. And he did it without so much as a blink. He didn't do it for me. He did it for you. All for you."

I wanted Patrick alive, true enough, but I never imagined it would come at any cost to Owen. I hadn't thought of him at all. I'd only thought of me. Of my sister. I'd accused him of being selfish. How wrong I'd been. And it was too late to take it back, to undo what I had done. Whatever it was, it was bad. I felt it to the depths of my soul.

"Hades wanted me to get a full picture of what could happen to Bennie with or without me. With me, she's amazing. But without me? She's nothing short of spectacular. She thrives on her own. It's as if I've always been a big weight dragging her down."

"Oh no, Patrick. You're wrong. She loves you." I squeezed his hand.

"I know she does. And I love her. But love shouldn't hurt so much. It shouldn't take so much work to get it right. She'll have love again. The kind she deserves."

"What about you?"

"I'll do my time in purgatory. With hard work and a little luck, I'll get out early on good behavior. Then it's up to me."

"What is?"

"My choices. I can go to Elysium, or I can be reincarnated. I can be a ball player. Isn't that great?" Then he sighed heavily, and I realized it wasn't great. It was a consolation prize. Baseball instead of taking his life back.

"But why?"

"I want Bennie and the kids to have the life they deserve. It's going to work out for them. You'll see. I wouldn't be able to come back as the man I should be. I know you want the best, and I'm so grateful you tried.

Thank you, Kate. But things don't always go as we hope. Even if I came back. I would try to change, yes, but how long would it last? I'm not that strong. Bennie is. She'll be happy again, in a way she'll never be with me. And I'll go off to a new life and a great career playing ball. Everyone wins."

I couldn't believe my ears. Everyone wins? I couldn't imagine a way that things could go badly if Patrick could only survive this. But how would I know? I didn't even know my sister had been so unhappy in the first place.

"The kids lose a father. I don't think they win. Bennie thinks you're the love of her life. I doubt she wins. And what about Hades? He made some major sacrifice to give you your life back. What happens to him?"

Patrick shrugged. "Maybe he can trade back with Zeus. I don't know. He knows about my decision. To tell you the truth, he seemed a little relieved. I don't know why, but for what it's worth, he said something about giving you what you really want."

"What I want?" I gulped hard. I wanted him. I wanted Hades, as Owen, at my side for the rest of my life. Was it possible? Could it really come true?

I dared not let myself hope for the best.

"Bennie'll be okay. I'm doing what's best for her. Trust me. Have faith."

Faith. I'd never been forced to have so much faith in my whole life as I had in the past month.

"Come here. Give me a hug. Have a great life. Look after Bennie, but don't forget to start looking after you. She's going to be fine. Tell her how much I love her."

I leaned across the bed to hug him, careful not to disturb the tubes and wires that worked so hard to keep his body going. "But wait, aren't you going to tell her yourself? She'll be here any minute."

I knew he couldn't actually speak yet, but to see his eyes open and responding once more might help her let go. I wanted her to have a chance to say good-bye.

"I'm almost out of time. It's easier this way. Before I go, one thing. There's an insurance policy. Look in my office, back of the top drawer. Bennie never knew. It's enough to take care of her and the kids for a long time. She'll be okay."

I tried to picture Bennie losing Patrick and somehow finding her way to okay. It seemed impossible. It brought tears to my eyes trying to imagine it. I could barely manage it myself. I'd been putting so much energy into trying to save Bennie from losing Patrick without much consideration to what he meant to me. We'd always been such good friends. My eyes welled up.

"Please, think again. Don't leave us." I even said it out loud, as if forgetting that he could hear my thoughts, and choked on a sob.

"I'll miss you, too, Kate. But we'll meet again somehow. Bennie's going to shine. Wait 'til you see her. Take care. Of her. Of yourself. Give the kids all my love. I'm so proud of them. Of everyone. Good-bye, kiddo."

He couldn't really smile with the tubes, but his eyes crinkled as if he were, and then he blinked for a second too long, giving himself away. Tears gathered. I gripped his hand. He gave my fingers a firm squeeze. He was sad, but he didn't seem frightened by what he had faced, or intimidated to face his new future. I saw tenderness and grief in his eyes, but not fear. He lowered his eyelids as if to blink away the tears, but then his eyes stayed closed.

"Patrick?"

His grip loosened on my fingers until his hand opened, letting go.

"Wait, Patrick. Come back." I shook him lightly, as if I could wake him. He may have been ready, but I wasn't. I wished I could see his smile one more time, the real Patrick smile, without tubes in the way. "Patrick, please."

No use. I realized he was well and truly gone. But his monitor continued to register a slow beat. He wasn't dead. Not yet. But he wasn't coming back again. I sank to my knees and sobbed. Unfortunately, that's how Bennie found me when she came in.

"Kate! My God." She ran to Patrick, checked his pulse. "He's okay. What's wrong?"

I inhaled slowly. "Nothing. I—the stress. I wish there were more we could do but sit and wait."

"The nurse said he might be coming around," Bennie said, rubbing my back as if to comfort me. "I got ready to come right back as soon as she called."

"She told me. But she may have been optimistic." I hazarded a glance at Patrick in case he opened his eyes after all. On the other hand, why give Bennie false hope?

It was a horrible feeling. I imagined it was how Owen had felt, knowing and not being able to say. My lungs constricted with sudden pain. When? How much longer did Patrick have?

As if in answer, his monitor started to beep. The nurse came at a run.

"It's okay," she said, adjusting the machine. "It happens if his oxygenation levels drop. It's probably just a glitch."

She checked the connections. I knew it wasn't a glitch.

"I thought he might wake up," Bennie said. "You called? You said he was getting better?"

"I said he'd been conscious." The nurse stared as if concerned. "I have to get a doctor. Could you step outside?"

"What is it?" Bennie grabbed the nurse's arm. "Something's wrong."

"Maybe nothing." The nurse gave a weak smile. "I need to get the doctor. We'll call you right back in."

I pulled Bennie away from the nurse and escorted her outside. "It's just for a minute. We need him to get the best possible care without us being in the way."

In my heart, I knew Patrick wasn't going to die without Bennie by his side. He would wait. He owed her that much.

The next few hours were the longest of my life. Once Patrick showed signs of serious distress, the doctors came in.

"Maybe it's too stressful for him, once you reduced his medications? It's too much pain." Bennie gnawed her lips. "Maybe you could just put him back on the Ativan?"

As if removing the stress and the pain would be enough to save him. But her hope was contagious. I stared at Patrick in his bed and prayed he could hear me, that he would change his mind and come back after all.

"We've tried everything," Doctor Chen assured her. "It's up to him." He placed a hand on Bennie's arm, gentle in a rehearsed sort of way, and asked her if she would sign some forms for his associate, Doctor Feldman. My gaze met Bennie's. She knew exactly what it meant, but she stayed calm, as if signing forms didn't change anything. She could agree to donate his organs and forgo extraordinary measures and all it meant was that the hospital needed to cover its bases.

"He's a fighter," Bennie informed them, swooping her pen over the last page with a flourish to her signature. "He's not giving up."

I put my arm around her. *She* wasn't giving up. It wouldn't be easy for her to let go, but she was not going to let it defeat her. Patrick had known as much.

She settled back in her seat at Patrick's side, took his hand, and started speaking to him again. "I know it hurts, and it's hard, but you have to hold on. Kate's going to bring the kids in to say hi."

"I am? You brought the kids?"

She nodded, not taking her gaze from her husband. "They're in the waiting room with Mom."

I didn't waste any time in going out for them. With increasingly longer intervals between blips from Patrick's monitor, I feared it wasn't long.

In the waiting room, the kids sat still like little statues at Mother's side, but their heads darted up in unison at sight of me.

"Aunt Kate." Sarah ran across the room.

Spencer took his time getting up, hands jammed in his pockets. "So, we can go in now?"

Mother covered her mouth with her hand, as if she couldn't bear to think about what was coming. We all seemed to know without being told. I knew, but I was surprised that I seemed to sense the knowledge in everyone else as well.

"Yes, Spence. I'm bringing you in." I put an arm around both children and led them to their father's room.

It was only as she looked up and saw the children that Bennie showed signs of wear. Her bloodshot eyes had bags underneath that seemed to come on in seconds. Still, she forced a smile. I hovered, unsure if I should stay or go.

"Please. Stay." Bennie said, as if reading my mind, but it was sisterly intuition, and not any supernatural trick.

"All right." I walked over to take her hand. The kids went to the other side of the bed, across from us. "I'll stay."

"I love you, Dad," Sarah said, putting her hand over her father's.

"Hey, Dad, you don't look so hot." Spencer had his mother's way with words.

Within seconds, Patrick's vital signs began to fade. No one spoke. I was surprised that the children stayed so calm, so mature, even as they realized what was happening.

"Don't stay if it hurts too badly," Bennie said to the unconscious Patrick, tears falling at last. "We don't want you to be in pain. We want you to have peace. Try to fight, but if you can't," her voice faltered, "we love you enough to let go."

I admired their peace and determination, even as I wanted to rage. I wanted to shout. Patrick, how could you? Patrick, wake up! See what you're doing? How could they be all right? How did he expect his wife and children to get through their loss and move on? I wished he could come back so I could tell him that he was clearly, terribly, wrong. But yet, he seemed right. They stood, accepting, full of peace and love, ready to let go. Not raging, not like me. I wanted him to come back and face his choices. Instead, he chose to fade away.

We all have a choice in the end. I understood Hades

so well now. It was Patrick's choice to get into a car after drinking so much, and his own decision in the end to leave.

I remained holding Bennie's hand, standing right beside her as Patrick's life signs ebbed. The children, standing next to Patrick's bed, held hands as they comforted their dying father. Occasionally, Sarah called out a soft "I love you, Daddy," as if she'd been afraid he would forget.

I'd never been so proud of my niece and nephew. I knew they could easily have given in to the emotion, but they didn't. They stayed strong for the sake of their mother. She stayed strong for the sake of the children. I stayed strong for all of them, ready to cater to their every need along the way.

"You know how much he loves you," I said to them. "He loves you all. He'll always be with you."

Sarah finally started to sob quietly. Spencer draped an arm protectively over his sister's shoulder. It was then, as if on cue, that Patrick's pulse dropped drastically and was gone.

"Good-bye, darling." Bennie wiped at the tears with the back of her hand, a gesture that reminded me so much of her in childhood. "Until we meet again."

I knew they wouldn't be meeting again. Patrick had chosen another route. A more selfish route. And just as I thought it, a wave went through me as if Patrick's very soul passed over me. Finally, I felt at peace with his passing. In that second, I knew that he was right. And for once, I wasn't afraid. He'd been to the underworld and back, albeit briefly. He knew what he faced on the other side, and still he went. How bad could it be? Instinct took over, and I knew that Patrick had made the very best choice for Bennie and the children. My sister would love, and be loved, again. Spencer and Sarah would carry on. It would take time, but eventually . . .

And though I wasn't frightened for him, the thought of him being able to go still made me sad. Patrick and Bennie had been the great example of love in my life. If things weren't perfect between them, how could things work for any couple, anywhere? It was as if my entire understanding of love and partnership had been a myth. A fallacy. Maybe there wasn't someone for everyone. Maybe deep down, we were all meant to be alone.

I didn't understand what Patrick had told me, how Bennie would be better off without him. Why couldn't she be strong and independent *and* in love with her husband? Was it so hard to believe that *love* could make her stronger?

Time and again, humanity stressed through art, literature, or any given medium that man became stronger through struggle. I'd always wanted to think that love, not pain, gave us the power to survive. But if Bennie was going to be better off without Patrick, what did it say? I'd been wrong the whole time.

Outside the room, Mother waited for Bennie with Hal, Gran, and Pops not far behind.

"I'm so sorry, honey," Mother said, reaching for Bennie.

Bennie waved her off. "I need sleep. I can't deal with any of this now. I just want to sleep."

"You can sleep, darling. All you want." Mother stayed close, so ready to play her role to the hilt that it was painful to watch.

"We'll deal with the arrangements tomorrow," Bennie said, walking on as if in a dream. The kids held her, one on each side.

"Come on, Ben. I'll take you all home."

She stopped. "Kate, what would I do without you?"

I held her tight.

The way things had worked out, she would never need to know.

Chapter 23

When I woke, for a terrifying moment, I didn't know where I was. I blinked and looked around, relief washing over me. I was in the guest room at my sister's house.

It all came back to me in a nightmare flash. Patrick was dead. Owen might be lost to me forever. Bennie and I were both widows in our own way. At least I was here to help her through the process. For now, it was comforting to play a role and worry about her instead of pining for my own loss.

I didn't dare hold out any hope that I could find a happy ending amidst all the pain of losing Patrick.

I sat up and looked around. The clock, a digital, said 6:30 A.M. Outside, the sun was barely beginning to light the early December sky.

I showered and dressed in my jeans and sweater, yesterday's clothes, sorry that I'd never thought to keep a spare outfit at my sister's house. I had a feeling I would be spending a lot more time here now. I wandered to the kitchen to see what the family was up to, if Bennie had slept at all. At my suggestion, she'd taken some Tylenol PM, but I wasn't sure it would hold her through the night.

"Aunt Kate." Sarah, an early riser, stopped me in the hall. She'd come from her mother's bedroom, where she'd slept for either her own comfort or for Bennie's.

I draped an arm around her.

"So how are you holding up?" I was so happy to see my smarty-pants niece, a reminder of the normalcy of life. They would move on from this. I would make sure. The children would make it.

She shrugged, but tears glistened in her eyes.

"It's not easy. I can't say it will ever get easier. You know I'm here if you want to talk." I knelt down to be more her size, but she was taller than me on my knees. I marveled at how quickly she'd grown, how fast the time had gone since she'd been born.

She nodded. "Grandma says that you and my mom lost a dad too, so you know what it's like."

Leave it to Mother. I sighed. "No, honey. I'll never know what it's like for you. My dad left, true. Yours, he didn't want to go. He loved you so much."

"I want to be strong for Mom," Sarah said. "Grandma said she'll really need my help, that it's worse for Mom than for any of us."

"Your mom is tough as nails, and even so, she has me. I can be strong for all of you. *You* don't have to be strong for anyone. You just have to be you. Let yourself feel whatever you need to feel. Don't shut it off. Never pretend to be something you aren't."

One tear rolled down her cheek, followed by another. She squinted up her eyes, nodded, wrapped her arms around my neck, and hung on as if for dear life.

After a few minutes, she let up, her sobs breaking off into sharp, broken stabs of breath.

"Thanks, Aunt Kate. You really know how to help."

"I try. Maybe you can help me now. How about you join me in the kitchen and we rustle up some breakfast?"

Before the rest of the crew got up for the day, Sarah and I had a hearty meal of pancakes, sausage, and fruit all spread outs on the table. I ate as I cooked. Sarah sat at the table with a big plate of pancakes.

"You know, no one else is going to eat this stuff," she said. "You made way too much."

"You never know." I poured myself a third cup of coffee. "People deal with grief in weird ways."

"It makes me hungry," Sarah said. "I always eat when I'm sad."

"You have the Markham gene. I bet you probably eat when you're happy, when you're mad, when you're nervous, oh, just about any time at all. Lucky you."

I sipped my coffee while Sarah dug into her pancakes. After a while, Spencer and Hal wandered in.

"We boys fell asleep playing *Rogue Squadron*," Hal laughed. "Still had the controller in my hand when I woke up."

Spence managed a weak smile. I was just glad that he'd found a distraction from his grief. Not enough of a distraction, I could tell by the dark circles that rimmed his red eyes.

Sarah said, "Mom cried, like, all night, but she tried to pretend she wasn't. She isn't used to sleeping without Dad."

Spencer took a seat that the table beside Sarah, but didn't attack the pancakes as per his usual routine. Instead, he merely looked down at his plate. Hal didn't even sit, but grabbed a plate and loaded up. I could always count on Hal.

Mother wandered in next, looking perfectly pressed and powdered despite the drama of the last thirty-six hours. She gave the kids a bright smile then gestured for me to follow her into the foyer, away from the kids.

"The funeral home is picking up the body today. We have to get Bennie there to choose a coffin and service." Wow. I had to hand it to Mother. I hadn't even thought of the details yet, but she was in full-on preparation mode, and I was relieved.

"No coffin," I said. "We'll need an urn. I have a good idea what Patrick would have wanted. I'll talk to Bennie when she gets up to make sure she's on the same page."

"Yesterday, your sister said she couldn't go to the funeral home. The finality of it all was too much for her."

I considered the information. It all seemed so harsh and too soon, but that's how it happened. Time marched on. Bennie had to be ready for it.

"She has to, Mom. If she doesn't face the finality, she'll never be able to move on. I'll talk to her."

Mom sighed. "Good luck."

"What about Gran and Pops?" I asked. "How are they holding up?"

"Mostly, they're worried about Bernadette," Mom said. "We all are. A widow before age thirty. It's going to be hard on her. After all, I know what it's like to be a single mother."

"Yes, Mother," I said, knowing what was coming next before she even said it.

"*I* may as well have been a widow," Mother went on. "Only I wasn't allowed to grieve."

I sighed. Clearly, I had my work cut out for me in making sure Mother's drama didn't overshadow

Bennie's need. It was the kind of talk that could drive Bennie nuts. The sooner Gran and Pops came over, the better. Mother never mentioned my father when Gran and Pops were around. They considered him ancient history.

Still, I couldn't help but wonder if Bennie could use a father back in her life now. If we *all* could use a father back in our lives right now. My father had been on my mind for weeks, ever since that weekend in Hilton Head. Owen said he'd been meaning to make contact. Why hadn't he? Maybe it was up to me to seek him out, to assure him that he was always a welcome presence. Mother meant well, but if she was his sole link to us on occasion through the years, who could blame him for feeling it was better to keep his distance?

I snapped back to the present. "I'm going up to check on Bennie. Why don't you have some breakfast?" I said to my mother. "It's going to be a long day."

"Who can eat at a time like this?" Mom said.

But on my way out of the kitchen, I couldn't help noticing Mom stacking her plate full of pancakes as she took a seat next to Hal.

Bennie, curled up at the very edge of the enormous bed she'd shared with Patrick, appeared to be sleeping peacefully. As soon as she heard me step in the door, she shot up like a bolt.

"Kate. Thank goodness it's you."

"I'm sorry. I didn't mean to wake you."

"I was afraid you were Mother." She rolled her eyes.

I approached the bed. "You slept well?"

"I had nightmares. More like worries. I guess they can't be dreams if I wasn't asleep, right?"

"Right. I'm here for you. Try not to worry. Just focus on what needs to get done."

"I don't even want to get out of bed. The sheets still smell like Patrick," she said, her eyes filling with tears.

"Oh. Bennie." I sat on the edge of the bed and rubbed her back.

"Patrick's gone," she sobbed. "He's really gone."

"Yes, Ben. He's gone. You know he wouldn't want you to cry over him." Instinct guided me to find the right words. "You remember what Patrick said when Dave Jackson's dad died?"

She looked up, the memory dawning. "He wanted a party instead of a funeral. Patrick said he wanted people to laugh and drink and have fun, to celebrate him when he died."

"To celebrate him, not to mourn him," I agreed. "That's right. So what do you want to do? We have to make arrangements. I don't mind taking over some of the planning, but I won't do it *all*. Patrick would want you to be the one to choose his final resting place."

"He wanted to be cremated," she said, getting herself together. "And have his ashes spread on the pitcher's mound at Fenway Park."

"I don't think Fenway will allow it," I said, "but I have an idea. We'll see what we can work out. I'm going to get changed and head out to run a few errands."

"Errands?" Bennie lifted a brow. "Are you going to see Owen?"

"No. Owen and I had what we had. It's over. I don't have time for men in my life. You know how I am."

"Unfortunately, I do," she sighed. "Kate, he even came to the hospital to check on you. Don't you think maybe this one deserves a chance?"

I smiled. If only she knew. "It was a mutual split. Don't worry about me now. I'm fine."

"Maybe you're better off avoiding serious relationships."

Ouch. Considering my past behavior, it wasn't an unfair comment. Still, it smarted to have her think I was commitment-phobic and better off for it now that I knew better. I knew what I was missing, and it ached.

"Better to have loved," I said, unable to add the rest, *and lost.* Loss hurt like hell. There was no silver lining.

"We had everything," she said, a whisper.

"You still do. He'll always be with you."

"But Kate," she said, her voice growing quiet. "What am I going to do? Patrick always took care of everything. I'm just—lost."

"I'm here to help," I said. "Patrick had insurance. It will get you through for a while. I have a great accountant, and I'm a whiz with finances. Trust me. We'll work it out. You and the kids will be fine"

I assumed she would feel better just to leave it all to me, but she still wore a troubled expression.

"I need to learn to take care of things," she said. "I'll probably have to get a job. A job." Her eyes rounded. "What could I possibly do? Who would hire me?"

"You could go back to school. I remember you thought about being a teacher once. You're good with kids. But hush." I patted her back again. "One step at a time. You can worry about that later. For now, let's just focus on getting through the next few days."

She leaned against me, as if relieved. "You're right. One step at a time. I guess that means I have to get out of bed."

"It's a good first step." I smiled and got up. "And then a next step would be to make it to the shower."

"You're right." She stretched and got up. "I can do this. It's not as if I have a choice, right? Thanks, Kate. You always know just what to do."

"Hardly," I laughed. "But I fake it well, don't I?"

"Still, it is nice knowing I'm not all alone."

"I know the feeling," I said. "We have each other. We'll get through this. Together, we can handle anything."

Chapter 24

With Bennie safely involved in the task of getting ready for the day ahead, I left Mother and Hal in charge of looking after the kids and went out to do some shopping and check in at work.

First stop, the mall. In the middle of the busy holiday season, I was lucky to find a parking spot right in front of Macy's. I didn't have time to mess around. I was on the hunt for black clothes for Bennie and the kids so that they would be prepared for the upcoming services.

In short order, I found a lovely black sheath with matching jacket for Bennie, on sale, and appropriate clothes for the kids in dark colors. I knew Bennie and Spencer had the right footwear. Sarah was another matter. She'd been headed toward a tomboy phase and I wasn't sure her last pair of Mary Janes would still fit. I found a nice pair of slip-on flats in the right size and moved on, ready to leave until my gaze caught on the sale sign hanging over the maternity department.

I hadn't had much time to consider the possibility that I could be with child, but I thought about it now.

Could I be pregnant? A small twinge of excitement coursed through me. How would it feel? Would my back be achy, my breasts heavier? I didn't feel any different.

I caught sight of my reflection in a mirrored pole at the corner, near a rack of smock-front dresses. My cheeks were slightly flushed, and my hair was a mess. How had I not checked what I looked like before I left the house? But my body was the same, no telltale stomach bulge that said pregnant any more than it marked me as having a love affair with Cheetos. I sighed and turned to the side to be sure. No belly. If anything, my jeans hung slightly lower on my hips than they had a week earlier.

I had practically convinced myself that it was just as well, when I headed for the exit and almost ran straight into a woman settling her newborn in a stroller. My heart beat faster. The baby was so sweet and tiny, barely a week old from the look of her, bundled all in pink. I shifted my own bundles and packages of clothes and quickly dashed out to the parking lot, shaking my head in an effort to shake off the baby urge.

At the grocery store, my next stop, babies were everywhere. It was as if they were giving them away in a two-for-one sale. Before I could stop myself, I was standing in front of the home pregnancy tests. It was too early to take a test with any accuracy, or so I thought until I began comparing brands. Some promised results right away. Others warned that it was better to wait until the day of a missed period.

I shrugged, loaded my cart with one of each kind, and moved on, all bases covered. I knew it was silly and that my new wave of baby yearning was most likely a direct reaction to losing Patrick, the urge to replace mourning with expectation of new life. He had only been gone for a day.

One day. And here I was rushing ahead with my life, picturing myself strolling along with an infant seat to block my view. I could just see me trying to multitask by amusing the baby with colorful rubber toy keys while I made the all-important choice between Pampers and Luvs.

At checkout, I looked for the cart with the whiniest toddler and got into line right behind him. He cried, fussed, and balled his chubby fists around the rolls of Lifesavers from the candy display, all to the frustrated sighs of his mother. But my yearning was not deterred. I wanted to pick him up and comfort him, to kiss the tears from his sticky little cheeks and buy him all the Lifesavers he wanted. What was wrong with me? I couldn't get out of the store fast enough.

Next, I headed for work, my grounding force, my reality. Working mothers had it tough, I reminded myself. How did I expect to map floor plans, coordinate moving schedules, manage the books, and restock inventory, all with a baby on my hip? I just assumed it would fall into place. And it would, of course. I took a deep breath. I was getting ahead of myself. For now, work was my baby. I'd made Curtain Call Designs a success all on my own, and I didn't want to neglect my first love for the sake of dreaming of what could, or might never, be.

Thankfully, I had Val. She had been a big help for the past few days, taking over things at the office so I could be at the hospital with Bennie. I'd told her about Patrick last night when she called to check in.

"I'm so sorry." Val was all sympathy and hugs the second I walked in the door. "I've got everything under control, but I've already contacted Deb in case you want to cancel next weekend's open house."

"No. We all need the income at this time of the year." I didn't, necessarily, but my moving men got paid by the hour, plus it wouldn't hurt Val to have the extra Christmas bonus. "Besides, I could use the distraction."

"What about Patrick's services?"

"Bennie's having the body cremated. She plans to put a memorial service on hold for a few weeks. I think she needs the time. We have an appointment at the funeral home in a few hours, so I'll know more after that."

"The poor thing. Can I stop by the house with a casserole?"

"Just bring your best wishes," I said. I had a feeling we would all be sick of casseroles in a matter of days. "And thank you. My sister will appreciate the concern.

"Have we had any interesting mail? Calls? Messages?" I asked, hopeful that maybe Owen had called. I could dream. I hated the way we'd left things. Me, realizing how much I loved him. Him, completely rejecting me. Yeah, that went well. I couldn't help but wish he would have second thoughts. But where would that leave my baby plans? Perhaps he knew I was pregnant, and it had something to do with him not taking me to the underworld? It was better than believing that he'd had a change of heart and didn't want me after all.

"A Marc Ramirez called. He said he wanted to send his condolences. I guess he must have heard about Patrick. That's about all. That, and some travel brochures from Vegas came in the mail. I chucked those, of course. I didn't think you'd be interested right now."

"Good call," I said. Actually, I was interested, but not

in travel to Vegas. In making a phone call. Owen had left my dad's number with me before I'd left Hilton Head, just in case, and it had been sitting in my wallet ever since. The brochures reminded me. I wondered if they had come through some sort of divine intervention. My father was out there with no idea of what was happening to the family he left behind. Maybe it was time he knew.

"Great," Val said. "So I've got everything under control."

"Good work, Val," I said. "I do have to get back to my family. Thanks for everything. I'll check in Friday to see how plans are going for the open house. Call me if you need me before then."

"That's three days from now." Val seemed to be working out the schedule in her head. "I can put together a kick-ass plan for the open house in three days. No problem."

Our usual MO was to hash out a plan together, go over it, get the movers to place the furniture, then take our time in trying it to make sure it all made for good flow, and, of course, eye-catching appearance. Between holidays and vacations, Val had handled the planning part on her own plenty of times. I wasn't worried. I was certain the business was in good hands. I wished I could have the same faith that my personal life would prove as easy to manage.

The sound of shouts from the kitchen reached me in Bennie's driveway as I unloaded groceries from the car. Uh-oh, crisis. I put down the bags and went in to see what was going on.

"You're happy that he died," Bennie said, spiteful. "Now I can be alone, just like you."

"Bernadette," Mother scoffed. "It's not like that at all. Of course I'm sad for you. I was only trying to comfort you. To sympathize. I—"

I stood in the doorway waiting for the right time to get between Mother and Bennie to stop the argument, just like old times. It might have been Bennie and Mother circa 1987, Bennie desperate to head to the arcade on a Friday night and Mother telling her that she couldn't go anywhere until her chores were done. It was always something between Bennie and Mother.

"Now I'll know what it was like to be a single mother? That's supposed to *comfort* me?" Bennie fumed. The kids were nowhere to be seen, thank goodness, probably in their rooms. Hal sat at the table, his gaze darting between them as if he was watching his favorite television drama.

I knew Mother had probably started on Bennie with the best intentions, but she had a knack for saying all the wrong things at the wrong time. I should have seen it coming. I stepped in at last, calling their attention by letting the screen door slam shut behind me.

"Bennie," I said, crossing the floor to reach out and calm her. "We're all devastated by the loss. You know Mom didn't mean to compare."

"I *wasn't* comparing," Mother said, defensive. "I was—"

"What, surprised I didn't chase him away sooner?" Bennie said. "Like you chased away Dad?"

"I didn't." Mom's lip quivered ever so slightly. "I— your father left. It wasn't my fault. He abandoned us."

"Over twenty years ago. Perhaps now *I* can take over as family martyr. Or wait, no, Patrick died. An accident.

That's probably not as bad as being left on purpose, right? You win, Mother. You'll always win. Congratulations." Bennie turned to me as if expecting me to take her side. "Can you believe her?"

"You know she didn't mean it that way," I said, torn between wanting to make it right but not wanting to take sides.

Tears streaming, Bennie looked at me as if I was a traitor and ran from the room.

"Oh dear, I guess we'd better go. She'll need her space." Even when confronted face-on with her own selfishness, Mother couldn't let it go.

"She's bound to have her moments," I said. "You and Hal should go home and get some rest. I can handle things here. By this evening, she'll have calmed down."

"We'll come back for dinner," Mother said. "I'll bake a lasagna."

"That sounds great," I said, pleased that Mother had found a way to satisfy her need to be helpful and still stay out of Bennie's way.

In the meantime, my best course of action was to make sure Bennie and Mother didn't end up together without my supervision.

Later that night, with the visit to the funeral home out of the way and arrangements planned, we gathered at Bennie's for dinner.

Despite the blaring television, the living room was too quiet with Patrick not being there to hand out drinks and make sure the conversation flowed. I stared at the bar and ached, missing him more than ever. I left Pops, Hal, and the kids in front of the television reruns and went to help in the kitchen.

"I'm a widow, not an invalid, Mother," Bennie was saying as I entered, as if trying the word on for size. *Widow.* I flashed Mom a stern look, and she stayed silent. Thank goodness. No further outburst followed.

I gathered the dishes to set the table while Mother peeked in the oven to check the lasagna and Gran sliced bread. I think the familiarity of routine helped Bennie. The kitchen had never been Patrick's domain. Out in the rest of the house, his absence was nearly palpable, but in the kitchen it was business as usual.

Bennie even hummed a little tune as she worked to put together a salad.

Then, out of the blue, she stopped sprinkling croutons over the greens and cried a little. I fought the urge to approach and stood back to let her cry. A second later, she wiped her tears, washed her hands, and went right back to salad. She really was going to be okay. It might take a little time, but she could get through it.

The real test came when we brought the food out to the dining room and took our seats around the table. No one sat in Patrick's chair. For a second, I wondered if I should sit there just to fill in the space and make his absence less obvious, but then I decided against it. Patrick was with us, even though he wasn't there. I could practically feel him in the room as we took our seats.

Bennie stared at the empty chair, her eyes filled not with tears but with a look of fond remembrance and acceptance.

"Patrick always enjoyed your lasagna, Mother," Bennie said, after a moment, breaking the tense silence. "I'm sure he would love to be here for it."

"We all miss him so," Mother said at last, blinking away a tear of her own. "It helps to be together."

"Yes, it does," Bennie said. "I'm glad you're all here." She addressed us all, but she looked pointedly at Mother. "Thank you."

I couldn't remember a time when Bennie had backed down from a snit with Mother and moved on with such grace. It seemed to be a new day for Bennie in so many ways. The healing had begun.

"Kate, would you like to select a wine for tonight's meal?"

"A wine? But maybe we shouldn't?" I hesitated.

"We should." Bennie shook her head, an argument at the ready. "It's too late to second guess the way Patrick lived his life, what he did, what he shouldn't have done. I would rather honor his memory in a way he would have liked. He liked his wine. He liked that it brought people together and made everyone talkative and merry. I don't intend to change the way I entertain."

"All right. You're the boss." I went out to the cabinet at the bar and selected a bottle I thought would do Patrick justice, a spicy red Zinfandel.

Over dinner, we toasted his memory, as if to assure him he would always be a part of our family.

Patrick, my brother, hit a home run for me.

By Friday, I was able to sneak away for a few hours and see the progress on my next open house. I arrived at the office to find Val panicked out of her mind.

"Oh. Shit. Kate."

"Thanks. Nice to see you, too."

"No, I mean, ugh." She brought her hands to her wild brown curls and acted as if she would tear them out. "I didn't want you to come in when it was such a mess here. I'll work it out. I've got everything under control."

"Of course you do," I said, taking a seat at my desk and starting to rifle through mail, bills, and messages, none. "I've got complete faith."

Val paced. "Don't have faith in me. I've blown it."

"What could you have possibly blown that we don't have time to fix. The showing is a week away."

"Right." She continued to pace then stopped and turned. "It's the movers. They've all quit."

"What? All four?" Now she had my attention. Val had occasional freak-outs, usually over nothing serious. I was sure we could work it out.

"Three. Nathan quit in September to go back to school, remember?"

"So what's wrong with Rock and Joe? And, who's the other guy?" I put the mail aside and leaned forward in my chair.

"Hank," she said, and stopped her pacing to sit at her own desk across from mine, as if to try to settle her nerves.

"Hank, that's right. So what happened? All three of them catch play-off fever at the same time?" The Patriots were having a great season. It tended to make Sundays hard to schedule.

"Hank quit last week. I didn't say anything. I didn't want to bug you. His band got picked up by a record label."

"Really? Wow, good for Hank." I'd been through a life-and-death crisis. I couldn't quite muster the panic that Val had worked herself into yet.

"Then Joe fell down his stairs two days ago. Broken leg. I've been looking for a replacement, but I'm coming up short."

"Okay, that's bad. We've still got Rock. Maybe he knows some guys?"

"Scratch Rock off the list." She propped her elbows on the desk and buried her face in her hands.

"But why? Rock's always been, well, our rock." Even as we spoke, I'd clicked on my computer, ready to begin an Internet search for capable candidates. How hard could it be to find new movers in a day? When Val didn't answer right away, I looked up.

Val went red to her roots. "Rock's got a personal situation."

"And this involves you?"

"Oh, God, how did you know? I'm sorry. I couldn't help it."

"Help what?"

"Well, I kind of hit on him."

"You hit on Rock?" I stifled a laugh. Just picturing the two of them together was an odd visual. Val, all five feet nothing with her every-which-way curls, with Rock— tall, built like a house, Rock. Stranger things had happened. "And?"

"We, um, we may have broken in the new sleigh bed you bought to display in the master bedroom suite."

Once I started laughing, I couldn't stop. It had been a few weeks since I'd had a good laugh and it felt great. "Val!"

"I know. It was so unprofessional." She went back to the pacing.

"Pfft. Who cares. Was he any good?" I wanted everyone to be in love. If I couldn't have it, someone should. No one was more deserving of a good time than Val.

"He was great." Val smiled at the apparent memory. "But now he says he needs time to think. He has a girlfriend. I had no idea."

"Wow. Any chance that he'll respond to begging or pleading?"

Val's cheeks colored again.

"I mean to come help us move furniture," I clarified before Val offered TMI.

"He took his girlfriend away for the weekend. He might use the opportunity to break it off with her. Who knows?" A twinkle lit Val's eyes.

"Don't get your hopes too high."

"Not to worry. I'm old enough to be his mother. I'm just glad to find out I could give the lad a good time."

"He's older than me, Val. You are not that old."

"Yeah, but it makes a good story that way. I guess the main thing is that I'm not unemployed. Thanks for understanding."

"You're welcome. Now let's put our heads together and see what we can do about movers for the open house."

Where were minions when you needed them?

But I didn't really want minions. I wanted the man in control of them. The idea of minions still scared me a little, but not as much after losing Patrick. Nothing scared me much anymore. If Hades could show such compassion to try to save Patrick for me, I could have a little more faith.

Right now, I only needed faith that Val and I could find replacement movers and keep the open house as scheduled. After hours of scouring the Internet and phone listings and following dead-end leads, Val and I still had no one.

"We have to cancel," Val said, giving up as it grew dark out. "I'm really sorry. I shouldn't have had so much confidence. If I'd called you a few days ago . . ."

"Val, truly, what difference would it make? Everyone's booked. No one's available. But I'm not ready to give up."

"No?" She looked almost disappointed. Clearly, she was tired.

"I'm going to keep looking here. Maybe I'll have some luck calling around to local college campuses," I said. "Christmas is weeks away. Tell me I won't find at least two burly young men eager to make some extra bucks for holiday shopping."

I hated to hire amateurs. Amateurs did some unflattering things to woodwork, especially around doorways and stairs. But anything was better than canceling on short notice.

"Or at least for beer money." Val brightened at the thought. "Great idea. Where shall we start?"

"Not we. Me. You go home, go over the mover's list, and make sure we have a solid plan in place. New guys won't know our routine, so we may have to spell a few things out. Then get some rest."

"Right," Val said, grabbing her coat, the checklists, and house plans. "But are you sure? I'm more than happy to make a few more calls."

"I'm sure. I would feel a lot better to know you got some sleep if it comes down to the two of us doing some heavy lifting tomorrow."

Once Val left, I called my sister to tell her that I wouldn't be home for dinner.

"Oh, too bad," Bennie said, but the sound of the kids laughing in the background took some of the weight out of her disappointment. "We're planning a make-your-own-pizza night. The kids and I were just making the crust."

"Making your own crust?" It seemed like a lot of work to me, but Bennie took delight in domestic tasks and I knew she preferred to keep busy.

"It's fun. You wouldn't believe how kneading dough

can ease the tension. Hang on. Kids!" She interrupted to tell Sarah to stop throwing flour at Spence. More giggling ensued. It was great to hear them getting back into routine and laughing. Actually laughing! It brightened my spirits despite my current dilemma. "Want us to make one and put it aside for you? We've got your favorite ingredients, sausage and mushroom."

"I'm going to have to pass on this one," I said. "In fact, I might be coming in so late that it probably makes more sense for me to crash at my own place tonight."

"Sick of us already?" Bennie asked.

"Hardly. It's a little crisis at work, actually. I need to find movers by tomorrow. Sunday at the latest." I filled her in on the situation, and had her in complete laughter with my recounting of the Val-Rock romance.

"Wow, Val and Rock," she said. "Who would have guessed? But good luck with finding movers. I hope it doesn't keep you up too late."

"Not too late," I lied.

"Oh, Kate, it's bad, isn't it?" My voice always gave me away. "You've been so great to have around this week, and I'm so grateful. I wish there was something I could do to help. "

"No need for gratitude." I said, my eyes tearing up, and I wondered if it was from PMS or pregnancy. I was dying to tell Bennie, but she didn't even know about the insemination attempt and it wasn't something to bring up now. "You've helped me this week, too. Some days, I don't know how I would hold it together without you and the kids. Enjoy your pizza," I said quickly, ending the phone call before I burst into a sobbing wreck.

I gave in to the tears for only a few minutes before I took a deep breath, got myself together, and started looking up phone numbers for local colleges. Considering the late hour, I made contact with a lot of answering machines and only one human, a work-study counselor at Boston College. She couldn't promise me anything but offered to make some calls and get back to me tomorrow. It was something. I hung up the phone and considered hanging it up for the night when the phone rang again.

"Hello?" I picked up immediately, hoping for the best. It was Bennie.

"Listen, Kate, I have great news," Bennie said.

"I'm listening," I said, trying to hide my disappointment that it was Bennie and not a college counselor calling back.

"Your moving problem is all taken care of. I've worked it out with Val."

"What?" My heart gave a leap. "How did you get in touch with Val?"

"She wanted me to call and harass you to come home if you were out too late. I guess she was worried about you."

It made sense. It was so like Val to worry. "She knows I've been staying at your house. I guess she didn't realize I was going back to my place tonight."

"Anyway, once she told me what was going on, I had an idea, and it worked. So not to worry. You can go home and get some sleep. Just be at your office bright and early. Say, eight A.M., okay? Oops, there's the oven timer. Gotta go."

"But how? Who? Bennie—" I stammered, but she hung up before I could get the question out.

So she'd hired movers? I felt a wave of relief wash over me. Who knew how Bennie had managed when I couldn't find movers to save my life, but she'd done it. Amazing.

I was too tired to make it back to her place for more of an explanation. I kept to my plan and headed for home, hoping everything would make more sense in the morning when I came back to work.

Chapter 25

The next morning, I showed up at work dressed in an old flannel shirt, jeans, and sneakers, just in case Bennie didn't come through with the movers. If it came down to it, I was prepared to move everything myself. No way was I canceling on my client.

But it wasn't Bennie who waited for me outside the warehouse. It was Owen. My heart did a loop. A triple toe loop, in figure-skating terms.

"Owen," I said, stunned.

I didn't think I'd see him again. Now here he was. I fought against the urge to fall to my knees and cry. *Here he was. For me. All for me.*

"I've got this incredibly strong human body," he said. "I've come to put it to good use."

"Wow. That's quite an opener," I said. "We should go up to my office. It will only take me a minute to clear my desk."

He laughed. "I'm here to help you *move*. The furniture? For your open house?"

"Oh." *Oh.*

"But maybe later, if the offer still stands?" He draped an arm around my shoulder. "I've missed you so much, Kate."

He'd missed me! After everything that happened! I had hope. "I've missed you, too." I threw myself into his arms and sat there for a minute just for the thrill of feeling him breathe. Then it hit me. I looked terrible. I reached out to pull my hair out of a functional but not flattering ponytail.

"You're beautiful." He laced his hand with mine. "It doesn't matter what you're wearing. Besides, we almost match."

I realized that he *was* wearing almost the same thing, a denim shirt over a T-shirt with faded jeans and running shoes. He even looked good dressed down.

I felt the wicked urge to dress him down even more.

"But how did you know about my mover problems? Oh, dumb question. You know everything."

"Actually, it was your sister. She called last night, worried about you."

"You're kidding." Even in grief, she couldn't help her matchmaking. Thank God!

"No, she really did. We had a nice talk."

"Nice?"

"Informative."

"Informative?"

"She thinks you might be a little in love with me. It gave me hope."

"You needed hope? But, you know everything."

"Apparently not where you're concerned. I really thought your choice was clear, that you wanted to be here for your family and it would be easier on us if I just left you alone. But your sister has other ideas. She said she thinks you're sad without me, that whatever we had isn't just going to go away."

"She said that? But I never really talked to her about it. Much."

"She apparently knows you better than you think. Unless she has it all wrong?"

He raised a brow. I searched his eyes for some glimmer of darkness hiding there, but found nothing. No shadows. Nothing sinister. Just a warm brown gaze. I felt the heat of him right down to my toes.

"Not wrong at all. I'm so glad she called. I'd thought you didn't want to see me again. I thought I'd let you down. That I didn't have what you needed after all."

He placed a finger to my lips. "Let's not talk about last time. I was hurt. I didn't understand a lot of things about family. I'm willing to try to learn."

"But it wasn't just you. I was awful. I didn't mean to hurt you. I just wanted—"

"To help your sister. I know. We can discuss it more later. After the move. For now, she's on her way. With reinforcements."

"Minions?" I struggled to raise that eyebrow. I think it actually moved this time, an eighth of an inch.

"Not minions." He smiled. "Family."

"Family?" I didn't understand. Until I saw Mother and Hal's van pull up and park across the street. "My mother?"

"And stepdad. Your grandparents are with them, too."

"So I see." I watched as Hal helped Gran from the backseat.

"Bennie's coming, too. With Spence and Sarah. Not a lot of heavy lifters in the bunch but with more hands to do the work, it should go by fairly quickly. And I have some tricks up my sleeve."

"Don't I know it." I blushed, remembering how he'd pinned me to my bedroom wall without even using his hands. And then when he did use his hands . . .

"I know what you're thinking, and I swear I'm not using any tricks for that." The wicked smile made its first appearance of the day.

"Feel free to use any tricks you like," I said, so only he could hear before turning to welcome Gran, Pops, Mom, and Hal to the scene.

"You know you only have to ask when you need help," Pops said. "I've got plenty of muscle to spare." He made a weightlifter's pose and I couldn't help but laugh.

"Thanks so much. But it's going to be hard work. I never would have asked you all to come." Especially not my grandparents. What was Bennie thinking?

"I'm so glad we can be useful," My grandmother said, as if to answer the question. "I couldn't take one more day of sitting in my recliner watching the TV. You know, they never play musicals anymore."

"Watch the TV? You watch the inside of your eyelids," Pops accused, then let out a hoot of laughter.

"So, Millie," Owen jumped right into the conversation. "I understand you're a fan of *South Pacific?*"

Bennie arrived next with the kids and I ran to meet her.

"Bennie." I threw my arms around her. "I have always teased you about being a saint, but I may have to be more careful. You've worked a real miracle for me here today. Thanks."

"You're thanking me? I've been trying to set you up with a guy for two years now. You think I'm going to get this close and let a prime candidate just walk away? Besides, he was more than willing."

I flashed a look at Owen, still in animated discussion with Gran. He caught my eyes for the briefest of moments, and I could swear I felt the heat of a kiss on my cheek. I rubbed the spot. Rubbing it in, not wiping it off. That's what my father used to say when my mother kissed him. Besides Patrick, Dad was the only thing missing to complete our family scene. I hoped that wouldn't be the case much longer.

"Okay, troops," I said, clapping to get everyone's attention. "We'll start with the warehouse tour, and then you'll be given assignments of what needs to go in the truck first."

We worked in pairs, the strongest of us tackling the heavier tasks while the kids and Gran loaded the van with boxes of the smaller trinkets. Within a few hours, we had the entire truck loaded, and no one could believe how quickly it went. I suspected Owen cheated when some of us weren't looking, but kept it to myself. The entire dining set complete with china cabinet had been loaded on the truck without anyone even being able to recall moving it. I might have been worried that someone would see something they shouldn't, like a table flying through the air, but after hauling three heavy mattress sets into the back of the truck, I was all for using any supernatural powers Owen could conjure. Plus, no one suspected anything. Owen worked his magic with the utmost discretion.

The men, particularly Owen, had handled most of the heavy stuff, to my relief. I didn't want to be carrying around heavy items in the off chance that I was pregnant, though I also didn't want to call attention to the fact that I was avoiding heavy things. I wouldn't get my period for another week, but I had taken one of the tests a few days ago to find a negative result. It could

have been too early. Still, I didn't plan on saying anything to Owen about the potential pregnancy right
away. It was possible he already knew, but I would wait
for the right time to bring it into the conversation.

"So this is what family's about," Owen said as we
moved the last item onto the truck. "I like it."

"You're always welcome in our family, son," Pops said
from across the room. "Anyone who's not afraid of a
little hard work is fine by me."

A part of the family, yes, but how big a part? I wondered if his reappearance meant that we were going
to take things slow. Manage long distance for a while? I
had no idea. But it seemed I had some time to find out.

While Pops and Hal came over to help Owen close the
truck, I found Bennie hovering near a canopy bed I often
used in houses that could handle more ornate décor.

"I wanted a bed like this when we were first married,"
Bennie said, swinging around the rail like a little girl.
"Patrick said no. Too frou-frou."

It reminded me of any number of their discussions
through the years.

I shrugged. "Canopy beds aren't much of a guy
thing. But you have a lovely bedroom. It's a nice mix of
the masculine and the feminine."

Bennie smiled, wistful. "He didn't like flowers either.
My next bedroom's going to be all lace and flowers.
Maybe I'll even get a canopy bed. On second thought,
I really like my bed. The mattress still has a slight
indent where Patrick used to sleep."

"Aw, Ben." I reached out and rubbed her arm.

"You two look good together." She nodded in
Owen's direction. "Do you think you'll give it a shot?"

"I don't know. I hope so. We'll see if it works out."

Before I knew it, he was behind me, his arm around

my shoulder. "How about you two lovely ladies ride with me in the truck?"

"Oh, no." Bennie begged off. "I've got my car."

"I'll drive your car to your house," Mom volunteered, joining us. "Your Gran's worn out and the kids are bored."

"I've got reinforcements on the other side," Owen explained. "A few very strong friends who owe me some favors. I've told Millie and Susan to go home with the kids."

"Minions?" I guessed. I felt up for it. Perhaps I could deal with a few minions.

"Friends," Owen emphasized.

"Anyway, your grandfather and Hal will drive the van," he said, "so it's you two up front in the truck with me. Unless, you're not up for it, Bennie?" He looked to my sister with genuine concern. It touched me to see him worrying about my family, and to see my family accepting him.

"Oh, I'm up for it," Bennie said. "As long as I get the window seat."

Gran came over to say good-bye, laying a hand on Owen's strong arm. "Now remember, you're going to rent *Carousel* and let me know what you think. The one with Shirley Jones."

"Yes, Millie," Owen said. "I've put it on my list of must-see musicals. But you'll be hard-pressed to get me to agree that it's better than *South Pacific*."

Any man who could win Gran over could definitely fit in with the whole family. I laced fingers with his.

Once you have found him, never let him go.

The rest of the move went well, especially since Owen had called in a local construction team to unload the trucks at the house. We were finished in no time, allowing Bennie to get Pops and Hal home for dinner with the family. I politely declined the invitation for the family meal, drawing a wink of support from Bennie before she got in the van to leave.

Alone at last, Owen and I kept quiet for most of the ride back to my office to exchange the moving truck for his car. But as we made the last turn, Owen broke the comfortable silence.

"You could have gone home with your sister. She needs you. I understand."

"I need you more." I hoped the answer was the same on his end, that he needed me. "I need to be with you."

"That's good." He parked in the garage. "I need you, too. We have all night."

He got out and came around to open my door. I hopped down the short step right into his arms and nearly melted. I missed his scent, a smoky, spicy male scent. I missed the feel of his skin on mine, that heat. He felt so right. I reached up to run my hands through his tousled dark curls. "I need to taste you again," he said, his lips grazing the line of my jaw.

"Here?" I had beds, more than one, but the warehouse was concrete and industrial, not inviting. I wanted to be somewhere with more of a domestic touch. I had no idea how long we would have together, and I wanted to indulge my fantasy, if only for tonight, of being a normal couple, man and wife.

"Not here," he said. "Come with me. I know just the place."

We walked to his car and got in. Within seconds of the drive, I knew where we were headed. And where else? It was the perfect choice. It was *our* house, I realized. *Our home.* It was only fitting that we would spend the night there.

Chapter 26

Lights dotted the driveway, lending an appearance of domesticity in a "welcome to suburbia" sort of way. The house was larger than I remembered. We left the car in the curve of the driveway and went in.

"It's really lovely in here," I said, taking in the décor once again.

"You do great work." He smiled. "Be right back."

He popped into the kitchen and came out with an open bottle of Cabernet and two glasses.

"Oh, that's nice." I sipped and allowed myself to slide down to the overstuffed sofa in the family room right off the kitchen. Just a few sips. What was the harm? I didn't even jump when the flame flared from the fireplace, a fire starting all on its own. Or with a little supernatural assistance. I met Owen's gaze as he sat beside me, head propped on his elbow as if to study me. His eyes mirrored the flame.

"Just the thing to unwind after a hard day," he said.

"God, was it hard. Every muscle in my body hurts. I didn't know I had some of them."

"Anything I can do to make them feel better?" He arched a brow.

"All kinds of things." I smiled, put my glass down, and scooted closer to him, reaching out to put my hand on his flat, firm stomach. "When you said we have all night, what did you mean?"

"That we have all night."

"And tomorrow? What then? How long do you have this time?" A night here, a week there, I would take whatever I could get. I was just so happy to have him with me again.

"I have tonight." He cupped my face in his palm. "Let's make the most of it."

"Tonight. And then?" When would I see him again? I wanted to know. I was willing to accept what he could give, but we would have to work out a schedule, to know when I could set aside all else and save my time for him.

"Tonight." His voice grew more insistent, but not sinister. No darkness passed between us. It was all light and warmth. I treasured the feeling.

He set down his wine, reached for my hand, and pulled me to my feet to lead me to the stairs. To our room. The master bedroom at the top of the stairs, to the left. I still remembered every detail. I'd done it in pure snow white, soft textures, warm woods. It was as if I'd known, even when I'd decorated it, that it was a room I would be at home in, a room for love.

At the top of the stairs, he leaned in for a kiss, his lips meeting mine in slow provocation. An invitation to the dance.

I drew his tongue to the hollow at the back of my throat and gasped at the delicate heat that scorched my mouth. Together, in each other's arms, we found our footing to the bedroom.

"Home," I said. I didn't mean the bedroom, though we'd crossed the floor to the bed, and I fell onto the downy white comforter. So soft.

"Home is where you are," he said, standing over me, tugging at the buttons of his shirt and stripping it away.

"Home is where we are together." I let my flannel slip off my shoulders, revealing my basic white cotton tank with the built-in bra. I'd dressed for comfort, never expecting to see him. I watched as he pulled his tight white T-shirt off over his head to reveal his rippled abdomen and the trail of dark hair that beckoned my eyes lower.

Not yet, I reminded myself. I peeled the tank top off in a slow roll over my breasts. They sprang free, nipples erect, begging for his attention.

He growled from low in his throat. His gaze caressed every inch of my exposed skin even as he unzipped his jeans and slipped them down his hips, the lower half of him a stark glowing white compared to his bronzed arms and chest. No underwear. Apparently, he'd spent the day commando. If only I'd known.

Without his clothes, he was all the more beautiful, as if sculpted in marble just for me.

My David. My own personal god. Hades.

He may have been a god, but his form was all man. I crawled to the edge of the bed and reached for him. I let my eyes drift to his large, swollen cock and held it in my gaze. I imagined stroking him, smooth silk over rock-hard marble, and bringing him toward me. Just the thought nearly toppled me. I couldn't wait to touch him.

"Oh, no." He backed his hips away. "Your turn."

He gestured with a tip of his head. Obedient, I kneeled on the bed and undid the button of my low-rise jeans. I let my hand linger, then dipped my fingers down into the waistband, watching his eyes follow along. I touched myself, so wet and hot for him, and slowly brought my hand back to my zipper.

"God, yes." His voice, hoarse and fragile, offered encouragement. "Let me see you."

I tugged my jeans down my hips, an inch at a time, as slow as molasses pouring down my body. I twisted my finger into the side of my panties and paused. "Yes?"

He didn't take time to answer. His hands, frantic, gripped my thighs and tugged me toward him. He pulled off the rest of my clothes in one solid rip and eased himself between my bare legs. My back settled flat into the voluminous white linens. I rubbed against him, so eager.

Still standing at the edge of the bed, he had the power to pull away. "Not yet. I want to touch you."

"All over." I agreed. "I want to feel every inch of you."

I sat up and smoothed my hands across his chest, paused at his nipples, and traced slow circles around the dark pebbled nubs. He started at my neck, palms down, and slid in one liquid motion to my breasts. He caught my nipples between his fingers and gave a light tug, then a more insistent pull. Following the exquisite sensation, I arched into him.

I trailed my hands around to his buttocks and cupped the smooth mounds. He slicked his hands to my navel and paused, letting the heat of his palms send wild curls of desire rushing through my body to my core.

I stroked a hand down the length of his erection, cradled the precious weight of his sac in my palm, and urged him to me. When I took him in my mouth, he trembled as if fighting the urge to buck. I pulled him deeper. Deeper. I rolled my tongue over the tip of his penis and savored his salty essence. I moaned at the wonder of taking him inside me as far as he could go.

He nudged me to the bed. His strong hands were tanned against the white flesh of my thighs as he coaxed my legs to open. For several seconds, he studied my pink, tender skin, then pursed his lips and blew his sultry breath all over me.

"So beautiful," he said, replacing his lips with his fingers, stroking an erotic rhythm that played me in expert time to his imaginary music. I reacted with an immediate and unstoppable moan. I started to move with him, pulse around him.

Tiny tremors rolled into cataclysmic quakes. He worked his tongue into the deepest heat at my core.

White hot and molten.

He touched me until I was mass of singing nerve endings, every touch bringing a new hum, sparkle, or fade. Every time he touched me fresh, I trembled, the sparks strong and alive. I moved with him; I couldn't help it. At last, he was inside me. I could feel every glorious inch. I gave in to sheer animal instinct to writhe, moan, and milk every elemental drop.

Sex, for me, had never been so completely physically challenging. Along with my body, my feelings were completely engaged.

So, finally, *this* was love.

In the middle of the night, I woke to the soothing sounds of Owen's deep breathing. I nestled against his chest and tried to drift back to blissful sleep. Something niggled from the back of my mind, keeping me from settling down. Things seemed too perfect. I wasn't used to perfect. Especially lately, with the tragedy of losing Patrick clouding the past few weeks.

Patrick had said Hades had made a sacrifice, a tremendous, life-altering sacrifice. My breath caught, a horrible feeling sweeping over me. What had he given up? I wanted to shake him awake to ask, but he looked so beautiful curled in bed next to me. I studied the perfect contours of his face, now dotted with the beginnings of a beard, and found no answers. At peace, he slept. Dark, fierce, and ethereal, my terrible angel rested while the world raged on.

I got up and crept quietly from the room, over the very same snowy wool space rug I'd laid carefully over polished oak floorboards hardly a month earlier, in anticipation of bare feet emerging fresh from slumber in search of a cozy landing. I'd done nice work. My feet barely felt a chill as I padded out and down the hall.

I had no idea where I was headed. Instinct took over. *The heart remembers.* I ended up outside the door of the corner nursery.

Gently, I pushed open the door and stifled a gasp. The room was filled with the nursery furniture. I distinctly recalled sending my men to pick it up because Owen hadn't wanted it. Now, here it was, just as I'd placed it, the crib along the back wall, set off by a gorgeous arched canopy, soft blankets draped lovingly inside by my own two hands.

The baby's room.

My hands reached for my stomach, cradling my womb. There could already be a baby inside. I thought of the negative test, but I wasn't ready to give up hope. If this one didn't work, would I try again? What would Owen think? Would he be there for any of it? Pregnancy, delivery? It would be so much easier with him at my side.

Over the crib, the mobile began to play. *You are my sunshine. My only sunshine.* A fluke? Sometimes wind-up things just went off. Or was it something else? I went to the crib.

My eyes played horrible tricks on me. I saw my baby there, a wide-awake gurgling little cherub. My heart surged.

You make me happy. When skies are gray.

I reached for her. A girl? I'd sworn I would have a boy. I ran my hand over her downy dark hair. Dark, like her father. Like Hades.

You'll never know, dear, how much I love you.

She kicked up her feet, reached for her toes, chubby baby thighs in the air as she cooed. Poor baby girl, she had Mommy's thighs, and also my nose, two things she would certainly not thank me for later. I laughed. Oh, darling. Sweet baby girl. I heard a shuffling in the hall, the creak of the door opening wider. But I couldn't move. I was transfixed by the beauty of my baby daughter's face.

"You want one, don't you?" he asked, and my fantasy faded instantly with the sound of his voice. *Don't go. Come back. Please don't take my sunshine away.*

I stroked the blanket. Still warm. I picked it up and smelled her delicate baby scent, powder and spring-fresh dew.

"I want one," I said. "I went to a doctor, I—"

"I know, love, I know." He wrapped me in his embrace.

It felt so right. So comforting. What we had between us was magic. Unique. Never to be imitated or repeated. I would never be loved by a man as I was loved by this god, my Hades. It seemed wrong we couldn't love each other all the time, every day. Wrong that I couldn't carry his child inside me.

"You've given me the sun, if only for a day," he said, backing away to look in my eyes. "Now I have something for you."

"We have more than a day." Instant panic swept through me. "Don't we?"

"In time."

"But—" He placed a finger to my lips. In time?

"I'll explain later. For now, let's go back to bed. I want to give you something you'll never forget."

He found my lips. I responded to his kiss. So tender. I leaned in to his embrace, nuzzled my hips against his erection. Arm in arm, we returned to the bedroom and made love with aching slowness, as if etching every movement into memory to last for all time.

For hours afterwards, I remained cradled in his arms, desperately fighting the potent urge to sleep. It would have been so nice to close my eyes, to find peace and complete release in his arms after loving him until we were both so thoroughly spent. But I knew. Deep in my subconscious, I knew what would happen if I slept: He would be gone, completely vanished as if he'd never been a part of me, a part so vital.

Eventually, I began to lose the fight. My eyelids grew heavy. Hades cradled my head, stroked my hair. The effect was more soothing than a lullaby.

"Pinch me." I shook my head. "I don't want to fall asleep."

"You have to sleep. It's the only way."

"Don't leave me," I said. "Stay. Please. Stay here."

"I have to go. It was part of the bargain."

"That you leave me? But that's unfair. It's horrible."

"You've never met my brother." He laughed. "I've

the terrifying reputation, but he's the one with the cruel streak."

"What else did this bargain entail?" My fingers tangled in the hair of his chest. I treasured every second of contact.

"For the gift of granting life, I exchanged my wandering rights. It's not so bad. It simply means that I'll spend the rest of eternity in the underworld. No more coming out to stir up trouble among the mortals."

"I'll go with you. We'll have each other."

"Not this time, love. I can't bring you back with me. Not now. You have so much to live for, so many reasons to stay. We'll have our time."

"I don't want to be apart from you. It's not fair. We've hardly had enough time." I laced my hand with his. I couldn't help thinking of all my reasons to stay. Maybe he was right. "Patrick didn't want to live. Don't you get to drop the bargain and stay with me?"

He sighed. "I'm afraid not. Zeus doesn't believe in refunds."

"So you end up with nothing, and stuck in hell to boot?"

"I ended up with the greatest gift in the world. You love me. That alone will get me through anything. Besides, there's something more. I can't tell you, but you'll know soon enough. You'll see."

"Tell me," I turned to face him. "Tell me now."

"I'm not allowed. You'll know in time. Now sleep. You need your rest."

"But I won't get to see you again."

"You'll see me. One day. We'll be together again."

"Soon?" My heart raced. I couldn't tell if I was eager or anxious.

He laughed again, the rich low sound lulling me to sleep. I startled. Still awake. He was still here.

"Not too soon," he said. "You have a long life ahead. Live well. Find love in the arms of other men. Embrace every moment, every chance, stay open to every opportunity. Then you'll come back to me, my one true love. We have eternity. In time."

"In time," I echoed, before I fell into a deep, immutable sleep.

Chapter 27

Christmas turned out to be a quieter affair than the Christmases we'd known in the past, but it was one of the most beautiful. We unwrapped presents at Bennie's and shared memories under the tree, memories of Patrick and of our childhoods. I thought of Hades watching over me. It was three weeks since I'd last seen him. Three weeks of grief and healing.

I'd been spending so much time at Bennie's that I put my condo on the market. Eventually, I would move into the house Owen Glendower had left in my name. It was a lovely place to raise a child. I missed my period, and didn't have the nerve to take another test. I didn't want to see a negative result when I'd finally been able to find such a positive frame of mind.

I had my family. Though I ached with the pain of our losses, Bennie's and mine, I'd never felt so blessed.

The best gift of the season actually came a few days before Christmas, a phone call from my father. I'd sent him a gift, a framed picture of Bennie and me posing with her kids, a candid shot snapped by Patrick at a family brunch earlier in the year. We talked for over an hour.

Dad told me about his life in Vegas, his desperate yearning to make things right, and his eventual score at a slot machine. He said he'd been wondering about us, thinking of calling but not knowing if the time was right. I explained about Patrick, and we concluded, together, that life was too short to put things off. My father was coming home. Maybe not to stay, but for a visit, and then we would see. I decided not to say anything to Bennie in case he didn't make it in time for the service, but I hoped Dad would be a welcome surprise to help take her mind off her grief.

It snowed on the morning of Patrick's memorial service, a light, cleansing snow. It seemed fitting, considering the date we'd chosen to remember him. Epiphany, January sixth, a day for new beginnings.

Bennie had wanted to scatter Patrick's ashes at Fenway, but the ballpark denied our request. Instead, we agreed on the high school ball field, but it would have to wait until spring when the field thawed. In the meantime, I arranged a service at Wellesley College, Bennie's alma mater, at Alexandra Botanic Gardens, one of her favorite places. It was a lovely setting, indoors but full of life and blooming plants and flowers. We'd needed more room for seating, so we'd set up services in the science center next door with a tour through the gardens and Hunnewell Arboretum directly following.

So far, so good. It hardly even looked like a science center with the decorative touches the children and Val had helped me place—bows at the end of every aisle and fresh flowers scattered and arranged throughout the room.

With minutes to spare before guests started arriving,

I tugged a forest green cloth in place over the lecture table and arranged photos of Patrick through various stages of his life. His kindergarten school picture, in a little league uniform, delivering the winning pitch at one of the high school games, graduations, marrying Bennie, holding newborns, and the most recent one from their family vacation with the four of them sporting mouse ears. The tale of Patrick's life as told through photographs, a story of success and love and so much happiness. A shame it had to end so soon.

I wished I had pictures of my relationship with Owen to look back on, but what I had of Owen I carried in my heart.

I wiped away a tear and joined the family and Val greeting guests out front. I found Bennie in conversation with the tall, kind-faced priest who was to be our first speaker. He'd been a friend of Patrick's family growing up. Val escorted him to the back to acquaint him with the program and where he would stand to speak. Next, some older family friends arrived. Spencer, looking so grown-up in his suit, showed them in and came back to greet more guests as they began to arrive. I hardly knew a quarter of them, but Bennie and the kids were gracious and friendly to each and every one.

A sudden wave of nausea overcame me.

"Mom, I feel sick," I said, taking her by the arm as she arrived with Gran, Pops, and Hal.

"I know," she said. "It's so sad."

"No, I mean, I really feel sick."

"You do look pale." She did the mom thing and felt my forehead. "No fever. But why don't you run to the ladies room and splash some water on your face? Bennie's doing fine out here. No one will miss you for a minute."

I ran to the ladies room and prayed Dad wouldn't arrive while I was away. No one else knew he was coming and I wanted to be there to greet him, reintroduce him, and explain. I had to deliver a speech once everyone sat down, which probably accounted for the nausea. I hated public speaking.

The water helped a little, but not enough. I leaned against the door of a stall, desperate to catch my breath and keep my stomach calm. After a few minutes, the nausea passed, but I was hit by another wave as I headed toward the door. I stared at my face in the mirror. I had to get it together. Finally, I resorted to Mother's age old remedy and freshened my makeup. I swiped on some blush, reapplied lipstick, and figured it was good enough.

I got back out in time to head in with Bennie and the kids. I looked out into the crowd, at the gathered friends and relatives I hadn't seen in years and the dozen or so faces I had yet to recognize—probably coworkers or business associates. The death of a man as young as Patrick brought in quite a few people eager to pay their respects, many of them unexpected. I searched the crowd for the one face that Bennie didn't expect, but that I eagerly awaited. What if he didn't show up? Bennie might be none the worse for wear, but I had begun to count on him again.

The service went very smoothly. Father Lawrence spoke briefly about Patrick as a young man. Paul Wiskowski took the lectern next to talk about Patrick's wonderful contributions to the community. I tried to listen. I couldn't concentrate with the nervous, sick feeling swirling around in my stomach. I would be speaking next. I gripped the edge of my chair off to the side of the lectern as I tried to steady my stomach—and my thoughts.

Before I knew it, Paul was passing the floor to me. I hoped the nausea would subside enough to let me get through the speech, which I planned to keep short and sweet. It was so hard to know what to say. I got to my feet and cleared my throat.

"When Patrick married my sister, he became my brother-in-law. But through the years, he became so much more. He became my brother." My gaze caught on Patrick's estranged mother, flanked by his two tearful sisters, in the front row. "And he was a wonderful brother. He always offered a shoulder to cry on and sound advice for whatever problems life was giving me. Moving forward without looking back was the way Patrick chose to live his life. He was very much about the moment, not about the past. In the spirit of Patrick, let's celebrate his life today. Together, we'll look back and remember, and then we'll move on, with Patrick in our hearts and memories reminding us to embrace life, to live every moment to the fullest."

In keeping with Patrick's wish for cheer in place of mourning, my tribute would take the form of a toast. I nodded to Val off to the side to start passing out the glasses of Patrick's favorite champagne.

Considering the way he'd died, I risked the possibility that some guests might find it inappropriate or tacky, but I couldn't think any more about his death. I wanted to focus on the way Patrick had lived. His glass was always full, and so were the glasses of his guests. I caught my sister's gaze from the front row, and she smiled.

I finished my speech with a portion of a Byron poem from Bennie's book collection.

I know not if I could have borne
To see thy beauties fade;
The night that followed such a morn
Had worn a deeper shade:
Thy day without a cloud hath passed,
And thou wert lovely to the last,
Extinguished, not decayed,
As stars that shoot along the sky
Shine brightest as they fall from high.

My words weren't for Patrick alone. I would never acknowledge my private loss to my sister or to anyone.
We'd all had enough grief. By the time I finished reading, Bennie, overcome, had joined me at the podium,
a spontaneous reaction.

"It was beautiful, Kate. Thank you." She hugged me.

"To Patrick," I said, raising the glass that I had set
aside in advance.

"To Patrick," everyone cheered, and raised their
glassed in return.

He would have loved it.

It was then that I spotted my father, standing in the
back of the room, strange yet familiar, like an aged and
heavyset Robert Redford. Late, but there. He met my
gaze and froze with instant recognition. He smiled, and
that was all it took. He stole my heart all over again.
Daddy, home at last.

People were already getting out of their seats and
slowly making their way to the front of the room to
look at the pictures and offer condolences, but Bennie's gaze had followed mine through the crowd.

"Oh, my God. Dad," she breathed. Never one to wait
for the right timing, she ran across the room, right into

our father's arms. I followed, close on her heels. "Dad! I can't believe it. You came. You're actually here."

I flashed a polite smile at an approaching guest and went over to join Bennie and Dad.

"Well, if it isn't my wee bonnie bairns," he said, tears glistening in his bright blue eyes. He pulled both of us close to him.

"It's good to see you, Dad," I said. "I'm so glad you could make it."

"I'm just glad I didn't miss it," he said. "I don't plan on missing anything any more. I've been a foolish man."

I couldn't disagree.

"You're here now, and that's what matters," Bennie said. "Oh, but you have to meet Spencer and Sarah." She looked around for her kids, and I was happy to see her beaming despite the underlying sadness of the day.

"Soon. You go off now," he said. "I know you have to attend your guests. I'll be around."

Bennie seemed hesitant.

"Come with us." I took charge and took his hand. "You're a part of the family, too."

Together, the three of us joined the rest of our family, near the photos on the lecture table.

"My God, you did show up," Mom said, her eyes widening with surprise before narrowing as if to take in every physical detail and assess how he had changed, or stayed the same.

"Now, Susan," Dad said. "You don't have to call me God. I still answer to Mike or Michael." He winked, his trademark smile spreading across his face.

Mother looked as if she would keel over on the spot. Hal, for the first time I could recall, was stricken speechless. Gran and Pops looked at each other as if neither one of them trusted their own eyes. I stood frozen in place, worried that all hell was about to break loose. Not that I couldn't handle a little hell.

It was Bennie who took control of the situation, surprising me with her presence of mind.

"Kids," she said, gesturing to Spencer and Sarah, "come and meet your Grandpa."

I smiled and hoped Hades could see us. I wanted him to know that I was moving on, but still holding him in my heart. Always. I felt him, an angel on my shoulder, and it warmed me to the bone.

The family reunion continued at Bennie's house after the service.

Spencer and Sarah stuck close to their grandfather's side, looking at him with apparent awe. My grandparents looked on with silent disapproval but said nothing.

And Mother?

True to her inner drama queen, she pretended to be completely unimpressed by Dad's appearance while making little digs like, "Oh is Mike still here? I figured he'd gotten restless and moved on by now."

There were still a lot of unanswered questions and a lot of missing information. After the loss of Patrick, neither Bennie nor I had it in our hearts to be bitter or hold a grudge. It was enough to know Dad loved us. He may not have been there for us, may not have been a dad in the ideal sense of the word, but he'd missed us and he wanted to be a granddad.

Now that he had all the money he would ever need, Dad planned to move comfortably back to Massachusetts and appropriately spoil his grandchildren. Bennie's kids could use a grandfatherly figure, and

Bennie was obviously more than willing to give Dad a second chance.

With everything that happened that day, the most impressive development, from my standpoint, was witnessing Bennie hugging Mother. I wasn't sure what was said between them, but I felt positive that it was a good, healthy mother and daughter exchange.

My family had weathered a devastating loss, but we were solid. We would come out okay. I'd learned to appreciate them all more than I ever thought possible. So we weren't perfect, not one of us. Maybe our imperfections were part of our charm.

With the exception of my occasional waves of nausea, the day had gone off without a hitch.

Before my eulogy, I'd thought the nausea was my fear of public speaking. But now, after the day had turned out all warm and fuzzy, I still felt sick. My skin was tender. I was warm all over. Maybe I was coming down with something. Or maybe—

Could it be?

There was still no sign of my period. Then I remembered the home pregnancy test I'd been carrying around for the last couple of weeks, but that I'd been too chicken to use. Suddenly, it was hard to think of anything else. What was I waiting for?

I excused myself and practically ran for the bathroom.

Twenty minutes later, Bennie knocked on the bathroom door. "Kate? What's wrong, honey? Do you still feel a little sick?"

I opened the door to Bennie's worried face. She was my sister. I could confide in her. There wasn't anything we couldn't share.

"No, Bennie. I'm not sick." I beamed. "I'm pregnant."

Epilogue

A steady stream of light beamed throughout the underworld, rays so strong he would have had to shield his eyes if he'd been a mere mortal.

His daughter's smile was nothing like the sun.

It shone far brighter.

The sight of her warmed him to the core. He kept near-constant watch over mother and daughter, his family. At last, the underworld reflected the new mood and temperament of Hades.

Brilliant, hot, alive.

He would never walk the earth again but he felt life coursing through his every pore, all thanks to her, his daughter. Her birth had rejuvenated him. He'd known he needed something. He never would have guessed it would come in the form of a delicate, gurgling, tiny baby girl. He could never touch her. No matter. She could never know the many ways she touched him.

By contrast, Kate was very much aware of him. She had a habit of speaking aloud when no one else was in the room as if speaking to him. Their connection remained strong despite their separation. Her happiness had become his source of joy, their daughter his light.

Like any proud father, he'd watched the birth. Kate never cried out or complained, though he could only imagine her pain. She had practically split in two. Her sister, a sustaining force, was at her side the entire time. Giving life was harder work than even he'd imagined.

Kate named the baby Eliana, Greek for daughter of the sun. He found it beautifully fitting.

On this midsummer day, mother and daughter were outdoors at a celebration. The sun reflected off Kate's golden hair. She'd cut it shorter so that it just skimmed her shoulders, probably to avoid the baby's endlessly grasping hands.

Eliana's hair was dark like his and hidden under a bonnet. Her eyes were the same green as Kate's. At nearly a month old, she was the perfect little combination of both of them. Kate's eyes, his hair. Kate's nose, his smile.

An idyllic summer scene: Kate sat on a blanket under a tree, cradling Eliana on her lap, occasionally bringing the baby closer to nurse.

It was a picnic. No, he realized, it was more. The sister was there with her children. Women and children, no men in sight. He liked it best that way, though he didn't mind the Marc fellow coming around more often. It was good for Kate to have a companion.

They were gathered at a ball field near a school, perhaps there to commemorate the sister's late husband. Patrick had recently passed to Elysium. Soon, he would be on to a new life. The sister cried as she scattered her husband's ashes across the pitcher's mound, but she smiled again not long after. It wasn't a day for lasting tears. It was a time for joy.

It was hard not to smile on such a beautiful day, surrounded by children and laughter. Hades sat back to enjoy the scene. Kate set Eliana in a baby seat on a blanket in the shade, a chance for their daughter to study her world and learn while the women laid out food and lemonade.

Hades loved to look at his daughter. He wished she could see his pride in her. With Kate, he had created life, created Eliana. What an amazing accomplishment. He would spend eternity content, and grateful to Zeus for the chance. It was worth not being able to spend time with Kate to have made Eliana. She was worth any sacrifice, worth all he had.

One day, they would all be together again.

In time.

When the women and children lifted their glasses to toast the absent Patrick, Hades lifted his own chalice as well.

"To life!"

About the Author

A 1990 graduate of Mount Holyoke College, Sherri Browning Erwin enjoyed a brief banking career before turning to writing full-time upon publication of her first book, a historical romance. A member of Romance Writers of America, she has been a frequent speaker at RWA National and local chapter events as well as Romantic Times and Writer's Guild conferences. Sherri lives in Massachusetts with her husband and their two children. Visit Sherri on the web at whinesisters.com or sherribrowningerwin.com.